The
Gutbucket
Quest

Tor Books by Piers Anthony

The
Gutbucket
Quest

Piers Anthony
& Ron Leming

TOR®

A Tom Doherty Associates Book
NEW YORK

THE GUTBUCKET QUEST

Copyright © 2000 by Piers Anthony Jacob & Ron Leming

This book is printed on acid-free paper.

A Tor Book
Published by Tom Doherty Associates, LLC
175 Fifth Avenue
New York, NY 10010

www.tor.com

Tor® is a registered trademark of Tom Doherty Associates, LLC.

ISBN 0-312-86463-9

First Edition: May 2000

Printed in the United States of America

0 9 8 7 6 5 4 3 2 1

The
Gutbucket
Quest

1

. . . the blues transcend conditions created by social injustice; and the attraction is that they express simultaneously the agony of life and the possibility of conquering it through the sheer toughness of spirit.
—Ellison, *Shadow and Act*

Born for the Blues (G-flat minor)

Some folks are born with a soul full of trouble,
And some are born just too poor to choose,
Me, I know, my time is on to comin',
'Cause this boy here was born for the blues

My daddy left before my life was seen,
My momma saw me as one more way to lose,
Doc said, "This boy a-comin' in blood and screams,
I know this here boy was born for the blues."

Poor man got no justice and rich man got no heart,
If you find somebody lovin', life tears you right apart,
When you just sit there a moanin', then you know you got to
  choose,
'Cause that's when you know you was born for the blues.

Folk say the road to hell is paved with good intentions,
But a poor man got no time to pay that much attention,
When you have to fight to live you either die or lose,
But you have to keep on fightin' bein' born for the blues.

The main color of the creek was green. Willow thickets closed and hid much of it, the water making only a small, narrow tunnel through the thin, knotted leaves and branches. Clumps of cottonwood grew spaced apart all up and down the bank, and catclaw bushed out in any place that wasn't filled with something else. Nature, Slim Chance thought, was odd and wonderful.

One of his first tasks, when he had settled here, had been to build a run of steps down the cliffside to the creek. Shaky, but fundamentally sound, the stairs had held up well, and he smiled as he hitched the guitar up on his shoulder and started down. He got nearly to the bottom, then paused. Something felt wrong, like a memory trying to surface. He started to look up at the sky, but then he knew.

There was nothing at all he could do to avoid or escape the bolt of lightning that exploded from the ground beneath him. It caught him fair and square and blew him up into the air. It hurt like hell, it scrambled his brain and nerves, but he twisted in his flight, trying to make sure the precious guitar was above him, so that he wouldn't land on it and shatter his dreams.

Then he hit the ground. He landed on his back, the guitar clutched to his chest. His head hit hard, and though he tried to avoid it, unconsciousness closed him into darkness.

When Slim woke, he was looking up at an old black man with a mouthful of gold teeth. His face was metallically black in the sunlight and he was smiling broadly, compassionately.

"What the—!" Slim mumbled.

"You all right, son?" the man asked him.

"All right?" Slim answered. "No, I don't think so."

"Why? Is you kilt?"

"No," Slim said. "I think I may be maimed, though."

"What about that guitar?" the old man asked. "Is that okay?"

Slim, becoming more and more conscious with every word, sat and held the guitar close, examining the body and neck. No new dents or scratches, and the neck was straight and tight; it hadn't been hurt.

"Yeah," he said. "Yeah, s'okay."

"Good, then." The man held out a delicate, white-palmed hand. Slim took it and stood up, surprised at the old man's deceptive strength pulling at him.

"That's a fine-lookin' guitar, son. I bet it plays real nice, too. You mind?"

Before Slim could object, the old man took the guitar out of his hands and proceeded to play the slickest, cleanest, smoothest B-flat blues riff Slim had ever heard. Even without an amplifier, he could tell it would sound true blue and beautiful as hell.

"Whoo," the old man huffed. "That maple neck's right nice. Never cared for 'em my own self, but you got a good one. Put some work in on it I 'spect."

"Wait just a damn minute," Slim said, frustrated. "Who the hell are you?"

The man laughed, his gold teeth flashing in the sunlight. *Sunlight?* Slim wondered. *What had happened to the storm?* The one whose lightning had launched him here.

"Me?" the man said, holding out his hand to be shaken. "Progress is my name. Progress T. Hornsby."

Slim took the proffered hand. "Pleased to meetcha," he said. "Did you see what happened to me?"

The man scratched his head. "Well now," he said. "I did and I didn't, you might say. Ain't sure atall. I was just goin' back to the house and *bang!*, there you was, flyin' through the air off my stairs, holdin' that there guitar."

"Yeah, I—hey, wait a minute. *Your* stairs? No, man, those are *my* stairs. I *built* those!"

Slim turned to point to the stairs, but they weren't there any longer. Instead, he saw a flight of well-poured concrete steps blended into the bank of the cliff. "What the hell?"

"Look here, son. I gots me a feelin' about you, somethin' I purely likes. Whyn't you come on up the house with me. I think you're more hurt than you maybe thinks."

"Yeah," Slim said, quietly. "Sure, whatever. Thanks."

He followed Progress up the steps, jumping up and down on each one, just to make sure they were real and not the product of his scrambled brains. He'd almost started to feel halfway normal when they got to the top of the trail and he looked down at the house.

"No," he moaned. "Oh no, that can't be."

It was like his house, but it wasn't. The shape was the same, but the adobe walls had been stuccoed and painted sky blue. Bricks had been laid in the walkways and instead of raw dirt and weeds for a yard, there was grass and a small garden. The deep wash in front of the house was filled with water and a quiet pump connected the water to the house. And there were real oaks surrounding the house. Not small, new oaks, either, but mature, double-trunked oaks that cast shade in all the right places.

"I do not *believe* this," Slim said.

"Believe what, son?"

"This was my house, man. I mean—it was before I went down to the creek and the lightning got me. It was nice. Well, it wasn't, but it was *gonna* be. I hadn't finished it. It was just adobe. No real yard or anything. No trees except for a few cedars. No pond. But this was just the way I thought I was gonna do it. Just like this."

Progress looked at Slim closely, looked deeply into his eyes, at his confusion, but he remained silent.

"Progress—"

"Yeah, boy?"

"*Where the hell am I?*"

"I ain't at all sure that's a question I can answer, son. But as far as *here*, you're at my house." Progress pointed south over the hill. "Over there, that's the city of Armadillo. And all this here is a part of the great nation of Tejas."

"Nation?" Slim said weakly. "Tejas?"

"Yep. Problem with that?"

"Oh no. No problem. Just that before I walked down to the creek, that city was called Amarillo, and this was the state of Texas."

"Texas?" Progress said. "What's it in a state of?"

"The United States."

Progress laughed. "You're foolin' me, ain'tcha? The United States? That's just a little ole country clear on over to the east coast. Nowhere near here."

Slim opened his mouth to say something, but nothing intelligible would come out of his tightened throat.

Progress laid a gentle hand on his shoulder. "Son," he said, "come on down to the house. They's somethin' happenin' here, but I don't know what it is."

Progress led Slim down the trail, through the yard, to the house. They went through the painted front door. The jarring, the dislocation, was total. The house was just enough like his own to throw his sense of existence completely out of whack. The walls were plastered and painted a clean white. Instead of the dirt floors he was used to, there was concrete and thick, brightly colored rugs. The furniture was wildly varied in style, but all of it was good stuff. Though different, a stereo and TV cabinet stood in the same place he was used to. There was a big, handmade table against the same wall he'd had his own. A different collection of stands and guitars stood beneath the same window his guitars had stood under.

"Nice," Slim said, trying hard not to act nonplussed. "It must have cost you a little bit to fix it up like this."

"Mmmm. Wouldn't have cost so much, but I did most of the work myself."

That made Slim laugh. He was overly familiar with the costs of self labor.

"That's better," the old man said. "You maybe got a hard shot here, but long as you can laugh I 'spect you be okay."

"Oh, man, Progress. This can't be happening. But it *is* happening. What am I gonna do?"

"What you mean, son? Do about what?"

"This isn't my house. This isn't even my whole world, I don't think. I don't know if I'm dead or crazy, but this just isn't where I should be. Where do I go? What do I do? I got a life I gotta try to live!"

"You any good with that there guitar?" Progress asked.

Slim shrugged. "Sometimes I think I am. Sometimes I feel like I'm not for shit. Depends on the day."

"Yessir, I hears that. We all like that. But do you have it inside you?"

"I think I do."

"Shore, son. I thinks maybe you do, too. I see me a man flyin' through the air, more careful about his guitar than his own ass, that there's a man I think maybe got hold of somethin' and tryin' to find out what it is he's holdin' on to. So I tells you what. You just come on and lives here with me awhile."

"Really?" Slim smiled. The offer, and the old man, made him feel better than he'd felt in a while, not just since the lightning, made him feel mighty good inside.

"Oh, shore. Look here, it gets pretty danged lonesome out here all alone. And I guess it's about time I took me on an apprentice. I ain't gettin' any younger, or so they tell me."

"Apprentice?" Slim was puzzled. "Apprentice to what? What do you do?"

Progress moved to the kitchen, not answering. He filled two glasses with ice, and then with brown-gold sun tea, and brought them back into the living room, handing one to Slim. Then he laughed. It was a deep, throaty sound that carried an honest joy. It had been a long time since Slim had felt so welcomed or liked by another human being.

"That's right," Progress said. "I forgot you ain't from around here. I s'pose you needs a proper introduction."

Progress walked to the stereo cabinet and turned on the power to the receiver and the turntable. He pulled an album from the shelf, pulled the disk out and placed it on the turntable. The needle hit the grooves and a raucous, sexy, beautiful twelve-bar blues song came from the speakers.

"Well, I woke up this mornin', to a rattle in my bed,
Said I woke up this mornin', to a rattle in my bed,
It was the loose shell blues, runnin' all round my head."

The voice was what Slim thought of as whiskey-soaked, full of the kind of pain and sorrow only the blues expressed. The electric guitar accompaniment was loose and slick and dirty-good, like a heat wave.

"Well, I shook and shivered, till I nearly cried,
Yes I shook and shivered, till I nearly cried,
Tighten me up, mama, give the good man a try.

My bones may rattle, but my mind is tight,
Say my bones may rattle, but my mind is tight,
And if I know one thing, it's where I am at night.

They tell me not to be impatient, every dog will have its day,
Say don't be impatient, every dog has its day,
But with these armadillo blues, I'm runnin' every which a way.

People talkin' 'bout hard times, tell me what they all about,
Talkin' 'bout hard times, tell me what they all about,
Hard times don't bother me, I was there when they started
out.

I been boobin' it and noobin' it, I can tell by the way I smell,
Yes boobin' it and noobin' it, I can smell that smell,
So come here, mama, put some oil on this here shell. "

It was a straight twelve-bar blues in E, but it went a long way down the road, was almost exactly what Slim himself wanted so badly to play.

The record went on to a slow blues and Progress motioned Slim over to the stereo cabinet, to a shelf filled with a short row of albums. Slim started pulling them out one at a time to look at them. *Fat Tuesday, Livin' Blue, Hook and Line, Two Finger Blues, Standin' Hard,* album after album. He counted: there were thirty-seven and Progress' name was on all of them.

"Wow!" Slim said. "You're a star. I mean—you must be a star."

Progress shook his head, smiling. "Some folks say so," he said. "I expect it's maybe true if I sit down and think on it. But it ain't what I thinks inside me. I ain't sayin' I don't enjoy it. I do. But here, where I live, I'm just an old man been around a while. Time has a wonderful way of cutting away the trivial, and you gives a person long enough, they can get to doin' most anythin'."

"But you're great!" Slim protested.

"Oh, come on here, son. You ain't listened to but a couple of songs."

"No, it's there. I can hear it, feel it. You're playing what I'd about give my left nut to be able to play."

"Come on, now. I bet you could play it without havin' to give up any body parts."

"Yeah, sure," Slim said. "I could play it. I can do okay. Technically I'm okay. But the feeling isn't there for me, somehow. I'm missing something."

"Well, son, like I said, you just stay on here with me for a while, I'll do my level best to teach you what I know, and we'll see can't we do somethin' about whatever it is you think you missed."

"Really? I gotta tell you, I'm pretty much a total idiot sometimes."

Progress laughed and clapped Slim on the back. "We all is, son. Every damn one of us is idiots in our own way and time. But you can learn to get beyond it most times. You stay on here. Like you say, you gots no place else to go to, so you just makes yourself at home."

Then Progress made Slim clean up and rest for a while, because he was dirty and bruised from the lightning strike and his fall. It was clear that the man didn't think any less of him for it, and indeed, was intrigued by the manner of his arrival here, but knew that Slim needed a bit of time alone, just to get his head halfway together.

And while Slim washed his face and arms, and brushed off his clothing, he thought about what had happened. He realized that he had somehow changed worlds, but had no notion how or why. So he forced himself to focus not on the moment of the strike, but on the hour before, when things had been normal.

2

*. . . I want to suggest that the acceptance of this
anguish one finds in the blues, and the expression
of it, creates also, however odd this may sound,
a kind of joy.*
—James Baldwin, *The Uses of the Blues*

It all began on one of those blistering days when the Texas plains
pant like a dying coyote, when the red dust lies heavy and the air
seems to scorch the flesh it touches. The white colleechee road
lay like a straight wound through the grass and mesquite green on the
hillside. Slim Chance walked slowly down the slope to the unfinished
adobe house he chose to call home.

Slim was, perhaps, average. Yet, there was a certain distinction
about him. He was nearly six feet tall, but chubby, so that in actuality
he appeared shorter. His gray-smeared brown hair reached to the
middle of his back, matching the swiftly graying beard that hid much
of his face. Metal-framed glasses, sad gray eyes and a particular swing
or sway to his walk were details that added up, in some definitive way,
so that an observer, seeing Slim for the first time, would say, "There's
a child of the sixties. An artist or a musician. Whatever, a misfit." And
the observer would be right. The only detail missing was the thinning

hair, or even the baldness that Slim had escaped, unlike so many of his contemporaries.

It was another day with no mail, no messages, no communication. A very dissatisfying sort of day, so Slim walked and studied the well-known side of the road, hoping for a glance at something new. A snake, a dust-brown tarantula, a bright wildflower, anything out of the ordinary half-mile sights he saw on his daily walk to the mall and back.

He took the walks, though his nature was to drive even the short distance, because he told himself it was good for him. If he could lose weight, he could have a better shot at getting work. No one loved a fat musician. Not out in front, anyway, where Slim wanted to be. He'd been there before, back when. But he'd been young and pretty, back when. Life and time and sadness had served to rob him of the strong, clean lines of face and body he'd once been blessed with. So he walked, waiting for the fat to go away, playing his guitar, planning, working when he could.

But he hadn't had a gig in more than a month. Even the welcome, if infrequent, royalty checks were getting thin. It just didn't seem to be the season for the blues. Not for playing them, at least. So he'd spent the empty time studying the wild Texas plains environment, trying to soak it in, make it a part of his playing, as if just by being there he could turn its existence into a sound, a style he was looking for.

He'd come to the plains first in winter, dug in against the chill and the snow and constant brownness. It had been worth the wait and the trouble. Spring hadn't sprung, it had exploded. It had been as if he'd woken up one morning to a world turned suddenly green. The land had been more alive each day that passed. The mesquite, the salt cedar, the cottonwoods and willows grew from skeletal barrenness to startling verdancy.

Quail hunted small prey in his front yard and the Godawful ugly crane that lived up the creek flew close to the house. Horned toads scattered from the paths his feet took. Millions of ants built their sand castles in the red dirt, hauling what were, to them, massive pieces of wood and branch to cover and conceal the entrances. The tarantulas were comfy in their holes awaiting unwary beetles whose empty shells were scattered on the excavated dirt like wilted lettuce leaves on a midden.

It wasn't until later, near summer, that Slim had seen the glittering black tarantula wasps that preyed on the beautiful, dignified spiders. They were flying black widows, parasites, poisonous and evil, in Slim's eyes. Over the course of the season, he had rescued several paralyzed tarantulas from their hideous fates, from the devouring wasp larvae.

His cat, Minnie, had, in her proper time, climbed up onto his bed at two o'clock in the morning, clambered onto his lap, panting, and presented him with three grandkittens. Then, once the kits were weaned, she had run away. Even the stupid-looking snake he had found and played with had escaped and was living behind the stereo cabinet where it seemed content to stay, maintaining a curious, uneasy truce with the rambunctious kittens.

Slim was most fascinated by the wolf spiders, the friendly, beautiful, fearless wolves that lived in nearly every window, nook and cranny of the house. He loved spiders, always had, but the wolf spiders were almost like a species apart from any others he'd known. They were frighteningly intelligent and, from observation and testing, he knew they had eyes that could see movement, at least up to ten feet away. He'd watched their stillness as they'd watched flies, their slow creeping and stalking, the massive leaps and pounces when moves were finally made on the unknowing flies. And he'd watched them eat, daintily, unselfconsciously, wondering at their sentience. They were the only spiders he'd ever seen that stalked and hunted, and he wondered if that activity was the cause of their obvious intelligence.

Slim had been absurdly excited when, one day, he'd spied a reclusive newt scurrying across a bare patch of dirt. And he'd been delighted, on his frequent walks down to the creek, to usually find an old box turtle or two to say hello to and pass a little time with. He was thrilled the first time he'd seen a dozen or more Fuller's hawks on their wild mating flight, and there was a deep contentment in witnessing the high, silent flight of the eagle that lived in the rocky cliff down the creek.

He knew that when outstaters though of Texans, his part of Texas, they thought only of dust and desolation, rednecks and rifles, oil wells and Alamos and flags. He'd been surprised, himself, upon moving there, unprepared for the wild beauty, the hundred-mile horizons. He'd also been unprepared for the savage glory of the Texas lightning storms, the rumbling travel of the thunder.

He'd moved to Texas to play the blues. Not the popular blues; homogenized, synthesized and zombilized. The real, down-home, gutbucket blues that caught hold of the primal skill and power the blues could hold in the right hands. But, in his ignorance of Texas, he'd ended up in a place so blue it didn't even have a blues scene, didn't have any respect for the music or the players.

"Damn!" he said out loud, tossing a rock down the road as he turned into the driveway of his house. "I wish I could get inside something for a change. Wish I could find a way just to play the music."

He truly didn't think he was asking so much. It had been so easy, back then, in the old days. It had come so fast he hadn't even had time to realize what was happening. He'd started the band in high school and, after graduation, had quickly gotten recording contracts, money and fame. They'd been San Francisco's own bad boys, even in the wild days of the sixties. Managed by a Hell's Angel, they'd been said to have the longest hair, the biggest amps and the baddest attitudes in the business. Named after a kind of LSD, they were the loudest band in history. Their first album had been recorded on a pier, the studio unable to contain the chaos of the blues they'd played. The only band to have been barred from the Fillmore for excessive volume, people said the music started shaking their guts blocks away from the halls and arenas.

But the money, the fame, the women had twisted his life and he'd left the business to try to be "respectable." But the women he loved always left him, no matter what he tried or did, and each time his heart broke it let more and more of the hunger escape. The hunger to stand onstage and sway to the music, to climb on the strings and lose himself in the sound and fury. Each crack in his seldom repaired heart let the hunger grow and begin to consume him.

After his last lover had left him—money, as always—he'd started taking side gigs he wouldn't have considered before, getting money together, planning his move to a Texas that had assumed nearly mythic proportions in his mind. A Texas where he thought he could find his blues, maybe even find himself. Perhaps find a love he could hold on to. But the hunger wasn't assuaged and the blues weren't to be found. Slim wanted to feel—well, he didn't know what he wanted to feel. There was just a brightness and a breathlessness inside him that didn't belong and often caused him to feel inept and ignorant.

He wanted to do something grand, something huge and heroic, wanted to pour his feelings, his loves and pains, his life, his small victories and little deaths into the thin silver strings of his guitar. He wanted to touch the magic of the blues and he wanted to love someone who would love him back the same.

But something was missing. There was something he didn't have a handle on. He didn't know what it was, he only knew it was there.

He was entirely alone, except for his animal friends, and he was dying of it, he felt. Twenty-some miles from town, he'd been unprepared for the isolation, the loneliness, the alienation of living that far up the country. Sometimes he wanted to scream from the hurtful need to touch and hold someone, to make love, to have someone else there;

to, for God's sake, *talk to somebody*. It was a summer of dreadful speculations, hopes and realizations. It was a summer of painful discontent and restlessness, a summer of hunger, a summer like no other he had lived.

Once inside the house, back in the coolness, Slim wondered what to do with himself. While thinking about it, he fixed a glass of ice water and petted the cats. He could sit down and work. Groups like Cities in Pain, Boots 'n' Jeans and the Oscars were all waiting with what he visualized as signed, sweaty checks for the songs he was supposed to be writing for them. He had a talent for songwriting that at least helped support his life, but the puerile rock-and-roll material the bands wanted didn't fit the mood he was in. He had, as he often did, the blues.

He loved rock and roll, sort of. But it didn't have the feeling, the emotional content of the blues. Rock and roll could make you dance, but blues could make you sweat. Rock and roll could talk about the pain and joy of loving, but blues could make you feel it. A good blues player could, with just his fingers and strings, express the sound of falling tears, the ripping of a broken heart, the poverty of being alone. A blues player could create the sound of hot, liquid sex, the swing and sway of a woman's walk, the curve of a breast, the tickling laughter of a feminine voice. And Slim hoped, someday, to be a good enough player to begin to find the voices he needed and wanted so badly, the voice it felt as if he'd spent most of his sad life searching for.

The sound of far-off thunder caressed the sky and Slim went outside again to look. Clouds were swiftly moving in, but it didn't look or smell like rain. A dry storm. Good. He went back inside and grabbed the black, maple-necked, Ibanez strat that was his favorite guitar. Then he headed down to the creek.

Slim had a dream. Or a fantasy, perhaps, though it seemed more possible of realization than a fantasy. He wanted to learn to play the lightning and the thunder, to capture on guitar the flash and crack and heat, the instantaneity of a close lightning strike, the rumbling rolling threat of the thunder as it moved from cloud to cloud.

He'd watched the lightning, loved it, studied it with the dedication of a scientist. He felt he knew things about the lightning that no one else in the world could know. Scientists had said for years that lightning actually started on the ground and flashed up to the sky. Most people didn't believe it, not really, and scientists, like everyone else, were too afraid of death to stand out in the light to actually study the phenomenon. But Slim had *seen* it, had truly seen it move upward, reaching to the angry clouds, a fern-frond of light and heat and potential destruction. And he knew, because of the massive Texas horizons, that it wasn't half the time, it really was all the time. Because he knew, he'd seen that lightning started on the ground and arced through the sky to strike downward at the Earth, ten or twenty or thirty miles away.

And he could look up at the giant sky cloaked with black thunderclouds, and he could feel where the next strike would be. It was a kind of magic, he thought. Testing himself, he had once stood within fifteen feet of a massive strikedown. He had felt the unbelievable heat, had been shaken and deafened by the bomb-blast of the sound, had seen, in aftervision, the ball of energy and radiation that had formed for an instant where the lightning had touched and moved through the Earth. It had almost knocked him over, and it had scared the shit out of him.

He could feel the pressure of the clouds above him as he walked down to the creek. Over what he thought were hundreds or thousands of years, the small creek had dug a respectable gully on his side of the bank. It was, in fact, the beginnings of a cliffside. But on the other bank, the land was flat and gently sloping. If one walked a little way down the creek, it took an odd twist and the cliffs grew on the opposite side, so that if one were to travel the creek from beginning to end, cliff and flatland would alternate sides.

And suddenly it had happened: the lightning strike. It had launched him not into death, not into the next county, but into what seemed to be another aspect of reality. And he still had no idea what to make of it.

3

*Blues is like a doctor. A blues player . . . plays for
the worried people . . . See, they enjoy it. Like the
doctor works from the outsides to the insides of
the body. But the blues works on the insides
of the insides . . .*
—Roosevelt Sykes, blues pianist

Progress wasted no time beginning Slim's education. After a ham-and-egg breakfast, he started in about the music and about Slim.

"I don't want to make no big thing of it, but I gots a feeling that you didn't just come here for no reason. Not just by chance, no pun."

"It was dumb luck that that lightning caught me," Slim Chance said. "If I had been walking just a little slower, or faster, it would have missed me. And it was dumber luck that it knocked me here instead of frying me."

"I don't think so. Things like that don't just happen. You came here 'cause you were destined to come here; how it happened don't much matter. And I'm not sure it's good."

"Progress, I swear I never planned this, and I mean no harm to you or anyone here!"

The man lifted a hand, smiling. "I know that, Slim. I know you're innocent. But there's somethin' else, somethin' behind this, maybe making you a pawn, or maybe a decoy duck, and that's what I'm frankly nervous about. Somethin' I don't understand."

"If you feel that way, I'll get right out of here! I'm not looking to bring anybody any mischief!"

But Progress' hand was on Slim's shoulder, firmly. "Don't you budge. Whatever it is, I'll figure it out by and by, and then we'll know what to do about it. But meanwhile, I don't think it's smart to waste any time, 'cause we don't know how much you got to know how fast."

Slim began to feel an apprehension. He had not known Progress long, but already he trusted the man's judgment implicitly. "Just tell me what you want, and I'll do my best. But I hope I can get to play the blues. Really play them, I mean."

"Son," Progress said. "Fore you can rightly play the blues, you got to know what they is."

"I've had the blues," Slim said. "I'm surprised my skin's not purple as much as I've had the blues."

Progress chuckled. "I can see that, son. But havin' the blues and understandin' 'em is two different things entire."

"Okay, so how do I understand them? What do I do?"

"Well, first you got to know that the blues is the facts of life, the true facts of life. The blues is the bone in the avocado, and if you got no bone, you got no avocado. Your quality got to grow from the ways you find to deal with havin' the blues. You can be broke and have the blues, you can be hungry and have the blues. If you has a good woman and she quits you, then you knows you got the blues. There's lots of ways to have the blues."

"My way is that one with the good woman," Slim said. "I have no end of problems with those particular blues."

"Yessir, that's just about the way it is with most men." The broad, golden smile never left Progress' face. As deep a bluesman as he was, as much as he obviously knew about life's pains, he seemed to be in constant good humor.

"Progress," Slim asked. "How do you stay so happy all the time?"

"Well, son, there's folk'll tell you you cain't have your cake and pizza, too. But I've done pretty good for myself, so I've had me about everything I wanted. I got a roof over my head, food to eat, good friends. But I ain't bound to anything except that groove in my heart. See, I loves people, but it's the groove that's happenin' for me.

"The blues is a vital and important thing. It changed my life, and I knows it changed lots of other folks' lives, too. Anybody says otherwise is just a fool talkin' trash. I know what it feels like to be down and alone and, *whoo,* that music got the power to make all that go away."

"Yeah, but how do I get there from here?" Slim asked. He was fascinated by Progress, awed by his playing and his wisdom, but he was frustrated by his own ignorance. "How do I find it and grab hold of it?"

"Way I figure it," Progress said, "maybe that's why you're here with me, now. I means to say, most things don't happen by accident, so you here for a reason, wishin' and hopin' maybe. I don't rightly know. But the blues is somethin' each person got to figure out for they own selves. A player, now, I never seen one yet couldn't use some help along the way to it. So maybe that's why you're here.

"You almost got the blues too hard, almost too sad and unhappy to play the blues. Remember, when you play a blues, when you hear a blues song, don't think the worst of it, think the best of it. 'Cause when I play the blues, I be feelin' good. But it got to come from inside you. Like a musk deer. That deer'll run ass over antlers trying to find out where the smell comes from, but all the time it's comin' from its own self. You got all your scales and chops and such?"

"Yeah," Slim said. "I got the technical side down."

Progress nodded in satisfaction. "Good," he said. "Me, I know the theory and all. Had enough readin' players explain it all to me to get where I understood why this or that works. And that's important, so your fingers know where to go without you havin' to tell em. But I don't think about none of it when I'm standin' up there playin'. I just go from the heart, from the gut.

"You see, son, you gots to understand. Blues is a thread that links experiences. If you listens to a blues player, you're listenin' to their lives. The only things you can take away from that are things that echo in your own life. Other than that, everything falls away. Most folks try to find their own lives. But too damn many people try to hide what their true life is and take on somethin' else. Now you, I don't think you rightly know what your own life is. I don't think you been able to find it, but you ain't took on nothin' to hide that. I think you been sent here to this world from whichever a one you came from so you can have a whole new life to find out who and what you are. You see?"

"I guess so," Slim said. "I don't know where to start though. I can hardly believe any of this is really happening. I don't know *anything* about where I am or what's going on. I just don't know where to begin."

"Right here, son. Don't be gettin' no attitude about any world where you're welcome is better than where you comes from. This here is a hard world. I 'spect any world is a hard world, like any other. It's all in how you walk it, how you talk it, the well of the cuff and the angle of the brim. You gets by the best you can just pluggin' it in, playin' it and shuttin' up."

"But that's all I want to do," Slim protested. "I just want to play the music."

Progress shook his head. For once, the ever-present smile left his face. "Don't whine, son. That ain't pretty. You got what you got. I know you wants to play, I can feel it inside you fightin' to come out.

But I thinks you got you a problem, whether you're here or wherever you came from. Blues got power, mighty power. I think you're scared of that power. I think you're afraid that power gonna take you over, gonna change you and make you a different man than you are. And it will, you know it will, so you back off from it. You run away and the feelin' never gets through you so you can stand up and say what you got to say. But you got to come out from under that shell and start kickin'."

"That may be right," Slim said. "*Something* brought me here, and I can feel it's all tied up in blues. I know there's power in it. The way you talk, the power's pretty big stuff in this world. It's not so much where I come from, but it's there. The only thing is, people that grab hold of that power, it seems like most of them self-destruct."

"You right. It does happen just like that. See, there's a big lie in this business that it's okay to go down in flames. But that don't do nobody no good. I've lost my own share of friends and players, don't think I haven't. Some of us can be examples about goin' ahead and growin'. But some of us don't make it there and end up examples because we got to die. I've hit the bottom a few times my own self, but I didn't have to die. You don't either, it don't always have to be like that. Not everybody goes down. After all, you got me for a teacher. I cain't save you from yourself if you're determined to go down. But I can show you how to sneak up on it and how to stay away from stupid mistakes. You can take on the power and still keep yourself alive, be better for it. But without the power you ain't never gonna find the heart of it."

"But shit, man, I don't even know where to start."

"You starts from where you is. You got no other where to start from. Life is just livin'. Now, I've done me some of that, so maybe I knows a little. You, you still got a lot of life left to live on out."

"Hell, Progress, I'm almost forty."

This generated the biggest laugh in Progress that Slim had yet seen. He blushed, but never felt the man was laughing *at* him. There was only the feeling that the laughter was in delight.

"Son, from where you stands, that may seem a long time, but from where I am, you're still just a kid."

"Just how old *are* you, Progress?"

"Me? Best I can recollect, if my momma and daddy told me the truth, I'm just about eighty-three. Comin' into my prime."

Eighty-three? Slim wondered how long people lived in this world. Progress looked, at most, like a worn fifty or a well-preserved sixty. Nowhere even near the eighty-three years he claimed.

"Yep," Progress said. "I know what you thinkin'. It's the power. It'll keep you young. Long as you understands that young years don't always mean pretty years. Blues power'll lift you right up off your feet. I got to say, though, I am about the oldest old timer left around. I been lucky, I guess."

"Man, I'll say. If that's what blues power is in this world, I have got to get me some."

"Well," Progress said, "don't be breakin' no trace chains just yet. It ain't somethin' that can be 'got.' It's there inside you to be found. Somethin' you got to fight about and suffer under and surrender to. It's there, I feels it. But you got to find it and figure how to get from the inside out. The gettin's gonna be easy for you. It's the right doin' of it and the surrender that's gonna give you the problem." Progress paused, his eyes serious. "You seen cold winters, ain't you, son? And you know how things get all slow and hard? How they break easy when they're froze up?"

"Yeah," Slim said. "Sure, I've seen that."

"Well," Progress said, "people's thinkin's about the same way. You stay hot and loose and play through the changes. But if you get all stiff and froze up, sometimes all it takes is a little push, or a knock and everything breaks apart. I be thinkin' you been stuck for a while. We got to warm up your mind and get you movin'."

"No, I—well, maybe, I guess."

"You see, now? You startin' already, changin' your mind and seein' the truth about it. You be okay."

"Yeah, sure," Slim said. His face looked sad. "Yeah, I'll be okay. I just don't know where I am or what I'm doing here. This isn't my world. I don't know anything here."

"You know who you are," Progress said.

Slim laughed. It was almost a healthy laugh. "Oh, man," he said, still chuckling. "I barely know that at the best of times. I've never been all that sure of who I am. I get to a point where I think I know, and some good-lookin' woman comes along and changes my mind. Hmmm—no matter. Listen, you got a map of this country? The whole country, not just Tex—er, Tejas?"

Progress nodded and went into the back room. Slim soon heard drawers opening and papers being shuffled. He looked more closely around the living room. Actually, like his own version of the house, the living room and kitchen were mostly one large room, taking up the entire front half of the house. They were effectively separated by a counter on one wall and a stone platform on the other wall, on top of which sat a wood-burning stove. He was glad to see that, even in this world, that hadn't changed.

The living room was filled with helter-skelter knickknacks and pictures, but Slim's attention was soon captured by a photograph off by itself, nestled between books on a set of shelves. It showed a young woman with green eyes, caramel-colored skin and very fine, very beautiful curly hair. Her eyes, even in the photo, drew him further and further in, wanting to be lost. Oh, he definitely had a feeling.

"That's my daughter."

Slim jumped at Progress' voice. "Wha'd you say?"

"That there's my daughter, Nadine."

Slim could see a pride in the old man's eyes, could hear it in his voice, as if he'd produced a work of art that had grown beyond him.

"She's beautiful," Slim said.

"Yep, that she is. She's a singer. Pretty good, too. Anyway, here's that map you was wantin'."

Progress handed Slim a folded map. It looked like a *National Geographic,* if they had that magazine in this world. The phone rang and, as Progress went to answer it, Slim unfolded the map and studied the new world he found himself in.

Like the land and the house where he stood, the shape of the country was the same, but the resemblance ended there. Tejas was still the largest state—country?—in what he was used to thinking of as the United States. But it was extended in all directions; down and west into Mexico; up, to the Canadian border; east, eating up half of what had been the south. From the Canadian border, into Central America, right off the bottom of the map, Mexico took up the entire west coast. Much of what had been the midwest was now the second-largest area on the map, the Indian Nations.

The rest of the map showed the east coast, divided horizontally by the Confederation in the south, and a very small United States in the north. Capping all of it was a Canada grown huge and detailless on the map, as if it were a nation of unexplored mystery.

Not Slim's world, indeed. All changed, all different. But there was something deep within him that liked the new configuration. Something in him that said it felt right. That it was more fair, more the kind of world he might like to live in.

4

> *The link between time and space is not lost in the*
> *blues. There is a realization that what is sought*
> *for in space, from North to South, must be sought*
> *for in time, from adulthood to childhood. At first,*
> *perhaps the suspension of movement is our only*
> *glimpse—after all, why travel if the goal is*
> *unattainable?*
> —Paul Garon, *Blues and the Poetic Spirit*

If You're a Viper

Dreamed about a reefer five feet long,
Mighty mezz but not too strong,
You'll be high, but not for long,
If you're a viper.

I'm the king of everything,
I've got to be high before I swing,
Light a tea and let it be,
If you're a viper.

When your throat gets dry,
You know you're high,
Everything is dandy,

Truck on down to the candy store,
Bust your conk
On peppermint candy.

Then you know your body's sent,
You don't care if you pay the rent,
The sky is high and so am I,
If you're a viper.

Progress came back into the living room shaking his head. The ever-present smile had disappeared, replaced by a serious sadness and concern. "That feeling I had about you—it's starting to come clear. I knew there was somethin'."

"Progress, I tell you I mean no evil to any—"

"Come on, son," he said gruffly. "We got to go to town, got to pay some dues."

"What are we doing?" Slim asked.

"We got to see a man. They done stole the Gutbucket."

"*Who* stole *what?*"

Progress was impatient, hurried. "Come on," he said. "Let's get goin'. I'll tell you about it on the way."

He bustled through the front door. Slim followed him out to a beat-up old pickup, the make of which was unknown to him. It started quickly and quietly, and they were soon on the driveway heading for the road.

The well-known side of the road looked much the same. There had been an old, ramshackle, frontless mobile home up the driveway from the house. It wasn't there anymore, but it had been replaced by a ramshackle, frontless house that filled its place perfectly. It leaked, and its wooden sides had been warped and bleached by years of summer sun and winter wind and wet. The land itself was greener, lusher, somehow. There were fewer houses and trailers than Slim was used to, not so many fences. The biggest surprise was the herds that roamed the free range.

"Buffalo!" Slim said. "Hot damn, this is okay." Then he sobered. He knew that something was very wrong, but its nature baffled him. He turned to the old man. "Progress, who stole what? What's the story?"

Progress' hands clenched tightly around the steering wheel. There was a grim look on his face.

"*Vipers,*" he said. "That's who I suspect anyway. Don't know as anyone else'd have any reason to steal the Gutbucket. As for what *that* is, well, it's twenty-two miles to town so I'll tell you the story best I can.

"See, back in the old days, there was a man named Luther Allrose. There was blues, but it was the ole country blues. Luther did a mighty wonderful thing. He invented the electric guitar. Took it to the blues and made a whole new thing out of the old."

Progress sighed deeply, caught up in the tight net of memory.

"I owes a lot to that man," he said. "That's where a lot of my ideas about how to play guitar came from—listenin' to Luther Allrose. Hey boy, I don't know nobody could play sassier than that man. Rosie. That's what we called him. He hated bein' called Luther. There's lots of different blues, lots of different styles, but the first time I heard ole Rosie I thought, *this is it.* Still do.

"It was my older brother first exposed me to the professional blues. We growed up with the blues, you know, but it was just around, what everyone did sittin' out on the porch Juggin'. But my brother, he started bringin' home all these records of Catchin' Vaughn, Sugar Box MaGee, Hound Dog Naylor, Black Bottom McPhail, Blind Black. And somewhere inside all that I ran into Rosie's music. I put his record on and it was unbelievable. All these other folks was playin' the same ole down-home blues we was used to. But ole Rosie, he'd electrified it, and *whoo!*, it was dirty and mean and low-down bad.

There wasn't nothin' else like it. Never had been. And he was writin' new kinds of blues that no one had ever heard before. That man had big mojo, and the people's knowed it good.

"'Bout that same time, I began hearin' him on the radio. I had me this little crystal set and I could pick up WDIA. That was an all-night blues station, and sometimes I could get the all-night stations out of Nashville, and some of the outlaw stations out of Mexico. I'd stick that little tinny crystal set under my pillow and listen late at night. Came a time they'd play Rosie's music a lot.

"I was workin' to the slaughterhouse at that time, so I had me the money to get some parts and all and make me an electric guitar. Just to learn about, you know, 'cause I kept stumblin' on Rosie's records here and there and they'd just make my hair stand on end. I couldn't get enough of him. So I began tryin' to figure out what he was playin', just listenin' to the records at night and kind of feelin' my way around the neck, figurin' out those bends and slides.

"I first seen him play live when I was just a kid. He was substitutin' for Blind Black who was in the hospital. Actual fact, Blind Black was s'pose to be openin' for the Armadillo Jug Band. But when the jug band found out it was Rosie, they insisted on openin' up for him. I had me a gig that night at a little dump called the One Night, on Eighth and Red River, 'bout a block from the police station. There wasn't no cover at this place, just a pass-the-hat situation.

"Anyway, that night someone came over and said, 'Hey, Luther Allrose is playin', fillin' in for Blind Black. You wanna go?' And I got on the microphone and said, 'Ladies and gennemens, I don't know about you, but I'm gonna go see Luther Allrose, and if you got any brains, so will you.' And I just packed up and left. Man, that was a night.

"There was only about seventy-five people there when Rosie played, but every single person was there to hear Luther Allrose, so the groove and the attitude were hot. During the show I went behind a PA stack and stood on a table right beside the stage. I just stared at him, you know. And partway through the show, he takes his mike stand and walks it over to my side of the stage, plants it down and stands there playin' and singin' to me the rest of the night. He didn't know me from a hole in the wall. I mean, here was this skinny little kid, all of eighteen. But I guess I yelled right or somethin', cause he really took a likin' to me. After he finished playin', he walked over to me, handed me his guitar and shook my hand. Said, 'That's yours, boy. I expect you to be playing that the next time we meet.' Then he left. I was stunned, walkin' around holdin' on to that guitar like it was made outta gold. I guess for me, it was. I'll never forget that evenin', though. Wasn't many of us there, but he gave it everything he had.

"Next time I seen him was at this place called Anthone's, down in Arsten. I went there early, carryin' that guitar, right around sound check time so's I could see everything from the get-go. And the first thing he did was, he walked up to me, started pointin' his finger sayin', 'I remember you, about three and a half years ago we met.' He never forgot nobody. Started callin' me by name, tellin' me where we met, what happened and everything, askin' me had I learned to play that guitar.

"Later on, I was out in the audience and he starts talkin' about this little kid, ninety pounds soakin' wet, you know—then all of a sudden I hears my name. He called me up on stage with that guitar, and I thought I was gonna play maybe one song with him. But I ended up playin' with him the rest of the night. It was amazing, you know. Nicest guy I ever met. After that, I just packed it up and he made me a part of the band and started teachin' me. And I tell you, I didn't never see him play but what he didn't *get* it. You'd watch him come alive on that stage and *man,* there wasn't nothin' like it.

"We played around—recorded some. Regular stuff. There was several things that we wanted to do, but they never came down. Just didn't happen."

"Why not?" Slim asked. "And what does it have to do with the Gutbucket?"

Progress shifted uncomfortably in the seat, and Slim could see his hands tremble on the wheel.

"Well, now," he said. "There's the question. Hurts some to talk about, you see? Rosie, well, he was a high flyer and a midnight slider. What we used to call a slywalker. He liked his women and his whiskey and his dope. We all knew it was gonna put him under. Few of us were stupid enough to try talkin' to him about it. But, you see, we'd all seen him when he didn't have none of it, and it wasn't the same. There wasn't no spark in it, like he was a burnt-out light bulb or somethin'. The women and whiskey and dopin', they lifted up his life while they was takin' it away at the same time. And he just up and fell over dead one day. Oh, it was a sad day then, I can tell you.

"Anyways, it surprised everyone, but old Rosie'd left a will and testament. Sort of. The man didn't have nothin' really. Spent his money on the sportin' life. But what he did have, he split up amongst his regular women. What he *did* have, though, was a last request. The man said he wanted his ole tired body to be cremated, but he didn't want no regular burial. Said his life had always been in the blues, and even if he was dead, he didn't cotton to that little detail stoppin' him from playin' on. So he asked for his ashes to be ground up real fine. He'd made up this special plastic compound he'd been usin' to make his guitars, and he said he wanted us to mix his ashes up in a batch of that and then make it into a guitar body. He'd already made up the neck special and all the electronics for it. I guess he'd been ready for it, you know, for a while, thinkin' what he wanted to do. Had it all planned up. So all his friends got together and did what he wanted us to. Once the guitar was made, well, he'd left it in his will that he wanted me to have it. I guess Rosie figured I'd be the one to use it best. Either that or it was his idea of a last joke."

"How long ago was this?"

"Oh, thirty, forty years, I s'pect."

"Why aren't you playing it?" Slim asked.

"Well, that there's hard to explain. I did try to play it for a while. Tried hard. But that thing was just too powerful. Some reason it didn't take to me. A guitar's a thing—it's alive and aware, son. A part of any song you create, your friend and company, sometimes your worstest enemy. It helps shape you into what you'll become. And just like a woman, you got to find the right one, the one that fits into all your curves and bends and matches your mind and your hands and your heart. The Gutbucket, well, it just wasn't right for me. The magic was too strong, too much power."

"So, what'd you do?"

"Well, I couldn't just lay it down. I mean, that was Rosie, sort of. When it was made, the magic took over. I don't know what Rosie *did* makin' it, what he had planned, but it was so filled with power that it became the heart of the blues in Tejas. I couldn't play it—maybe no one can play it. But it seemed like everyone who was playin' was drawin' power from it. We was all goin' to the same well, but we was all comin' back with different water from the heart of it.

"I had to do somethin' to keep it safe, to preserve the heart of the blues if it was gonna be that almighty powerful. I had to have it some-place it'd be appreciated and cared for. So I took it to Charlie's, where we headed now. Friend of mine, name of Orville Wilbur, works there. He's a genius with guitars; makin' 'em, fixin' 'em, settin' 'em up. I knowed he'd take good care of it, keep it clean and intonated and all, so's it'd be in good shape. So's the heart of the blues would stay healthy and strong. He's been keepin' it for me all these years. Now it's done been stolen."

"These—Vipers?" Slim asked. He'd listened to the story, but it seemed hard to believe. All this was about a guitar? A week ago he'd have said he didn't believe in magic, that it wasn't something that could exist. But that was in his world. That was before he'd been blasted into Progress' world. Now, he couldn't be sure what to believe.

"Yep," Progress said, answering his question. "I s'pect it was the Vipers, all right. No one else hardhearted enough to want to do it, not when everyone knows it's the heart."

Slim didn't ask any more questions, though he was curious. Who were the Vipers? He had, though, enough to digest for the moment, so he remained silent, staring out the windows of the truck. But he also wondered exactly what it was that he, Slim, was supposed to have to do with all this. Because surely he did, as Progress said, and even if he meant no harm, he could be part of some larger thing that did mean harm. He didn't like that feeling at all.

They were coming to the outskirts of town proper. The transition was abrupt like that of so many cities wrested out of the desolation of the high plains. One moment they were passing through green and gold open range, and the next they were in the middle of buildings and houses. Stores and businesses passed by, carrying names like Sierra Hotel, Karloff's General Store, Donut Center, "It's a Real Hole," Knuckles Bros. Salvage, Killus' Party Supplies and Novelties, Stop-N-Shoot-'Em, Onan's Gas. The town wasn't that different from what Slim had known, except nothing was the same. There were grocery stores, Laundromats, real-estate offices, all the endeavors that small-town entrepreneurs were prone to attempt. There was, though, no single thing that he recognized from his own world, and, all in all, the streets and buildings were cleaner and brighter than any he'd been used to.

Progress turned down a street that Slim felt he should recognize but didn't, and they quickly pulled up in front of a small yellow building with nothing but a sign that read CHARLIE's.

Progress shot out of the pickup and Slim quickly followed. Once they were inside the building it was obvious what the business was. Hundreds of guitars, of all shapes and sizes, stood belly to back, body to body on racks on the walls and hanging from hooks on the ceiling. Amplifiers crowded the floor and a young, skinny blond boy sat on one in a corner, noodling with a black Danelectro. A flash of guilt crossed his face when he looked up from his playing and saw Slim and Progress walk into the store, but it was quickly replaced by a smile as he put the guitar down and crossed to stand behind the counter.

"Howdy, Progress," he said. "How's it going?"

"Hey, Wanger. It's still goin'. Heard there was some trouble I need to know about."

The kid's face darkened and his eyes turned down. "Yeah, guy," he said softly. "Sorry, You know?"

Progress sighed. "I know," he said. "Orville in back?"

"Yeah. Go head on, he's been waiting for you."

Progress and Slim walked behind the counter and went through a small door in the back wall. They entered another room filled with tables and amplifiers and parts of guitars, both whole and mutilated. A small, sad-looking black man sat on a stool before a felt-covered table, working over an acoustic guitar. His hands were laid on the strings and he was humming to it, vibrating the body.

"Orville?" Progress said.

It had been almost a whisper, but the man looked up slowly. He stood, just as slowly, and seemingly in pain, then walked over to Progress and Slim.

"Howdy, Progress," he said, shaking the old man' hand. "Who's your friend?"

"This is my new apprentice," Progress replied. "Name's Slim. Slim Chance. Slim, this is Orville Wilbur. Best guitar man in Tejas. A wizard of the string and plank and pickup."

Orville shook Slim's hand. "Good to meet you," he said. He turned back to Progress. "Don't feel much like a wizard today," he said. "Not with the Gutbucket gone and all."

"What happened?" Progress asked.

"Damned if I know," Orville replied. "I came in this morning like always. Opened up and came back here to get started working. The back door was all busted up, the alarm was unhooked and the Gutbucket was gone. Just gone. See."

He pointed to an open guitar case. Slim looked. The blue velvet interior was empty. *No,* Slim thought. It was more than that. It wasn't just empty, it was as if its condition expressed the very meaning of *emptiness,* of loneliness and loss, it felt wrong, very wrong, and Slim was surprised when he felt an urge to cry or yell or hit something in reaction to the desolate emptiness that now existed where the Gutbucket had been.

"Vipers?" Progress asked.

Orville shrugged his shoulders. "I guess. I can't say. Don't know anyone else around here that would do it. No one in the business would touch it. No one would take the chance of screwing everything up."

Progress patted Orville on the back; and the man straightened up. A half smile crossed his face. "It's not your fault," Progress told him. "I s'pect it would have happened sooner or later. Listen, you want to go over to Mitchell's and get some chili? I want to stay around for Nadine's gig tonight. Why don't you come on along and have a bowl or two?"

Orville shook his head. "Nah, got work to do. You know me, always got work needs doing. You go on and take care of business. I'll be here if you need me."

"Okay," Progress said. "You call me if *you* needs anything, too, you hear?" Progress turned to leave.

"Yeah," Orville said, turning to Slim. "Nice to meet you, Slim. You hang in there with Progress and you'll go someplace. Come on back in here and see me, too. I do good work setting up and all."

Slim shook the man's hand once more, then nodded and followed Progress back out to the pickup. The old man wasn't smiling.

Slim cleared his throat, then asked, "What do we do now?"

Progress looked at him and let a tiny gold smile interrupt the seriousness. "Now," he said, "we go to Mitchell's Domino Lounge and have us five or six bowls of the best chili you ever ate. Mitchell's, it's kind of a player's hang. All the folks collects there after their gigs, talkin' and jammin' and eatin' that chili. It'll be slow now, during the day. Mitchell don't come in till dark. He stays open all night, you know. You play a gig and then you say, 'We go to Mitchell's. We *know* Mitchell's be open.' Then you have you a bowl of that chili and you knows you straight. People's be eatin' five or six bowls of that chili, one behind the other."

"But what about the Gutbucket?" Slim asked.

"Oh, I ain't forgot about that." He frowned for a moment, and Slim realized that indeed, the matter had not left his mind for a moment; whatever faint cheer there was was despite the gravity of the situation. "But Nadine's got a gig tonight, so we gonna hang at Mitchell's, then we go along to Nadine's gig. After that's over, we'll go back to Mitchell's and talk it all over." Progress sighed deeply as he drove. "It ain't no easy problem, son, and right at the moment, I don't feel like explainin' it to you no more. You just gonna have to be patient with it. Besides," he said, a small twinkle in his eye, "you want to see Nadine, don't you?"

Slim recalled the picture in Progress' living room. Yes, indeed yes, he *did* want to see Nadine. But it was strange. In a way, it was this which convinced him that magic *did* exist in this world. Because, in some way, he'd almost swear he was in love with this woman he'd never met, whose photograph was the only thing he'd seen or touched. It shouldn't be, it couldn't be, but he'd been in love too many times not to recognize the feelings inside him. Yes, he wanted to see Nadine! More than anything else he could think of. And if there *was* magic in this world, maybe for once in his life, it would work for *him*.

5

There is a music which underlies all things. We dance to the tunes all our lives, though our living ears never hear the music which guides and moves us. Happiness can kill people as softly as shadows seen in dreams. We must be people first and happy later, lest we live and die in vain.
—Dr. P. M. A. Linebarger

House Blues (A-flat)

Woke up this mornin', blues came walkin' in my room,
Woke up this mornin', blues came walkin' in my room,
I said, blues please tell me, what you doin' here so soon?

They looked at me and smiled, but they refused to say,
Said they looked at me and smiled, but they refused to say,
I came again, but they turned and walked away.

Blues, oh blues, you know you been down here before,
Said blues, oh blues, you been on down here before,
The last time you was here, made me cry and walk the floor.

Blues on my brain, my tongue refused to talk,
Blues on my brain, my tongue refused to talk,
I would follow 'em down, but my feet refused to walk.

Blues, oh blues, why did you bring trouble to me,
Say blues, oh blues, why did you bring trouble to me,
Oh, death please sting me, take away this misery.

If I could break these chains, and let my soul go free,
Yes if I could break these chains, and let my soul go free,
Well, it's too late now, the blues have made a slave of me.

Later on that evening, after hanging at Mitchell's and talking blues, they drove to the club where Nadine was scheduled to appear. Slim was knocked back, again, to see that they were on Sixth Street, and it was much as he remembered; antique stores, used-book stores, collectible and consignment places. Different names, of course, but still much the same. Cleaner, but the same.

They pulled into the parking lot of a club called Dillard's. In Slim's world it had been a popular spot, called Banger's. He'd even played there a few times, filling in for various musicians who had gotten sick or tired and given it up. It had been a hard-rock and heavy-metal place, and while Slim didn't much enjoy playing the speed riffs, he did enjoy the playing and the crowds.

But in this world, it had turned into a righteous club. They walked up to it, and Slim smiled to see a sign painted on the entryway that said, PLEASE DON'T KICK THE DOOR IN. They walked in, and he was instantly comfortable, at home. It was the smells, the familiar smells of alcohol, smoke, sweat and electricity. The sound of blues rose from the air like steam from raw flesh, and the club was dark and smoke-filled like a good one should be.

Slim looked around at the people. He saw a mixture of black and white faces across all the tables. It was strange for him to witness the easy mixing, though it was exactly what he had always hoped it could be like in his world. But, there, clubs stayed one or the other pretty much, particularly blues clubs. It made him feel good to have come to a world where race, at least, seemed to be a forgotten subject.

It seemed as if everyone in the crowd recognized Progress and had a few words each to say to him, but they soon found a table. Progress slapped Slim on the shoulder and said, "Have a seat, son. I'll go get us a couple beers."

He walked to the bar, leaving Slim to look around the club. The band on stage was playing a slow blues. There was nothing outstanding or exceptional about them. Just a hardworking house band.

Every bar that put on live music supported at least one house band that played when no one else was scheduled. Usually, the bands had a small but loyal local following that brought good enough business to pay the bills, and they were talented enough at comping to be able to back up solo performers the bar managers brought in. Blues was a complex musical form, even though it sounded simple to people who didn't know the inside. But it was built on basic foundations, so that if a performer told a band a song was in I-IV-V in B-flat, a decent player would know it was a twelve-bar in B-flat, E-flat and F. The only thing to do after that was figuring out how to play through the changes, and a good workmanlike player could always find those.

Slim's fingers itched to play, which to him meant the band wasn't coming up to his standards. Progress came back to the table and set two bottles of beer down just as the band kicked into a good version of "You Can Have My Husband but Don't You Mess with My Man." They both listened for a while. Progress tapped his foot on the table leg, and Slim was relieved to hear that, even if the world he was in was different, much of the music had stayed the same. Standards were standards anywhere, he guessed. Still, the music here, in this world, seemed to have more life, more vitality.

"What you think of the band?" Progress asked.

"They're okay," Slim said. "Nothing special. House band?"

"Yep. They don't have much power on their own. It's there, but they don't get to it. Probably wouldn't know what to do with it if they did."

"Progress," Slim said. "I don't really understand what you mean by power. I can hear that the music here is more—more *something* than it is in my world. But I don't get what this power is."

"Well, son, the power of the blues ain't somethin' I can rightly explain. You wait till Nadine comes on for her gig, then I think you'll see what I mean."

The band on stage stopped for a break, slowly moving off to the bar for the free beers and towels the management provided as perks. Progress waved at them, inviting them to the table. They waved back, and one of them, a skinny, dirty-blond, intense-looking man came over.

"Hey, Zarb," Progress said. "Soundin' all right tonight."

The man shook his head. "Nah," he said. "Sound just the same as we always do. Straight stuff, nothin' big. Pays the bills, you know." He seemed to notice Slim for the first time. "Who's this?" he asked Progress.

"Name's Slim Chance," the old man said. "My new apprentice."

"You took *him* on?"

"Yep. What's wrong with that?"

"Nothing I guess. Not with *him* anyway. I'm just surprised." He turned to Slim. "My sympathies," he said. "I'm Zarble Marz."

"Glad to meet you," Slim said, shaking the man's bony hand. "What do you mean, your sympathies?"

"Hah! Progress here, he's had a hard time with apprentices. Or they've had a hard time with him. Hasn't he started teaching you yet?"

"Yeah, but there's nothing hard about it, except maybe my own ignorance."

Marz looked at him in surprise. Then he smiled and turned back to Progress. "Sounds like you caught hold of the right sucker this time, old man."

"He's a good boy," Progress said. "You watch out for him. He'll be comin' along right quick."

The man laughed. "We'll see, we'll see. Look here, I gotta get goin'. Nadine should be about ready to get started." He took a drink of his beer, smiled at Slim, waved and said, "See you." Then he walked away.

Slim was left with a slightly sour feeling. "He always talk to you like that?" he asked.

"Sure," Progress said. "Nothin' to it. He got an attitude, but way down deep he's solid. He just ain't found his groove yet."

"What's he got to do with Nadine?"

Progress raised one eyebrow and studied Slim for a moment. Then the gold smile reappeared. "No worries, son. He plays in Nadine's band, too. And to answer the question you're too scairt to ask, no, Nadine don't have any men in her life at the moment."

Slim blushed, but he was relieved. Was he really *that* easy to see through. And if so, how had it happened? Was it truly possible to be so deeply involved from just seeing a face in a photograph, from just an idea?

"What would you say," he asked, "if I told you I think I'm in love with your daughter?"

Progress laughed loudly, slapping his knee and choking, wiping tears from his eyes. When he'd recovered, he said, "Well, son, I'd say you got yourself mighty good taste but a hunger for danger."

"What's that mean?"

The old man's laughter kept resurfacing. "You'll find out," he said. "The three of us, you and me and Nadine, we're gonna be spendin' a lot of time together till we get the Gutbucket back."

"You have a plan?"

"Plan? No, no plan. An idea, though."

"What is it? Can I help?"

"Don't want to talk about it yet. Just wait till Nadine's with us, so I don't have to repeat myself. As to whether or not you can help with it, that's somethin' we'll have to find out along the way. I got me a feelin' you're a real deep part of it, though." He waved his hand at Slim. "You hush, now. I s'pect it's about time for Nadine. Let's have us a couple more beers."

Progress went once more to the bar for the beers. Slim suspected it was because Progress knew he didn't have any money and didn't want him to be embarrassed. Slim watched him, saw that Progress apparently got the beer on the house. On the way back, the old man stopped to talk with a couple of smiling people, exchanging handshakes and backslaps. Then, he set the beers on the table and sat down. He reached into his vest pocket and pulled out a tightly rolled joint.

"Friend of mine gave me this," he said. "You like smokin' herb?"

"*What?*" Slim said, suddenly panicked. "I mean, yeah, I do. But right, here, in the open?"

"What you mean," Progress said, puzzled. "Smoke it if you like. No big deal."

"Progress," Slim said. "In my world, this stuff is illegal."

For the first time, the old man looked surprised. "*This?*" he said. "This a weed. Grows all over around here. They make weeds against the law where you come from?"

"Yeah, they do. Major bad news."

"Son, that's downright ignorant."

"I always thought so. Hey, wait—you mean it's okay to smoke it here?"

"Sure thing. Light it up and relax. Fall into the groove."

"Progress," Slim said, "I'm liking this world more and more all the time. What about you? You want some?"

"Nope." Progress shook his head. "Don't mistake me, now. I've smoked up more than my share, startin' with Rosie and movin' right along. But nowadays I only smoke if I can't sleep. Puts me right away. So you go on, now, enjoy yourself. Here comes Nadine on stage."

As Slim lit the joint, he could smell the sticky sweetness of it from all around the club. But his attention was quickly captured and held by the small figure that was walking around the stage as the band set up.

She was short, perhaps 5'2", wearing a black leather miniskirt and a purple blouse so sheer that Slim was sure he could see her small breasts through it. When she smiled, hard white teeth met the fullest, softest-looking, most inviting lips he'd ever wanted to kiss. She had thin, to-die-for legs and a small ass that Slim would have sworn was the most perfect, kissable ass that could be found. She was the most perfect woman he'd ever seen, as if someone had taken every feminine quality he'd ever loved and lusted after and put them all in one compact package.

He was oddly surprised, as well. He had never before been attracted to a black woman. Not the way he was to Nadine. But he could almost imagine what her caramel skin would feel like against his hands, how she would smell and taste and move. The desires and unfamiliar emotions that were blasting through him came close to making him holler. He knew he should repress it all, should forget it, or try to. Why would such a beautiful woman be interested in a fat, forty, burnt-out bluesman like him? But he'd always been a fool for women. They broke his heart every damn time, but he could never seem to find the strength to just say *fuck it* and leave them all alone.

Nadine was going to be the worst yet, he could already tell that. He felt as if he'd never been in love before. Maybe, he hadn't, not really. And maybe Nadine would be different. As he finished the joint, he decided that, this time, he would be very careful to try to do the right thing so maybe it could work. After all, if this was a new world, maybe he had a fresh new chance.

Nadine stepped up to the microphone, stood straddle-legged, in control. Slim would have sworn he could hear the crackling of electricity in her movements. Her eyes were closed and she didn't speak. The normal audience noises of talking and laughing and clinking glasses and bottles were absent. Nadine stood ready in a small sea of silence and expectation. Slim was impressed by the control she seemed to hold on the audience waiting for her to perform.

The band jumped straight into "Come to Mama," and it was the absolute hottest version of the song Slim had ever heard. Nadine's voice was low and smooth like the brown flow of Texas sugarcane syrup. It drew him in, reached into his gut and made him want. When the band kicked down on the whole-step grace note from B-flat, Slim felt his heart skip a beat.

The experience of the music was unlike anything he'd ever felt. He'd played music, seen it, listened to music stoned, drunk, straight, and while he made love. But nothing had touched him like this. The club, Progress, everything else in the world had vanished into a haze of rhythm and sound. Only Nadine and the song existed at that moment.

Then, the song ended.

Progress, the club, the rest of the world came back to Slim's sight and consciousness. *"Damn!"* he nearly shouted.

Progress chuckled. His eyes crinkled in amusement.

"Got you, did it?" he said. "That's what I was tryin' to tell you, about the power. And that's just a small taste, a spoonful. Nadine's good, you see, but she don't let it out much. Myself, I think she's about as afraid of it as you are."

The band started up with "Roadhouse Blues," but Slim's attention was on Progress, so this time the power didn't capture him, even though he could feel its pull.

"You mean *I* could do that?" he said.

"Son, I gots me a feelin' you could go way beyond that. Maybe further than me. Don't get lost here, though. What Nadine's doin' seems big to you, now, because you ain't never seen it and knowed what it was you were seein'. And I s'pect it caught hold of you real bad because of what you think you're feelin' about Nadine. There's more to it than just catchin' a person up in the music, though. Way far more."

"But I can learn it, right?"

Progress shook his head and took a drink of his beer. "Nope," he said. "'Tain't somethin' you can learn."

"But—"

"Hold on, son. I told you before, it's somethin' you either got or you don't. You cain't learn it, it's there. Everybody has it, some more and some less. Some peoples can use it, some can't. Most folks don't really want to. It's all filled with risks and chances and responsibilities, you see. You, you got a whole big soul full of it. And you believe me, son. When the time's right, it's gonna all come bustin' right out of you." Progress' shoulders slumped and he sighed. "That's what I would have said," he continued. "Now that the Gutbucket's missin', though, I don't know what's gonna happen. You might not get your chance."

"What do you mean?"

"Well, all the power, it was just sorta runnin' loose before Rosie was made into the Gutbucket. The Gutbucket focused all of it, seems like, gave it a center to work around. You listen to Nadine, now. Get yourself past the power, get to the heart of what she's doin', what the band's doin', and then you tell me what you feel."

Slim listened again. But instead of listening with his heart, he listened with his own musical skills, with his fingers, as if he were the one performing. Nadine was singing a slow, jazzy blues, a train song. Slim let himself get caught by the power once more, let himself fall further and further into the song, reading each change, each note, until he came out the other side and realized Progress was right. The song was *wrong, chaotic.* It wasn't as simple as a mistimed beat, sour notes or getting behind on the groove. It was a sense of being out of place, being lost or confused. Somehow, the joy, the intrinsic lifting quality of the music had gone out of the song. It made him sad, not least because it was happening to Nadine. He could see it on her face as she sang, see that she, too, knew it was wrong.

"You can feel it, can't you?" Progress asked.

"Yeah," Slim said. "It, uh, it *hurts*. Somehow. It doesn't feel good, anyway, like it's supposed to."

"That's why we gotta get the Gutbucket back. Would *you* want to play if you knowed it was gonna hurt like that?"

"I see what you mean. No, I wouldn't be able to stand it. It'd take away all the reasons I want to play in the first place. It'd take away one of the only two joys I know anything about."

"That's it, right there, son. And I know Nadine's feelin' the same thing. I s'pect she'll be callin' me up on stage to play any minute now. Maybe I can part fix it."

Indeed, when the song was finished, Nadine did step up to the microphone.

"Come on up here and play, Daddy," she said. Progress walked strongly up to the stage and took the guitar the lead player handed him.

"Ladies and gentlemen," Nadine said. "What do you call the force exerted on pure nickel-wound strings by one hundred and seventy pounds of muscle, heart and ornery will?"

The audience, having heard the introduction before, answered with a yell, *"Blues power!"*

"I call him my daddy—Mister Progress T. Hornsby."

The audience applauded as Progress stepped up to the mike, noodling on the guitar, getting the feel.

"Muscle, heart and ornery will, huh?" Progress smiled. "People, it's just six strings, three notes, two fingers and one asshole."

The audience laughed and applauded even more loudly.

"I wanna thank my fambly before I start on this here song. Thank 'em for savin' me a place at the table. Okay peoples, work the body, drive for real, eat ethnic and play them blues."

Progress started out slow, picking loose, rhythmic notes up and down the neck, almost like a snake hypnotizing a bird. Then he settled into A-flat and started a single-string swing that the bass player and the drummer quickly picked up on. Once the groove was established, the rhythm guitarist jumped in on the backbeat to give the thing some quick slide and jump.

In Slim's world, he would have said it was funk meeting ZZ Top, but the way Progress did it made it something wholly different, hot, blue and righteous.

After playing with the groove for a while, settling in, Progress made a slight shift to a twelve-bar form and started to sing.

"Hey, hey, hey, hey,
Bullfrog blues is on my mind.
They're all in my bedroom,
Drinkin' up all my wine.

Hey pretty mama, hey pretty mama,
Can't stand these bullfrog blues no more,
They're all in my cabinets,
Hoppin' over my best clothes.

Have you ever woke up,
With those bullfrogs on your mind . . ."

As Slim listened and watched Progress perform, he was drawn deeply into the music, further than he'd ever been before. Progress' age had dropped away and he stood there wide-legged, humping in the air, filling his soul, shaking in the cast-off rags of his eighty-some years, screaming through the guitar. And it was right, it was so right. It felt healthy, and there were images of young girls, playing in the cane breaks, lifting up into the light of a nice summer's day and a young girl's freckled skin pressed against his own.

He looked longingly at Nadine, dancing gracefully near the edge of the stage, looked around at the rapturous faces of the audience, all lost in private dreams and visions, caught up in the power that Progress was weaving with the strings. And there was no sense of wrongness about it, as there had been before. The power was sharp and clean and bright. It cut through everything.

Slim was half-stunned by it, but he was able to get past it. The power affected him, but he was able to keep a part of himself clear and free, able to observe. Then, the song was over and Progress handed the guitar back, walked over to Slim's table and patted him on the back.

"Come on, son," Progress said. "Let's go."

"Go?" Slim asked. "Now? Isn't Nadine gonna sing any more?"

Progress looked sharply at him. "Would you?" he asked quietly. Slim shrugged. "I guess not."

"Nadine knew once I played, that'd be about it for the night. I think she wanted to cut it short's why she called me up so soon. I don't think too many of the good ones gonna be playin' till we gets the Gutbucket back. If it hurts to listen, how do you think it feels to play?"

They left the coolness of the club and went out into the warm summer night, headed for the pickup. Slim saw other people heading for cars and trucks. They walked slowly and had expressions of confusion on their faces. They weren't talking.

"Why didn't it affect you?" Slim asked.

"I was around before the Gutbucket came to be," Progress said. "I already knew the power, how to use it. And, to tell the truth, the Gutbucket's just got too damn much power in it for me. So it bein' gone don't touch me none, leastways, not in any important way. Ain't many like me, though."

Slim thought to himself that that last might be the truest thing he'd ever heard. "Where do we go, now?" he asked.

Progress started the pickup and backed it out of the parking lot. "Back to Mitchell's," he said. "Nadine'll meet us there."

6

*Appreciation of this accursed tradition . . . can
only enhance the contemporary appreciation of the
blues. For the blues singers belong to the same
heroic company. Their work . . . is emblazoned
with all the colors of the future. Held in check by
the repressive forces of the past, they are reborn
today in the fever of our wildest dreams. They are
anticipations of that which will be.*
—Paul Garon, *Blues and the Poetic Spirit*

Boogie and Yowl (A)

*Just got a bellyful of boogie and yowl,
Now I'm flyin' like an ole night owl.
That hot blue rhythm got ahold of me,
I gotta live, I gotta be free,
Nothin' takes it to you and lays it down,
Like gettin' you a bellyful of boogie and yowl.*

*Boogie and yowl, boogie and yowl,
The land of Tejas is on the prowl,
Kick it in and kick it out,
Boogie is a thing you can't do without,*

So if you wanna take it with you when you go,
Boogie and yowl is the thing to know.

    I knew a woman, a real good pal,
She had a bellyful of boogie and yowl,
A real good woman, she drank with the men,
And when she loved you would come again,
She put it all together in the strangest way,
Talkin' boogie and yowl till her dyin' day.

    Boogie and yowl, boogie and yowl,
The women of Tejas are on the prowl,
Slide it in and slide it out,
Boogie is a thing you can't do without,
So if you wanna take it with you when you go,
Boogie and yowl is the thing to know.

    So if you wanna get it all right now,
Get yourself a bellyful of boogie and yowl,
Break it up and shake it up and let it all go,
There ain't a thing about lovin' you won't know,
Everybody's lookin' for a real good ride,
Boogie and yowl gets you deep inside.
Boogie and yowl, boogie and . . .

Mitchell's was more crowded in the darkness of the night, tables filled with black and white faces in deep conversations, the sound of soft guitars jamming in the corners and back rooms, dishes and odors of cooking seasoning the air. But Slim and Progress were left alone at their table. Progress was eating his way through a spicy, green bullet, snake and harp, South of the Border concoction, smacking his lips and liberally pouring an even greener sauce over his plate. Slim worked on a meal he thought of as more normal, a cheeseburger. They weren't talking, just eating and waiting for Nadine who, at that moment, walked in, hair and breasts bouncing and causing Slim to miss the bite he was ready to take from his cheeseburger.

She kissed Progress on the cheek. "Hi, Daddy." She pointed at Slim. "Who's this fool?"

"Hey, girl," Progress replied, "you ain't so big I cain't whoop your butt, so you put a hold on that mouth. This is Slim, my new apprentice."

Slim was, frankly, staring at her wide-eyed. She arched one eyebrow, then the other as she checked him over. *Wow,* Slim thought, *a woman who can make an M with her face.*

"Him?" she said. "Why him?"

"What's wrong with me?" Slim asked softly. "Why is it every time Progress tells people I'm his apprentice, everybody says, *'Him?'*"

"It's that long hair and that look on your face," Nadine said. "You look like you died a year ago and haven't had the guts to lie down."

Slim hurt. But, at the same time, he wanted to smile. At least she'd noticed him.

"Shut up, Nadine," Progress said. "Wouldn't hurt you none to be a little more like him."

Nadine laughed. Slim thought it was lovely. "You want me to be more like him?" she said. "Fine, schedule the lobotomy."

Progress sighed. "Nadine," he said, "I'm not gonna bust your ass, but you and me, we're gonna have us a little talk later on. The boy's had a hard time, so you let him be."

Slim knew Progress was serious, but he wondered how much, seeing the old man's cantankerous, mischievous laughing face. It seemed to make a difference to Nadine, however.

"Okay, Daddy. What do you need? What's the prob?"

Progress told her about the Gutbucket.

"Man," she said. "I knew something was wrong when we tried to do the gig and it soured. I didn't think it was that bad, though. I just thought it was me. What are you going to do?"

"It ain't a matter of what am I gonna do. It's what *we're* gonna do. I s'pect you and me and Slim better stick together."

"Why him?"

"Look here, girl. He's a part of it. You just accept that. I'll explain it to you later on at home. My home, if you can manage to be free to stay out there with us."

"Sure, Daddy," Nadine said. "That's no problem. But what then?"

"I guess we'll all three go to see T-Bone. Not that I s'pect it to do much good."

"Who's T-Bone?" Slim asked.

Nadine was about to say something snappish, but Progress laid his hand on her arm and she remained silent while Progress continued speaking.

"T-Bone Pickens. The man. I s'pect he's the bad guy in all this. The newspapers call him an industrialist. I got other names for what he is. He started out wantin' to be a player. But the boy just never could get no handle on it, so he started makin' money other ways— buyin' up property, startin' businesses. Now he owns the helium mines, the beef processing plant, the power company. I swear, sometimes I think the man owns about everything in Armadillo. Maybe half of Tejas if you believe the stories people tell."

"What does he have to do with the Gutbucket?" Slim asked.

Nadine couldn't hold it in any longer. "Daddy!" she said. "This fool's about smart enough to get out from under a falling tree. Why are you telling him all this stuff everybody already knows?"

Slim blushed and felt about as incompetent as he'd ever felt in his life. He knew that, maybe, he wasn't all that likable, but Nadine made him feel incredibly stupid and he knew he'd do about anything if she'd just be nice to him.

"Hush up, girl," Progress said. "Slim ain't from around here. He don't know anythin' at all about all this except what I already told him."

Nadine looked at Slim with what seemed to be interest. "Sorry," she said. Slim could see it had been a struggle for her to say it, but it made him happy just the same.

"T-Bone's head of the Vipers," Progress explained. "Or maybe that's not quite it. The Vipers are his, they're his boys, do all his dirty work. You see, T-Bone lusted after the power. He didn't want it for the blues, he wanted it for what he could do with it. Some people are like that with the power, wantin' it for its own sake." He shook his head sadly. "That's real wrong," he said. "That kind of wanting twists people. It did T-Bone. He couldn't get his power from the blues, so he's gettin' it with money and machines and fear. Truth is, like I done said, the sumbitch owns about everything around. And if he don't own it, people just like him do. They ain't so bad, though. They're greedy, but T-Bone's the only one trying to get the power. The thing is, no matter how much money and machinery and property he gets, he ain't never happy with it. He wants everything. He's still bitter, you see, about not havin' the blues. So he can't be happy if people are free just to play and enjoy the blues, he wants to control it. Wants it to be done *his* way. It ain't exactly that he's a bad man . . ."

Nadine laughed and said, "Shit!"

"No," Progress continued. "Truly. He thinks what he's doin' is good and right. But he cain't see that it ain't the good and the right that anybody but him wants. That never seems to matter to him, anyway. He wants all the blues folks to make it into some big business, industrialize it. He don't know that goes against everything the blues is about, that it would kill it. And we all know that he's the only one would make any money on it, and if there was someone he didn't like, well, they just wouldn't find no place to play, 'cept on their back porch, if he didn't own that, too."

"Could he do that?" Slim asked.

"I s'pect he could—with the Gutbucket. That there ain't a thing to be messin' with. It's like a bomb, waitin' to blow if it's handled wrong. I don't have no idea atall just how much power that thing's got inside it. It could destroy him, I guess, but it could back up and destroy us at the same time. That's why we got to go see him, try to reason things out with him."

"Daddy," Nadine said. "You know you can't reason with that man. He hates you more than anything."

"Why's that?" Slim asked.

Progress looked a little abashed. "Years ago, when he was just gettin' started, I thought I saw something in him. Took him in as my apprentice and tried to teach him. When I finally had to tell him he wouldn't never be no good, he took it real hard. Other folks tried to tell him the same thing, but it's me he blames and hates for it. The boy never was too awful big on carryin' his own load."

"So what do we do if he won't listen to you?" Slim asked. Nadine pleased him by agreeing with his question and nodding her head.

"I don't think he will listen," Progress replied. "But I got to try. What I think will be, is that we'll set us up a big blues festival out at the Canadian River."

"What good's that going to do?" Nadine asked.

"Think about it. That man's wantin' to spoil the heart of the blues. Now, you just know if a bunch of us gets together for a festival, he's gonna be out there with the Gutbucket tryin' to make it turn bad. That's when we'll go after it. We just got to get the right folks to set it up and the right people to play. Remember, it's the early worm what gets eaten by the bird. We gots to trick him."

"Won't he try to stop us?" Slim asked. "He doesn't seem like the kind of man who would let it go down that easy."

Nadine reached over to Slim's plate and grabbed a handful of french fries. The unconscious familiarity pleased him immensely. And when she looked at him and smiled, he almost wished for a tail to wag to show his pleasure.

"I didn't say it wouldn't be dangerous," Progress replied. "But we gotta do it. We got to go after the people we need, personal like. He's liable to go after them, too."

"Who are you thinking of?" Nadine asked.

"Elijigbo and his bunch. Belizaire, Mother Phillips, Sonny Early, folks like that."

Nadine whistled. Slim thought it was a beautiful noise.

"The big guns," she said. "You aren't fooling around, are you?"

"Cain't afford no foolin'. We needs the power, need people he cain't touch with the Gutbucket."

"Are all these people old timers?" Slim asked.

"Nope," Progress said. "Some are, but, see, there's some folks got their own way of power. Had it all their lives, before they came to the blues. So the Gutbucket don't touch 'em much one way or the other. That's what we need."

"Any rock and roll people?"

Progress and Nadine looked at him in puzzlement, saying, nearly in unison, "Rock and roll?"

"Yeah," Slim said. "Come on. Elvis Presley, Chuck Berry, Little Richard? You know."

"No, I *don't* know, son. Never heard of 'em, or of, what is it— rock and roll? I seem to remember a skinny kid named Chuck Berry or somesuch, 'bout twenty years ago. But he couldn't play worth a nickel and he wrote weird songs about cars, so he didn't last long at all. What's rock and roll?"

"I'll tell you about it sometime," Slim said. *Damn!* Every time he started to get comfortable in this world, something got knocked loose or turned up missing, different. He enjoyed rock and roll, sort of, sometimes. How did the blues keep from evolving into rock and roll in this world? Was it the racial equality? Had it prevented ghettos and doo-wop singers? He didn't know enough to even think about the causes. On the other hand, if it wasn't here, maybe he could "invent" it right. That would be something, for sure.

Progress stood up. "You finished eatin' Slim's food, Nadine? About time to head home, I'd say."

Nadine blushed and threw a couple of uneaten fries back on the plate. Then she stood. So did Slim, following after her as she followed Progress out the door to the pickup.

"You sit in the middle," she said to Slim. He did, and she got in after him and hung her arm out the open window.

As they drove the dark road to the house, Slim didn't know if he was in paradise or being tortured. If so, it was a sweet torture. On one side of him sat a man who was becoming a hero, a teacher, a father fig-ure he'd never had, with his smells of honest sweat, beer and blues. On his other side sat the woman he was now sure he was irretrievably in love with. Her leg was pressed tightly against his, and he could smell a slight perfume, the odor of her hair, a sweat and woman smell that reached right into him. When she reached into the center glove-box, her breast brushed his bare arm. He could feel the summer night sweat and the large, erect nipple like a shock. Forty-year-old men were not supposed to get instant erections, but Slim had never been quite normal and he realized he had. It made sitting unadjusted rather uncomfortable, but Nadine didn't seem to notice.

She lit up a joint and passed it to him as they rode in silence. It was passed back and forth until it was done. Nadine then leaned her head back against the seat and let her left hand rest on Slim's thigh. He didn't know whether to scream or cry, but he did know he wasn't going to move and risk her taking it away. He knew that it didn't mean anything, that Nadine simply expressed an unconscious comfortable-ness, but it had been a long, long time since anyone had touched him with anything nearing affection, and he wanted to enjoy it for the small pleasure it was.

It wasn't that Slim was a bad man, he was just a lousy husband. Any one of the women from his past would freely admit that he was a hell of a nice guy, a great lover. Just about anything but a decent moneymaker. He was a dreamer and he had a weakness for women in pain and need, women who had problems, who hadn't found themselves yet. Sad women. He fell in love with them, and in return, he tried to wake them up, teach them to be strong and independent and sure of themselves. Tried to teach them to be free. Unfortunately, once they'd learned all that, they discovered, as well, that he was a weak man with problems of his own. A man who didn't know how to do much of anything but love, desperately. And knowing how to love didn't support any relationship. So they ended up abandoning him, going on to better, more successful things, leaving Slim with a badly broken heart and a total lack of understanding.

His biggest problem, his secret problem, was the hurt and rage he felt for women. He couldn't understand why they all left him, why they all broke his heart. And, not understanding, he was hurt that much more, and the hurt turned to rage and bitterness. Yet, it all stayed inside him. He loved women so intensely, needed them so desperately, that he had never said a cruel word, never struck a blow, was absolutely terrified to even argue.

Arguing, even expressing his feelings, wasn't something he could do very well. His father had been an alcoholic, a cruel, manipulative man who couldn't stand to be contradicted. And Slim never knew what would be seen as argument. In his home, emotions were stifled, repressed. The failure to do anything but hide and remain emotionless resulted in getting beaten, punished, put down and put out.

So he swallowed his rage, repressed his hurt and anger. Inside, though, was a gentle man who wanted to ask why, why wasn't he worth loving forever? Why did they all hurt and betray him? Why were they always so heartless and compassionless? Why, why, why? He'd never found any answers because, in his soul-deep need to love and be loved, he'd never even think to broach the questions, except inside himself. He just wanted everything to be nice.

But Nadine was different. Slim could tell that she knew who she was, that she didn't need to wake up to anything at all. If he could just do right, maybe he could find a way she could love him. He'd never believed in love at first sight. It had happened to him a thousand times with a thousand women, but he'd always put it down to lust. But here was Nadine, knocking his heart for a loop. He would find a way, he determined. He would find a way if it killed him. Maybe this search for the Gutbucket was the perfect way to prove himself to her.

He sighed when they pulled up to the house. Nadine took her hand off his leg and got out of the truck. He felt a distinct loss as they all went inside.

"You mind sleepin' on the couch?" Progress asked. "Gonna be a little crowded with Nadine here. Only got the two bedrooms."

"Nah," Slim said. "No problem." It looked like a big, comfortable couch, and Slim had slept on worse.

"Nadine," Progress said, "go get some sheets and all for Slim, would you, please?"

To Slim's surprise, she went off into the other room, bringing back sheets and a thin cover, and even put them on the couch without a word. Then she and Progress went into the bedrooms and Slim was left alone.

It had been one hell of a long, strange day. His body and brain were both tired out, so not many minutes went by after he undressed and lay down before he was fast asleep, dreaming of a caramel-skinned woman running beside him in the cane breaks . . .

. . .

It wasn't quite light outside as Progress and Nadine whispered in the bedroom.

"Daddy, why do you want that long-haired fool around here? What good is he going to do you?"

"Don't rightly know as yet. But deep down, he's a good man. You can see it in him, see the boy's been hurt, and hurt bad. But he don't be pushin' it off on nobody else. Just as nice as he can be. There's somethin' shinin' inside him, fightin' to get out."

"But you don't even know if he can play."

"No, now, I do know. I ain't heard him yet, that's true, but I knows. You gots to understand that he came here from a completely different place, holdin' on to that guitar of his like it was more impor-tant than livin'. That there tells me somethin'. Besides, the boy's heavy in love with you."

"Oh, that's great! That's just what I need, some long-haired beat-up old fool sniffing after me like a stupid puppy."

"Give the boy a chance, Nadine. I know right now he don't seem like he's much at all. But he's growin' more than you or he knows. Don't go breakin' him down till you see what it is he can build up to. I know he acts kinda stupid sometimes, but he ain't. He just never learned how to act. And you know he so scairt about bein' in love with you that it's gonna make him that much more stupid."

"I know it. And you know I can't stand it when men act like that."

"Nadine, don't torment the boy. I ain't sayin' you got to put up with nothin', but don't torment him. Be fair. His heart's real break-able. Don't you be the one does it to him. It's a good heart."

"Daddy? Are you *wanting* me to love him back?"

"I'm hopin' you will. I don't wanna force nothin'. Just hopin' you'll find somethin' in him worth lovin'. I think he's the right man for you."

"You know I can get along just fine without a man."

"Didn't nobody say no different, girl. But Slim's the right man for your life. I feels it."

"So what is it you want me to do?"

"Just try to be nice to him. I know that's a hard thing for you to do. I know how you is. But be fair to the boy. He's carryin' a heavy load he don't yet know even the half of. Don't you pile on more weight. Give the boy a chance."

"Okay, Daddy. I'll try. But he'd better find a way to get better, or I'm not going to be able to stand it."

"He'll find a way. I got faith in him."

She looked at him sharply. "Daddy, what are you keeping from me?"

Progress did not pretend to mistake her meaning. "I'd rather not tell you."

"Well, you'd better, if it made you so urgent to put me on to this man. I can just about see that dark cloud looming behind your head."

Progress sighed. "You always could, Nadine. It's the Glory Hand."

"The Glory Hand!" she exclaimed, shocked. "You don't have anything to do with that evil magic!"

"Not by choice, for sure! I found this one in the bathroom. Must've been tossed through the open window in the night. Wasn't there yesterday."

"Who would put one of those filthy fetishes in our house?" she demanded indignantly. "The whole region knows you have no truck with those things."

"That's what bothers me. I don't think it was for me or you. I think it was for Slim. He's from elsewhere; he may not know about such things."

"So he's a nonbeliever, so it shouldn't affect him. So what's the point?"

"That's it: I don't know the point. I don't trust it. Somethin's goin' on here, Nadine, and it concerns this man. But I be not ready to tell him about it yet—not till I know what he knows about hostile magic."

"Point taken," she said thoughtfully. "If it's for him, and he doesn't know it, something strange is going on, and we'd better keep it quiet for now. What did you do with it?"

"I hooked it with a wire and carried it out and threw it in the river. I don't care if it sinks or swims; it's gone."

She nodded soberly. "Who do you think sent it?"

"I don't know, but I think maybe it's another reason it's time we saw T-Bone. Just to let him know we's on to him, or make him think we is."

"And you want me to find out what Slim Chance knows, without him knowing I'm prying?"

"Maybe. But that don't change what else I said. So maybe he has a bad enemy; that don't speak bad for him."

"If T-Bone doesn't like him, I'm getting interested," she said, smiling grimly.

"Don't go lookin' for no wrong reasons, girl, when there's good ones to be had."

"I was fooling," she said.

"Not entirely."

She didn't argue.

Progress went to take a shower while Nadine went into the kitchen to start breakfast. When she passed through the living room, she looked down at Slim, still asleep on the couch. He'd thrown the sheets off and lay there uncovered. She took the time to glance at his body, his erect morning dick, then looked back up at his peaceful face. He was kind of cute, she thought.

7

While the history of the blues is the history of the individuals who perform it, the danger lies in these performers becoming isolated from their richest traditions, and from the people as a whole, resulting in a total fragmentation of the blues.

This, of course, is the tendency of an advanced industrial society, wherein any attempt at creative activity on a mass level is inevitably short circuited and smashed.
—Paul Garon, *Blues and the Poetic Spirit*

Slim woke to the smell of frying ham. He sat up and looked sleepily over the back of the couch into the kitchen, rubbing his eyes. He could see Nadine working at the woodstove, felt the heat of it in the room. She was wearing cutoff jeans and a white T-shirt and she was so pretty that Slim wanted to lie back down and moan.

She turned and saw him looking at her. "Morning," she said.

"Mornin'. What time is it?"

"About eight."

"You always get up so early?"

"Yes, I guess we do. Daddy and I got into the habit a long time ago. It doesn't seem to matter how late we stay up, come six or seven, our eyes open up on their own and after that, it's no use to stay in bed. You hungry?"

"I probably shouldn't be, but I am. Sure does smell good. Where's Progress?"

"He's outside, messing around with the garden and feeding the birds. Get your clothes on. Breakfast will be ready pretty quick, now." She moved back to the stove and dumped a big pan of biscuits onto a plate. She shook flour into the ham grease to make gravy, and her hands were white with it as she poured in the milk and began to stir with a fork.

Slim watched her ass jiggle in the shorts as she stirred the gravy. He was embarrassed. He slept naked, so it was a trick to get his pants on without Nadine seeing him. He managed, looking over his shoulder frequently to see if she was watching him. He got up to go to the bathroom, and when he came back, Progress was inside and three plates of ham, biscuits and gravy were sitting on the big table.

"You want some coffee?" Nadine asked him as he sat down.

"Yeah, thanks."

She brought him a cup and they all sat down and started eating. The ham was sweet and hot, the biscuits and redeye gravy as good as he'd ever had. Slim ate with real relish. It was far better than his own cooking, though he considered himself an excellent cook. There was no talk until the food was gone and the coffee drunk. Only the crunch of chewed food and the slurp of coffee and the scrape of biscuits soaking up the last dregs of gravy off the plates. When they were finished, Progress leaned back in his chair and patted his belly.

"Well, chillen," he said. "We got a busy day, today. I think, first-est, we should go and get Slim some clothes."

"But Progress—" Slim started to say.

Progress waved his hand lazily. "No, son," he said. "All you got's what you got on. Man needs more than that to get by. Now, you go on in and take yourself a good shower. When you're ready we'll go on into town, get some pants and shirts and socks and such. Then we'll go to see T-Bone, see what can we do."

"What do you expect, Daddy?" Nadine asked.

"Truth?"

Slim and Nadine nodded.

"I ain't expectin' nothin' from him. I just want him to know that I know."

"You think he'll do anything to us?" Slim asked. He was scared, but not badly. He'd always been able to take care of himself, martial-arts training had insured that, though he'd never been in an actual fight.

"Not while we're on his property," Progress replied cynically. "Once we leave, though, and while we're on the road gettin' to the people we need, I s'pect he might put a few folks on us."

"How?" Slim asked.

"Don't think he'd try to kill us, though I ain't at all sure of it. That's too easy for him, and it ain't what he wants. He might beat on us, or try to. But you a big healthy boy, and Nadine, she can take care of herself if she got to. I thinks we can stand on our own there. What I'm worried about is how he'll try to use the power against us."

Nadine got up to clear the dishes, as if she didn't want to hear or be part of the discussion.

"I thought," Slim said, "that he didn't have any power."

"Yes," Nadine said from the kitchen. "Just like Daddy doesn't go to the sno-cone stand three times a week to get his horrible frozen pickles on a stick."

"Nadine, now. I likes those. I don't tell you what kind of junk food to eat, do I?" He turned to Slim, a serious look on his face. "He's got power. It ain't blues power, but it's power just the same. He's got the Gutbucket, and he's got all his machines. I don't know how, but he draws power from them machines. And we're at a disadvantage. The magic of the blues is more powerful, more natural, but it's a slow power, like wind and water. His power is quick, like fire. We got to build up, he destroys. Always easier to tear somethin' down than it is to put it up. We gonna have to draw on the deep power, the lightning and the rain, the trees and the land. That ain't nothin' easy. It's why we got to have the right people at the river."

Slim nodded. "I'm gonna take that shower," he said, getting up from the table and going into the bathroom. All the talk of magic and power disturbed him. He'd wished for a chance to play, to be on the inside of something. There'd been a saying in the fantasy novels he'd read, something about not wishing because you might get what you wished for. Well, now it looked as if he'd gotten it. This—it was too far inside to be comfortable. He'd lost his home, his world, everything he owned except his guitar and the clothes on his back. He wondered too, if his kitties were still okay without him.

But there was Nadine, and there was Progress, both as a friend and a teacher, teaching him the true blues. And it looked like, scary as it might be, there was going to be some fun and adventure, as well. Maybe it was a fair trade, after all, he thought, stepping into the shower.

Yet there was something weird and awful too, as if he'd just caught a whiff of a ripening corpse. Something close but faint. He couldn't pin it down, but he felt it right here in the bathroom. Probably his imagination, but—

He was going to ask the others if they smelled anything here, but since he couldn't actually smell anything himself, he let it go. They had enough to do without concerning themselves about spooks he tried to dream up. But whatever it was had sent an ugly chill of horror through him.

Later, driving into town, with Slim sitting by the window this time, he said, "Progress, talk to me about the blues." Maybe that would take his mind off the phantom in the bathroom.

Nadine snorted and elbowed him in the ribs. Progress just asked, "What you want to know, son?"

"Everything. I dunno. What's it like to be a star?"

"*Star?* Son, I'm just another Tejas guitar player. Oh, I got somethin' different to say with my music, I guess. But I have to keep it in its place. It's a gift. It's all a gift, and I have to keep givin' it back all the time or it goes away. If I start believin' it's all my doin', it'll be my undoin'. So I commit myself to doin' the most I can with the gifts I have, so's they can do as much good for as many people as they can.

"Comes right down to the bone," he said, sighing, "I likes to fish. I veg out. Sit there with the line in the water, thinkin' of riffs. It's the most relaxin' thing. I go into my own world and think of lots of riffs. Yessir, pretty soon now, when we get the Gutbucket back and I see you and Nadine gettin' along, I'm gonna pack it up and head down on the Brazos. Do me some *real* fishin'.

"I'll just get in my old pickup, throw some clothes in the back, drive cross country. Get me two good poles and lay down on the fishin' bank. Might could drive my bus, could I ever get the time to fix it. Put a cookstove in it, cook right on the river, catch 'em and cook 'em. That be the life. Course, I'll keep a guitar or two around, practice a bit, write some songs, maybe play a gig now and then."

"Oh, Daddy," Nadine said. "You know you'll never retire. You can't give it up."

"That's what *you* say, girl. Might be I have me some different ideas."

"How'd you come up?" Slim asked.

"Whoo, son! You wantin' to know ancient history. Lessee. I growed up with the blues. Never knew nobody that didn't when I was a kid. It was just the natural thing, porch players sittin' around doin' it all the time. Back then, us kids made guitars out of cigar boxes and saplings. We'd use strands from wire whisk brooms for strings. We couldn't play much of nothin', but we'd get a sound, you know. Later on, my mama and daddy got me an ole guitar from the pawn and I started learnin' to play it."

"You just had to ask, didn't you," Nadine said, poking Slim once again.

"Hush up," Progress said. "The boy ain't heard it before, even if you has. Anyway, son, when I was, oh, 'bout twelve, I guess it was, McPhail's Medicine Show come through town, sellin' medicine for rheumatism, arthritis and everything that ailed you. He liked to have him a little show, and he liked to have a home boy for that, so I played and sang a little song and he paid me five cents and all the medicine I could use. I swear, my mama had bottles of that medicine till her dyin' day. Made me take it when I was poorly, too, which made me get *right* back up on my feets.

"Later on, me and my buddies put a little band together. Wasn't but three of us, and when we started out we didn't know but three songs. But we played 'em fast, medium and slow and we got over, somehow. After a few years of that, I met Rosie, like I told you, and everything else just growed out of that. He taught me how to play, to really play, without sayin' anything or tellin' me what to do. He'd just look at you and play a little thing, and you'd know how he was feelin'."

"Do you sound like him?" Slim asked.

Progress laughed. His laugh and those shining gold teeth still made Slim feel good. Maybe because it never sounded as if Progress was laughing at him.

"Nope," Progress answered. "Or only a little. It's both, or least-wise it's mostly not. Them were crazy days. We used to have us a Nash Rambler to drive to the gigs. Zero to sixty in twenty-eight seconds. Fake whitewalls that would fly off like flat donuts anytime you got over forty. But while we'd drive, Rosie'd talk about women and the blues. And he spent a lot of time tryin' to show me how to find my own groove and not be jumpin' into his.

"You do take somethin'," he continued. "You get an idea or a groove from somebody. You don't necessarily got to hear them play, right there. You knows what they play like and just bein' with that person give you a little thing, so that when you pick up your own guitar again, you might could come up with somethin' different. That's 'cause you got a different feelin' in your body about bein' with someone. You catch a vibe from someone and you goes back to the shed to find out what it is.

"Oh, I knows there's some people who try to take on another player's groove, steal his riffs and all. But the music ain't *real* that way and you can't take someone else's power. The music got to be an expression of your state of bein', not just somethin' you done took on."

"Well," Slim said. "I feel like I got my own thing going. I always thought that was important. See," he continued, blushing a little, "I was kind of famous once, myself—a long, long time ago. I didn't know what I was doing. Still don't , I guess. But at least I have an idea of when to stand forward and when not to."

"You've got some attitude," Nadine said.

"Nah. I gave up attitude a long time ago. See, what I'd do was practice in my bathroom with the door closed. I'd turn it up and when my balls would vibrate I'd know I had it right. The hair on my arms would stand up and I'd hear that air movin' and I'd just scream. But when I played, and I played good, I'd feel like *somebody*, I'd feel all together."

"That's the power," Progress said.

"Yeah, I suppose. It's nothin' like it is here, though. I was doing good just getting up on stage and making sure whatever I was wearing was funnier than my body, and going out after the gig for fifty-two ribs and left-handed cigarettes. But, see, I always felt I was missing something. That's why I moved here—er, where I was before I came here. Trying to find it."

"How did *you* start out?" Nadine asked him. She seemed more than routinely curious, but Slim wasn't sure that her interest was really in him. It was almost as if she was trying to ascertain something else, something to which he was only peripheral.

"Huh? I started out with nothing. Still got most of it left, too. No, okay, okay. I grew up in this dinky little farm town called Ducor. It was real close to another little no-horse town called Pixley. There was this minister's son, named Roy Buchanan, used to come around my house. His dad didn't like the school in Pixley or something, so he went to the school in Ducor. I was younger than he was, so I don't know why he let me hang around, except my dad had horses. He'd been playing guitar for a while, and he started teaching me. The blues.

"He moved away a few years later, to Canada. He started playing with a top band, making his name, but he'd gotten me started and it was something I loved. I kept on playing, started a band in high school and we made it big, real big. But what with the women and the drugs and the money, I got all fucked up, so I put down the music entirely for a long time."

"Why are you back playing, now?" Nadine asked. Still it seemed that she was after something else, as if Slim were carrying some hint of a larger mystery, some more important thing behind him she was trying to see.

"A few years ago, I just got hungry for it, so I picked up my guitar and started playing. Side gigs, sessions, jamming. I thought about getting in touch with Roy again, and I'd just gotten ahold of his address when I heard that he'd died. After I heard that, I knew I had to play again. It was like I'd be disloyal to him or something, if I didn't. And here I am. But there's still something missing from me. That's why I keep asking you stuff, trying to get hold of the idea."

"That's fine," Progress said. "You ask all you want. Far as I ever knowed, that's the only way a body ever finds anything out."

"Yeah," Nadine said gruffly. "But shut up now. We're at the store.

Let's go get your clothes and see if we can't get you looking a little more respectable."

Later, with Slim dressed in new jeans and the kind of floral shirt he liked, and with the empty tool box of the pickup filled with packages, they drove to the part of town where friendly, one-story buildings changed to tall, imposing edifices. An almost invisible haze of steel-blue smoke colored the sky. Even the sun seemed hotter in this part of town. They paid a lot attendant two dollars for a space, and got out of the truck to walk.

"Can you beat that?" Progress said. "Chargin' a man money just to park his truck. That's T-Bone's doin', tryin' to make more money. That man'd charge for air if he could."

As they walked the sidewalks, Slim noticed that things here were opposite to the world he'd come from. In his world, the downtown areas were always clean, nearly polished. But here in Tejas, at least Armadillo, downtown was the *only* part of the city he'd seen that *wasn't* clean. On the contrary, it was gray, dingy and depressing. The glass in the tall buildings didn't shine in the sunlight and anonymous trash blew through the streets and gutters.

The sidewalks were empty. They headed for the tallest building of all: a black, seemingly windowless tower of stone. The only indication that it was more than a column of solid rock was the glass front doors and a bright red sign at the very top that read T.B.P. UNLIMITED.

They walked up the short flight of stairs and went through the streaked glass doors into a bare lobby, devoid of life. They went quickly to the elevator, which opened to them almost immediately. It was empty, and smelled faintly of urine or cigar smoke. Slim couldn't identify the odor except as stale and bitter and unpleasant. Nadine wrinkled her nose and glanced significantly at her father, as if the smell was proving a point. But Slim couldn't figure what that point could be, except that something disgusting must have been there recently. Something like—whatever might have been in the bathroom, in the morning. But that didn't make any sense.

They were going to the very top floor, and it was an excruciatingly slow and bumpy elevator, almost as if it had been designed to keep the riders in suspense as to the safety of the metal box and the cable that held it. No one interrupted the ride, and Slim wondered if there were actually any other people in the building.

The three of them stepped from the elevator and were faced by a uniform gray entry office. Against one wall sat a gigantic desk and at the desk sat a gigantic woman who could easily fulfill every preteenage boy's nightmare of the ultimate authority figure: a combination of the wicked witch of Oz and Grendel, with traces of bigfoot and the Marquis de Sade thrown into improve her looks. A formidable woman who glared at them with obvious hatred for disturbing her important task of doing nothing.

"Can I *help* you?" she sneered.

Progress, unintimidated, walked right up to her desk and looked her in the eyes. "We want to see T-Bone," he said sternly.

"Do you *people* have an appointment?" the woman asked. The expression on her face showed clearly that the entirety of her job was to ensure that no one, ever, got inside.

"Nope. But T-Bone will see me. You just tell him that Progress is here to talk to him."

"I'm sure," she said, her tone derisive. "Just a moment." She lifted the receiver of a red phone and pushed a button. After a few seconds, she mumbled into it, making sure that no one but the person on the other end could understand anything she said. Then her eyes widened and she hung the phone up quickly. As if Slim, Progress and Nadine had ceased to exist, she waved her arm in the general direction of a wide door behind her and said, "Go in, go in." Then she began shuffling and studying the papers that lay on her desk.

They walked through the door she'd indicated, into an office that, to Slim's surprise, was totally, brilliantly white. Behind a high desk sat the man they'd come to see. He was thin and fishbelly white, as if his life was lived completely within his office. He had little pig eyes, a thin, scraggly mustache, and stubby fingers. He was dressed in a white suit with a red tie, and seemed intensely preoccupied with counting the several bundles of filth-covered money that lay on the desk before him. He was using a dirty handkerchief to clean the bills as he counted them, and he ran them lovingly through his hands and before his eyes as if drawing power from their existence.

He looked up as they entered the office. "Progress," he said, smiling crookedly, twitchingly. "Come in. Come in." He nodded and added, "Nadine. You look mighty good."

Nadine pointedly averted her gaze.

His porcine eyes scanned Slim carefully and his smile broadened into a leer. Slim felt violated, the way a child would by the touch of a molester.

Pickens turned back to Progress. "Who's this?" he asked.

"My new apprentice," Progress replied. "Slim."

Pickens seemed to flinch for just a moment; then the nasty smile returned to his face. When he spoke, a venom had entered his already unpleasant voice. "What? Did you find yet another poor fool to humiliate?"

"No," Progress said calmly. "This one can play."

Slim saw Pickens' hands clench tightly around the already crushed bundles of money as the piggy eyes turned and seemed to try to burn through him. "Well, I'll have to keep an *especially* close eye on you."

"Don't go to any trouble for me," Slim mumbled. The man made him feel dirty and afraid.

"No trouble at all," Pickens said, turning back to Progress. "Well, *Mister* Hornsby, what's you business here?"

"Don't be playin' no games, T-Bone. You know what I'm here for. Where is it?"

Pickens ignored the question. "Nadine," he said. "Why don't you dump these losers and come in with me?"

Slim hadn't had a reason to hate the man until that moment. But the feeling flared up inside him like a lightning bolt, shaking him and causing his fists to clench. He was going to say something, but Nadine spat on the white rug and said, "You? Don't even think about me, you slimeass. I'd rather fuck your slave out there."

Pickens growled and the affable mask slipped once again. Showing clearly the greed and hatred that consumed him, he pointed his finger at Progress and shook it. "Old fool, you'll *never* get the Gutbucket back. It's mine, now."

Progress wasn't fazed. "Take your finger out my face," he said. "I s'pected that'd be your attitude. I guess there's nothin' for it. Come on, chillen. Time for us to be goin'."

They turned and headed for the door. Just before they reached it, Progress turned.

"By the way," he said. "We're havin' us a friendly little blues festival out at the river in a few days. Whyn't you come on along and see some folks with *real* talent do it right."

That didn't seem like much of a barb to Slim, but it scored on Pickens. "Get out! Get out!" His voice was high-pitched and filled with rage.

They left, quickly closing the door behind them. They heard something hit it on the other side, and Progress laughed all the long way down the elevator.

8

*These brief flashes bring with them a great joy, a
great beauty and a great uplift. They are, for most
people, their first vivid awakening to the existence
and reality of a spiritual order of being. The
contrast with their ordinary state is so tremendous
as to shame it into pitiful drabness. The intention
is to arouse and stimulate them into the longing
for re-entry into the spirit, a longing which
inevitably expresses itself in the quest.*
—Paul Brunton,
Introduction to Mystical Glimpses

*After an hour or so in the woods looking for
mushrooms, Dad said "Well, we can always go
and buy some real ones."*
—John Cage

After another hearty breakfast, Slim and Nadine were traveling alone in the pickup. Progress had said that there was important work he had to do in his garden. After a stop for gas, and ice and sodas Nadine packed in a chest, they headed west. The roads were rural and twisting. Sometimes Nadine, driving, took dirt roads, or paths that didn't look like roads at all. Slim was glad of the sodas when he could wash the invading red dust from his throat.

"Where are we going?" he asked nervously. It was the first time he and Nadine had been alone, and he wanted very desperately to try to start a friendship, a relationship.

"We're going to Tralfaz, to see Mother Phillips," she answered. There was a strange smile on her face that spoke of things she wasn't saying. "Daddy wants her to bless the festival."

"I don't understand."

Nadine whoofed, exasperated. "Can you really be that stupid and live?"

"Hey—"

"Never mind. Sorry. I know you don't know anything. I grew up here all my life, so I don't take well to explaining things I think everyone knows. Daddy wants to call on the deep powers at the festival. So he has to start out with a blessing so that everything builds up the way he wants it."

"Why are we taking such a hard way to get there?"

"In case anyone tries to follow us."

"Oh," Slim said. "I guess that makes sense."

Nadine whoofed again. "Oh thanks," she said. "I always appreciate a man that knows absolutely nothing telling me I know what I'm doing."

It wasn't going well. Slim could tell that. No matter what he said, it seemed to be wrong.

"Nadine?"

"Yes?"

"I'm sorry."

She sighed. "It's okay," she said. "But tell me something. How do you manage to be so inept?"

"It's easy," Slim said. "I practice."

They both laughed then. It was the first time Slim had seen Nadine really smile. It was a beautiful smile.

"Did Progress tell you where I came from?" he asked.

"No. Just that you weren't from around here."

Slim told her his story. He might have gotten a little carried away in his desire for her. Started a little too soon, told her a little too much about his problems with women and life. But he wanted her to know, and he soon got to the point where he'd been exploded into her world, and how confused he was about it. He almost told her he loved her. He wanted to, badly, but he was afraid.

"That explains a lot of things," she said, when he had finished.

Slim was surprised. "You believe me?"

"Daddy does, so I do, too. I've never known him to be wrong about a person. And you may be a lot of things, but I don't think you're a liar. Besides, you're not used to this world. A lot of strange things happen here. Stranger than you."

They were suddenly driving through trees, not a common sight on the plains. The woods he had known in Texas were certainly not lush enough or green enough to give the impression of a forest like the one they were now in the middle of.

"What the—"

"It hits everybody that way when they first come to Tralfaz," Nadine said. "They found an underground lake under the property. And there are streams and creeks all through here, so there's always enough water to grow all this. Hey, it still gets brown in the winter, so don't sweat it."

They followed a narrow dirt road through the trees. Slim was amazed to see small antelope and buffalo in the brush, along with what looked to be hundreds and hundreds of cats. "What's with all the animals?" he asked.

"Oh, Tralfaz is a kind of safe place. Mother Phillips doesn't allow hunting here at all, and they'll take in any kind of strays. The animals know it somehow, and they migrate here from all around. The people in town know it, too, so if they can't keep their animals they bring them out here."

"That's outstanding," Slim said. "I like that a lot. You come out here often?"

"As often as I can. I'm not exactly a member. But I like the people here. It's a good place to be. I agree with the beliefs and I like the attitude."

"What do they believe?" Slim asked.

Nadine smiled that mysterious smile again. "I don't really want to tell you," she said. "Once we get inside, you can ask Mother Phillips. She'll be happy to tell you."

"Why didn't Progress come with us?"

Nadine's smile turned to chuckles. "Daddy wouldn't come out here for anything in the world. Mother Phillips has been after Daddy for years. I guess she's been in love with him since they were young. Daddy likes her and there have been a few good times between them, but he isn't looking to get connected with her just yet."

Nadine drove the pickup to what looked like a group of domes that had grown from the earth. Instead of wood or concrete, they were covered with soil and grass and wildflowers, surrounded by the oldest trees of all. They were huge, but not imposing.

"Reference stop," she said. "Everybody out." She was still laughing, and Slim couldn't figure out why.

They walked through a doorway in the nearest dome, pulling a buffalo-skin cover aside, and were in a small bare room.

"Take your clothes off," Nadine said.

"*What?*"

"Take your clothes off. No clothing allowed in Tralfaz." Nadine was already undressing, so Slim did so as well. He had a difficult time because he couldn't take his eyes off Nadine. She seemed totally at ease and, as she slipped her panties off, she stood and turned to look at Slim.

"Come on," she said, still smiling wickedly. "Get them off."

Slim took his pants off, and as he wore no underwear, was exposed to view. The sight of Nadine's small breasts, her legs, her stomach, her puss, had put him into an embarrassing condition. He knew he had a nice face, and women had told him many times that he had a beautiful dick, but there wasn't any other part of his body that he felt was attractive and this casual intimacy both excited and disturbed him. He wished adamantly that he could exert control over the single part of his body he knew it was useless to try to control.

Nadine, however, was looking him over carefully, unselfconsciously as he stood there wondering what to do with his hands. She spent, he thought, an inordinate amount of time looking at his protruding dick, but there seemed to be a look of approval on her face.

She walked up to him and patted his stomach. It made him jump.

"Don't worry," she said. "I like big men. Come on, now. Let's go see Mother Phillips."

She walked through another door. Slim followed, which did nothing to abate his embarrassing condition. It made it, in fact, even worse. But she had said she liked big men. That meant he had a chance. At least his rotundity wouldn't stand in the way. Now, if only he could overcome his personality, he might have it made.

He'd heard that people who spent time in nudist colonies soon got over the immediate sexual attraction. But as long as a naked Nadine was around him, Slim thought it highly unlikely that that condition would ever occur to him. As long as he could see—*everything*—it just got more desperate.

They walked through several doors and buildings, following an increasing scent of earth and water, but Slim couldn't have said what, if anything, the rooms contained. His attention was totally focused on Nadine's shoulders, back, ass and legs and the way they all seemed to move so gracefully together. So he was unprepared when she stopped. He almost ran into her, which he thought could have been a wonderful disaster. When he was together enough to look around, he realized he was in a large, dome-shaped greenhouse. It was filled with young trees, plants, flowers and naked people who paid no attention to him and Nadine beyond an initial identifying glance. Most of them were working with the plants. Some were playing. The energy and attention seemed to circle around a very short, wrinkled old woman who sat on a small grassy hummock just ahead of them.

The old woman looked up at them. She dismissed a little girl she had been talking to and stared at Slim as appraisingly as Nadine had. Then she smiled widely and genuinely. It made Slim uncomfortable in a way Nadine's smile hadn't. This old woman had power. He could feel it, but he didn't understand it. It didn't frighten him, but it was discomfiting.

"Nadine!" the old woman said with delight. "Welcome. Welcome. Who's your handsome friend here?"

"This is Slim Chance, Mother. We've come for an important thing."

Mother Phillips stood up easily and walked over to Nadine and hugged her. Then she walked to Slim.

"Give me a hug, boy."

She reached out her arms and Slim hugged her fearfully. To his amazement, she reached down and slapped her hand around his dick, which by this time felt gigantic and obvious. He would have pulled away, but Mother Phillips seemed to exude an aura of goodness, mixed with a subtle threat, as if this were a test that Slim had to pass or go no further, either with Nadine or with this world.

Mother Phillips released him with a smile and returned to her seat on the hummock. "Sit down, you two," she said.

Slim sat first and he swore that, if Nadine sat cross-legged, he would explode. She did. He didn't, but it was a close call.

"Nadine," Mother Phillips said. "This is a good man. He's a little desperate, but he's got a good heart." The old woman looked at him and her eyes seemed to pierce him. "Do you know he's in love with you?" she said.

Slim groaned out loud. Did *everyone* see his feelings? Nadine looked at him harshly.

"Yes, I know," she said. "But that doesn't do me any good at all until *he* tells me."

Slim wanted to protest, to say something to turn the conversation away from himself, but Mother Phillips put her hand over his mouth.

"He can't," she said. "I can feel inside him. He's been hurt too bad, too many times. And he feels that he has something to prove to you."

"He *does*," Nadine said, looking straight at him. "He's a little slow, and I haven't even heard him play guitar, yet."

"Is he a player?"

"Daddy says he is. He took him on as his apprentice. But I have to see it for myself."

"That's fair," Mother Phillips said. "How is your daddy? Still ornery as ever?"

"He's good," Nadine replied.

"Tell him I said hello and he's welcome here," the old woman said. "I'm glad you're giving this boy a fair chance to make it. For a minute I though you were being your mean old self."

"She *is*," Slim blurted.

Nadine turned on him angrily, but before she could say anything, Mother Phillips broke in and stopped it. "No, boy," she said. "If she was, she'd never have brought you here. You're the first man she's *ever* brought here."

"Oh," Slim said. "Sorry. Do you people always talk so—*personal*, here?"

"Yes, I guess we do, at that. Without clothes, there's little need to cover up other aspects of reality and life, so we do tend to get right to the heart of things. Our beliefs don't allow for any other attitude."

"What is it you *do* believe?"

Mother Phillips smiled and closed her eyes. "That's a hard question. Basically, we believe in the two Mothers, the Goddess Without Name and our Mother the Earth. We celebrate life and love and lust, all the growing things. We believe in what we can see and feel and know. Past that, it's hard to say. We're just a community that loves life and freedom, sex and love and the enjoyment of the natural human being. Does that explain it for you?"

"As well as anything," Slim said, more confused than ever. "It's at least something I can halfway agree with."

"Good," the old woman said, turning back to Nadine. "Now that the air's clear, tell me why you've come."

Slim and Nadine told Mother Phillips about the Gutbucket and about Progress' plans. They told her about their meeting with T-Bone. The old woman hmm'd and scratched and oh my'd throughout the story, and when it was finished she shook her head sadly.

"That's bad," she said. "That's very bad. I don't talk about it much, but Pickens has been after Tralfaz for years, trying to buy us out. He hates us, I think. Hates anything good that doesn't make money. Wants to put more tall buildings here, I guess. So, yes, I will be more than happy to bring the whole community out to give the blessing for you."

"Thanks," Slim said, feeling he needed to. He wasn't sure why, but it felt an important thing to say at that moment.

"Yes, thank you," Nadine added. "You be careful, Mother. Daddy thinks T-bone's liable to pull some tricks."

"Like the hand?"

Nadine jumped. "You know?"

"Caught a whiff of it."

"Am I missing something?" Slim asked, perplexed by this interchange.

"Better tell him, girl," Mother Phillips said gravely. "He has a right to know."

Nadine looked uncomfortable. "Daddy felt it best not to, right away, anyway."

"Tell me what?" Slim was getting uneasy.

"Something ugly," Nadine said. She looked at the old woman. "T-Bone can't touch you, can he?"

"No problem. We're safe here. Can you kids stay for dinner? We have fresh corn and some good buff tonight."

Slim wanted to find out what buffalo meat tasted like, and he would have liked to spend more time talking with Mother Phillips, not to mention enjoying his view of Nadine. But Nadine shook her head and said they had to go.

She and Slim stood up and started back the way they had come. They didn't talk, but Nadine took his hand and, again, Slim was oblivious to the surroundings. When they got back to the small room where they had started and began to put their clothes on, he was surprised to discover that his embarrassing condition had ceased to be a problem some time before.

Nadine took a different route leaving Tralfaz. Slim could think of nothing to say to her. The image of her body was burnt into his mind, into his memory, his being. And she had acted as if she really might like him a little, as if he had a chance to earn her love. But she scared him, too. She was so strong, so independent, so clear on who and what she was. And Slim was so unclear on all those things. And what was this business about a hand, that made even Nadine nervous? He wanted to ask, but thought he'd better wait for her to tell him on her own.

Remembering the conversation with Mother Phillips, Slim thought that a whole lot was depending on one thing he had, at the moment, a singular lack of confidence about. His playing. In *his* world, he knew he could hold his own. He was competent. Maybe not the best, but above average. But here in Tejas, where blues seemed to be the heart of the culture—where would he stand here? He knew that his playing rarely came from inside. It was all technique, all chops, little feeling. He wanted to express his feeling. Once in a while a note or two would linger and seem to go beyond him. But he needed to let himself out before he played for Nadine, or she would never love him. As they rode, he tried to remember something Progress had told him.

"When you play it right," Progress had said, "this hurts." He'd grabbed his foot. "And this hurts." He'd grabbed his heart. "And this hurts, too." He'd then grabbed his crotch. "If it don't move people, if it don't make 'em feel, then it don't work. The most important thing is emotion. It's easier to sit down and figure out what notes go with what chords and how fast you can play 'em than it is to be askin' yourself why you're playin' that song or what feelings you're tryin' to express or even why you're playin' at all. Them questions require that you be real honest with yourself. It ain't about what you play, it comes down to what's in your heart."

Be honest with himself. That was hard. There was so much he'd prefer to keep hidden. And how could he be honest with himself when he wasn't sure, anymore, who he even *was*? There was so much hurt piled over him, much of it his own fault. But pushing him on was Nadine, and the hope she offered. Maybe, he thought, he could wrap himself around that hope, center on it and stand out from there. He'd find a way to put his playing through that hope and have it come out saying what he wanted it to say.

"Slim?" Nadine said suddenly.

He was jarred out of his thoughts. "Yeah?"

"We have trouble, I think."

"What you mean?"

"There's a car that's been following us at least the last few miles.

I've been going nowhere and back trying to lose it, but it's been staying right on us."

Slim turned and looked through the rear window. A black sedan was close behind them, matching their speed, seeming to make no attempt to conceal its pursuit. He couldn't identify the car or see the driver, but it gave him a bad feeling. As he watched, it put on a burst of speed and began to catch up with the pickup. Before he realized what was happening, or could warn Nadine, the car rammed into the rear of the truck. The jolt knocked his face into the window and he could feel the pickup wobble and slew on the road as Nadine tried to get it back under control.

"Shit!" Slim said. "I think they're tryin' to kill us."

The car hit them again and the truck's rear wheels slewed around on the dirt road. Nadine stepped on the gas and the truck jumped forward with more power than Slim would have expected. He looked over at Nadine and saw a look of intense concentration and rage on her face.

"Sons of bitches!" Nadine yelled.

As incongruous as it was, Nadine's yell made Slim laugh. He was holding on to the back of the seat, his arm around Nadine. When the car hit the rear of the truck, the seat was forced back, pinching his fingers. He didn't move his arm, but he held on more carefully.

"What do we do?" he asked.

"Hold on."

Nadine turned the truck. It slid sideways on the soft dirt road, but she held on to it, even as two wheels came up off the ground, then slammed back down. They drove straight off the road, tearing through a flimsy barbed-wire fence, into the open field. Slim looked back and saw the car attempting to follow them, hitting a bump wrong and rolling over. Then they hit their own bump and both of them bounced up off the seat and hit their heads on the roof. Nadine slowed down enough to navigate through the mesquite and cactus, traveling through the field for a mile or so until they burst through another barbed-wire fence and onto another dirt road. No one was following them.

"Hell of a ride," Slim said, relieved it was over.

"Nothing to it," Nadine replied. "Daddy had this old truck built up special so it could go anywhere. Remember, he *really* likes his fishing."

"Who were those guys? Vipers?"

"Sure. Who else? That was a cheap trick, though. I *know* this country. I know every rock and tree and back road. I can steer around a snake in the shade. Pickens is an ignorant man. None of the local people would work for him, so he brought all the Vipers up from Arsten or Hewstone, down south. They don't know their way around these old bumpy back roads."

"Do you figure we're safe, now?"

"Right now, yes. But tomorrow's another day. We won't really be safe until we get the Gutbucket back and whip Pickens."

Slim thought about that. He was surprised, in a way, at the involvement he had felt growing in himself. He really cared, and he'd never been a man that cared for very much outside himself and the women he loved. It wasn't just Nadine, this time, though. She was a big part of it, that was true. But it was Progress and all the other players. It was the blues and what they meant and what they were. It was too late in the world he had come from. One man's actions didn't matter, there. There was no more room for any individual to be important. But here, in Tejas, he felt like he could do something that would matter, that would make a difference. What he did could be important, he could be important, be a part of the blues and part of the world.

He wondered, for a moment, if his motives were purely selfish or egotistical. But maybe something was only selfish if he wanted it without working for it. Maybe if he worked hard for something, then the motive was something better. And he did care. He loved Nadine and Progress and the blues. And he couldn't bear the thought of never hearing Nadine sing again, of never watching her strut the stage. Or worse, of never being able to play with her.

"Let's go home," he said.

Nadine nodded.

9

*In the flow of a phrase, as well as in the
mysterious wind of blues, reveal to me your plans
for the coming revolution.*
—Andre Breton, *Introduction to the Discourse
on the Paucity of Reality*

Alligator Social

*Folks, I'm tellin' you something
That I saw with my own eyes,
As I passed the pond one day,
The gator was teachin' his babies
To do the Georgia grind.
And I heard one of them say,
This is a social, but the alligator's pond's gone dry,
Yeah, it is a social, but gator's pond done gone dry.*

*Now ole Mister Gator, got himself way back,
He said, look out chillen,
I'm throwin' water off my back,
Aww, it was a social, but alligator's pond went dry.
Say it was a social, but the pond went dry
And it must have been a social, for gator's pond to go dry.*

Now, Mister Alligator, he got himself real hot,
He said, "We're gonna have that function,
Whether there's water or not."
Aww, it was a social, but the gator's pond went dry.

Now if you don't believe what I'm sayin'
Ask ole Alligator Jack,
Wasn't a drop of water in the pond
When he got himself back,
Oh it must have been a social, but gator's pond went dry...

Breakfast, the next morning was, again, an involved production: steak and eggs and potatoes.

"Do you always eat like this?" Slim asked.

"When I'm out here with Daddy I do. By myself, I normally just have cereal for breakfast or something. I don't really like to cook very much. Even for dinner I usually end up going out to Mitchell's."

"You sure do cook good, though."

Nadine nodded as she watched Slim shoveling in the food she'd made. "Mama taught me everything I needed to know," she said. "She taught me all about cooking. Being good at something, and liking to do it, are two different things, though."

"What about your mother?" Slim said. "Progress hasn't said anything about her at all."

"He probably won't," Nadine replied. "She was from the Indian Nations. She never told me the whole story, but she'd gotten into some kind of serious trouble with her tribe. They exiled her. I guess, rather than stay with her own people, she came here. It's not something she talked about.

"Daddy found her out at the river, half starved, feet worn out from walking. He brought her home and I suppose it just went from there. It wasn't light, though. I've never seen two people love each other as much as Daddy and Mama did."

"So what happened to her?"

"Oh," Nadine sighed. Slim could feel the sadness inside her. "About ten years ago," she said, "Daddy was playing a gig in Arsten. Mama decided to fly down and surprise him. The zeppelin crashed and killed everybody." She turned away from the table, wiping tears from her eyes, her small shoulders hunched and tight. "No one ever figured out what happened," she continued. "The zeppelins were safe. The helium came from mines right here around Armadillo."

"Wait a minute," Slim protested, his sense of reality jarred, "helium's a gas. It doesn't come from mines. Even I know that."

"That's where it comes from in *Tejas*," Nadine asserted. "I mean, once it's exposed to sunlight it's a gas. But while it's underground or in the dark, it's like some kind of rock. That's how they control the zeppelins."

"But why use zeppelins?" Slim asked. "We gave those up in our world a long time ago. We fly in airplanes." Slim had actually always rather liked zeppelins, seeing them in a romantic light, but he felt he had to try to understand the logic of this world he found himself a part of.

"They tried airplanes. They didn't work too well. For one thing, they were way too expensive. Mostly, though, they just weren't safe. In the last sixty years, there have only been three zeppelin crashes in Tejas. Unfortunately," she said, sadly, "Mama was in one of them."

"Oh, gosh," Slim said. "I'm sorry."

"It's okay," she said, taking his hand in her own. "It hurt when it happened, but I'm okay, now. It's just a sad memory."

They heard Progress' pickup turn in to the driveway. "Hush, now," Nadine said. "I don't want to talk about Mama when Daddy's around. It still hurts him."

Progress had left before either Slim or Nadine had woken, not telling either of them where he planned to go. When he came into the house, he was leading a wrinkled, dilapidated hound and there was a sad look on his face.

"This is Stavin' Chain," he said. The look on his face made it clear that it was hard for him to say, that there was a pain just below the surface.

Nadine picked up on it immediately. "What happened, Daddy?"

"Well, I went to see Bonehack Sissibone, to get him to play at the festival." His eyes had a faraway, painful look as he talked. "I got out to the house and everyone was gone. All their clothes and stuff was there. His guitars and amps and all, just sittin' in the empty house. I knowed he was gone for good though." He handed them a slip of paper, stained red, as if by blood. "I found this stuck to the front door," he said.

The note was simple, just a few words scrawled in a shaky hand. DON'T FUCK WITH THE VIPERS, it read.

"The hound was still there, lookin' all beat-up and worried. I figured he could help, so I brought him along."

"Help how?" Slim asked.

Progress shook his head. "After what happened with you two comin' back from Mother Phillips, I though maybe he could give us a little protection for the house."

Nadine nodded, but Slim was still puzzled. "Protection?" he said. "How? He didn't protect this guy you went to see, did he?"

"Nope," Progress replied. "But that was physical stuff, nothin' for it. Hounds are pretty powerful in the blues. Bonehack was a good ole boy, had a reasonable amount of power. But the Vipers was too much for him to fight, belly to belly. If they come after us, the dog probably couldn't do no more than bark and hide. But it's the power he can help with. If T-Bone tries to get to us with the power, Stavin' Chain'll stand in the way and it won't be able to get around him. He cain't do nothin', you understand, but you just can't use the power in a bad way when there's an ole hound around."

"That's right," Nadine said agreeably.

"Okay," Slim said. "If you guys say so it's all right with me. I can't say I understand it, but I'll buy that it works. What do I know?" He shrugged his shoulders and went on. "So what do we do today?"

"We gots us a hard road today," Progress replied. "We gonna go see the gris-gris man, Belizaire Cajon. He's a player from the swamps down south. He's a powerful man, but a strange one. There's no tellin' if he'll play at the festival or not. He plays with me now and then, but, these days, he pretty much goes his own way. Folks come to him for healin' and dehauntin' and such."

"You think he'll help us out?"

"I thinks so, son. But you cain't never tell with the gris-gris man."

"If we're going," Nadine said, clearing the table and piling the dishes in the sink, "then let's go."

But as Slim went for the door, the hound dog whined nervously, setting himself between him and it. "He wants to come along," Slim said, smiling.

"No he don't," Progress said. "There's something he's afraid of. Best not use that door right now."

"You mean—?" Nadine asked, looking at the door with apprehension.

"We'll find out soon 'nough." Progress led the way out the back.

They walked around the house and peered at the front door. There was something hanging before it on a string, burning. "Damn!" Progress swore.

"What is it?" Slim asked.

"What I should have told you about," Nadine said tightly. "The Glory Hand."

"The what?"

Progress went up to the thing, reached up, caught the string between his fingers, and yanked it down. The object now dangled from his hand. "The Glory Hand," he said. "The hound smelt it and gave us warnin'. You'd have walked smack into it."

Now Slim saw that the thing on the string was a severed human hand that must have been dipped in wax; the fingers curled up, glistening with the stuff, and the nails projected. Each nail burned like a separate candle, so there were five little flames. The smell was sickening. Indeed, the thing sent a current of apprehension through him, as if some nameless menace were reaching out from it.

"I smelled that before!" Slim exclaimed. "In the bathroom—and the elevator!"

"Then it has power over you," Progress said. "If you'd walked into it—"

"It's disgusting," Slim said. "But I can survive a little burn."

"A Glory Hand doesn't just burn," Nadine said. "It's a fetish, doom for the one it's meant for. Daddy and I can handle it, but you—"

"Get me a tight box," Progress said.

Nadine hurried inside, to emerge in a moment with a cookie tin. Progress dangled the burning hand into it, then clapped the lid on and pressed it tight. Then he took the sealed tin inside and set it on the floor. "You watch this, Stavin' Chain," he told the hound. "Don't let nobody take it out." The dog growled, seeming to understand. He was no longer afraid of the hand, now that it had been contained.

"That's twice they've tried to touch you with that thing," Nadine said to Slim. "What's the worst that could happen to you, right now?"

"To be forever separated from you," Slim said without thinking, still shaken by the horrible fetish.

"Then it must be primed to send you back to your own world," Progress said. "One touch, and you're gone. T-Bone's getting occult help. Figures if he can't get you one way, maybe he'll get you another way. Now I *knows* you's important and we better keep you safe till we finds out *how* you's important."

Nadine nodded. "I'll stay close to him, Daddy."

Slim tried to mask his delight. Clouds did have silver linings! But what could be so important about him that a man as powerful and unscrupulous as T-Bone Pickens was desperate to get rid of him?

They took the highway out to the river. In Slim's world, the Canadian River had been a state park and a paradise for off-roaders. But here in Tejas, while it looked as if it were still a popular location for camping and partying, it was wild and mostly untouched by civilization.

Progress turned on to a road paralleling the river, a road that hadn't existed in Slim's world. It wound through the huge cottonwoods and oaks, around boulders and close to the water, seeming to go on for miles. It was a dark, rough road, covered over by the tops of the trees, sheltered from the hot summer sun.

"Your man lives out *here?*" Slim asked, daunted by the unfamiliar wilderness they were traveling through.

"Yep," Progress said. "He likes his privacy. Says if anyone wants to find him for somethin', they should be serious about it. So it should be hard to get to him. Then he knows they're not just foolin' around."

Slim wanted to ask another question, but Nadine took his hand and held it, which served effectively to shut him up. Maybe she was just doing it to protect him from a Glory Hand, getting him used to her close presence, but he was glad for it anyway. The pickup bounced on along the road and he just looked out the window, trying to spot wild turkeys. In a while, they came upon a steep hill. Progress gunned the motor and the truck clawed its way to the top.

Once over the hill, they began passing through a line of junked cars and trucks and vans which stood on the side of the road in various states of dissolution. They lined both sides of the road and pointed the way to a space cleared of trees. Ahead of them, Slim could see a potpourri of logs that some people might call a house. It looked like a box, to which rooms and outbuildings had been haphazardly added. When they pulled up in front, he could see that the whole construction had been shingled with Prince Albert tobacco tins that had been cut on one side and flattened. They were rusty brown on the side of the house where they'd been started, and as they went on to the other side they got redder and shinier.

Plants and herbs grew unplanned around the house, and seven children playing with seven dogs were scattered around the yard under the watchful eye of a small woman Slim assumed to be their mother. Her beauty had been worn away by work and childbirth, but there was a joy of life shining inside her that gave her a beauty Slim could feel, even from a distance.

The woman and the children and the dogs paid no attention to the three of them as they got out of the pickup. A fat man walked out the front screen door. He was half bald and bearded and jolly-looking. A wide smile crossed his face as he saw them.

"Papa!" he said to Progress, shaking his hand vigorously. "What you come all de way out here fo', eh?"

"Came to talk to you about a thing," Progress said.

The man's smile never wavered. "Me," he said, "I got time for de talk. Welcome my home, you. Nadine," he said. "Cherie, come in, and your fren', too."

"This is Slim," Nadine said. "Daddy's new apprentice."

"Me, I tink he mo' dan dat, eh?" Belizaire winked at her conspiratorially. "But come in de house. I knock de pain out dis mornin', so me, I know dey no moonstroke, no sunstroke, so you come in now, yes?"

They followed him into the house, into a room filled with chairs and tables and little else. They all sat down in places that looked comfortable to them.

All but Belizaire. "Me," he said, "I'm hongry, some. I gotta get dis. You maybe want someting to eat?"

"Nope," Progress said. "We just had a big breakfast. You go on ahead."

Belizaire walked out of the room. Progress lit a cigarette he had taken from a box on the table next to his chair, coughed, but seemed to enjoy the thing. Slim leaned over and whispered to Nadine.

"Tell me again what we're using this guy for?"

"He's a bass player," she said. "He plays with Daddy sometimes. He used to anyway. Not so much anymore. A few years ago, he dropped out of sight and moved up here with his wife and kids. But Daddy wants him to back us up at the festival."

"Us?" Slim choked. "You mean me, too?"

"Yes, you," Nadine snapped. "Of course you. What did you think, that you weren't a part of this? That Daddy just kept you around to talk to?"

"Yeah, I mean, no. I didn't think Progress would want me to *play.*"

"Sure. You're just a mass of quivering sensibilities, right? Look, I don't care if you fart or blow a tin whistle, but you're a part of this and you're going to be right up there with us, so you get your shit together, you hear me. If you can't do anything else, just act stupid and no one will know the difference."

Every time he thought he maybe had a farfetched chance to get somewhere with her, she set him back with something like this. "Why do you say stuff like that, Nadine? It isn't fair."

"Hey," she said. "The *world* isn't fair."

"Yeah, I know, but why isn't it ever unfair in my favor?"

"Shut up, chillen," Progress hissed. "This ain't no time for none of that."

"Just like him to interrupt our repartee," Slim said, grinning.

Nadine smiled wickedly, her mood shifting. "Just when I had you wriggling in the crushing grip of reason, too," she answered.

"No." Slim shook his head. "I was getting my second wind."

"And me without any antacid," Nadine quipped. "Oh, well."

Slim and Nadine were laughing and holding hands when Belizaire walked back into the room chewing on a submarine sandwich that looked as big as his arm.

"Tigalo, tigalo," he said, through mouthfuls of sandwich. "I'm gonna axe you, me, what you do here?"

Progress told Belizaire the story, stopping only occasionally to shush Slim or Nadine as they poked one another trying to make each other laugh. The man continued eating, but it was clear that he listened carefully as Progress brought him up to date, telling him, at the last, about Bonehack being gone and the second appearance of the Glory Hand.

The man radiated power, even as he sat thinking and taking immense bites from the sandwich until it was gone and he had wiped his mouth on his sleeve. "But, papa," he said. "De gris-gris, she's fo' heal. I don' touch no Glory Hand. What I do in dis business?"

"Well," Progress said. "You could look on it as a healin'. Healin' the blues. Maybe we can get rid of Pickens, too."

"Oh, him, he got nottin' fo' me. He not interes' in me at all. But de blues. Me, I tink dat maybe important." He turned to face Nadine. "What you tink, cherie?"

Nadine looked back at him, shrugged. "Daddy wants you to play," she said. "We've never had to go up against T-Bone before. I guess we can use all the help we can get."

Belizaire then looked at Slim. "What you tink?"

Slim felt a push against him, felt the big man's power turned onto him. But, at the same time, he could see goodness in the man's eyes, and, as with Mother Phillips, he felt Belizaire was no threat. Still, he thought about his answer.

"I'm not sure what to tell you," he said. "I'm involved in this, but

I'm not sure how. I love the blues, and it didn't take long to learn to hate Pickens. Progress is teaching me about the blues and Nadine's teaching me, well—"

"Why you back away from her, you?"

Belizaire's eyes burnt into him. He could feel that Nadine was looking at him, too, waiting for an answer. Again, it felt to him like a test he *had* to pass, and he knew that this was a very deep question. One he would have to answer honestly, or not at all.

"I tink I broke something," Belizaire said after Slim's silence. "Say de answer, you. I can see, me, dat you come from de other worl'. Don't be 'fraid, tell Belizaire what de problem."

It was something Slim hadn't wanted to talk about, hadn't wanted to think about. It was hard enough trying to love Nadine without a shame from his own world getting in the way. But, now, here it was, coming out in the open where he couldn't avoid it.

Did everyone in this world discuss their personal lives like this, he wondered, or were they just picking on him? He was being made to constantly feel as if the success or failure of all their plans depended directly on what he said and did, on answers to questions he was reluctant to even think about.

"You see," he said, slowly. "In my world, where I come from, black people and white people don't get along very well. There's a lot of them that hate and kill each other. I don't like it or agree with it," he was quick to state. "I honestly don't even understand it. But when you grow up with something, you kinda get used to it. It gets to be a part of you without your even knowing it. You fall into it, into the patterns of it. You might hate it in yourself, but it's still there no matter what you do. So now, with Nadine, there's a distance, a fear. I kind of back away from her. And it isn't her, it's *me*. I can't seem to get out of the habit of being afraid that she won't take me seriously or she won't like me, or we won't get along because I'm white."

"Oh, Slim," Nadine said, squeezing his hand. "I don't take you seriously *now,* but it doesn't have anything to do with your color."

Belizaire shook his head sadly. He looked piercingly at Progress, whose expression was one of surprise, then he looked back at Slim. "Sound to me," he said, "like dat a powerfully unhappy worl'. You like it, being here mo' better?"

Slim held Nadine's hand tightly and looked at her. She smiled. She probably meant it about not taking him seriously, but if that enabled her to be friendly, it helped. "Yeah," he said. "Right now, there's no place I'd rather be."

"Bon," Belizaire sad, a smile once more lighting his face. "Me, I tink I help you out with dis problem of de blues."

Just then there was the roar of a motor being overworked. They all sprang up and rushed out the front door. A black car was topping the rise, spraying dirt, dust and gravel behind itself as it struggled with the grade.

A growl came from Progress' throat. *"Vipers,"* he said angrily.

Belizaire turned to his wife, who was gathering herbs. "Mama," he yelled. "Get de chillen inside de barn. Don't come out till I say."

The woman quickly gathered up the children and the dogs and Belizaire began to chant low in his throat. Slim could hear the vibration of it inside himself. He watched as the man pulled a worn drawstring bag from one of the many pockets in the overalls he wore.

The black car stopped in the road, between the lines of junkers. It looked like a standoff, or as if the driver of the car was studying on just what to do upon finding Progress and Slim and Nadine here instead of finding the gris-gris man alone.

Slim could feel a darkness pressing down on him, on his mind. He wondered if the others felt it as well. It was a sensation full of unhappiness, oppression and depression.

He had trouble seeing clearly, and there was a feeling growing inside him that all was hopeless, that the best thing to do was just to give it up. Nadine would never love him. Progress could never teach his clumsy fingers to wrap themselves around the blues. And Belizaire—how did they know that the gris-gris man was on their side? He almost started running toward the black car, had even taken a step. But Progress grabbed his arm and held him.

"It's the power," Progress said. "It's gettin' inside you, pullin' at you, takin' the blues away, takin' *your* power from you. You got to fight it."

Progress let his arm go and started humming. Slim tried to fight. At first, he didn't know how, didn't know what to do to battle the oppression that was sucking at his soul. He looked at Nadine, and saw her looking wan and worn, just as depressed as he felt. It was affecting her too!

But Progress' humming gave him an idea. If the blues had magic, maybe he could use them to fight. Timidly, unsure of himself, he started singing one of his favorite old standards:

"Going to the bottoms, to get me a mojo hand,
Yes, I'm goin' to the bottoms, get me a mojo hand,
To try to stop the men, from takin' my woman.

The hoodoo told me, to get a black cat bone,
Ole hoodoo told me, get you a black cat bone,
And shake it over their heads, till they leave your woman
      alone."

The feeling of oppression slowly lifted as he sang. His voice grew clearer and he was filled with a sense of strength and freedom. He looked to the others. Progress was smiling at him and nodding his head, Nadine was looking at him in wide-eyed amazement.

Belizaire, at that moment, opened the bag he held and poured a fine reddish powder into his open hand. He yelled out something in Cajun that Slim couldn't understand, and then he blew the powder into the air. Instead of dispersing, the red cloud seemed to grow and move until it settled over the lines of junked vehicles on the roadside. Slim heard motors turn over, cough, stutter and start. To his astonishment, the vehicles he had thought were derelicts began moving, fast.

The black car was trying to escape, but it had been blocked, both front and back. Two by two, the driverless heaps of rusted metal smashed into the driver and passenger sides of it until, eventually, it was a worse pile of flattened junk than any of the cars and trucks on the sides of the road. Then they pushed the demolished vehicle into a space that had been left and, one by one, they moved back into their own places in the lineup. Then there was silence.

"Shit!" Slim said, looking at Belizaire. "How'd you *do* that?"

Belizaire grimaced. "Long time ago," he said quietly, "I zombilize dose cars. Dey go on dey own, now. But I'm no killer, me. I don' like dis, not any. Dose bad men, though, I tink dey try to kill us, me. So I figger some, and I tink dis only ting to do."

"It's been serious," Progress said. "I don't know if they done kilt Bonehack. But I knows they was tryin' to kill us."

Slim couldn't see it quite that clearly. "But they didn't really do anything, did they? Nothing to die for."

Progress patted Slim's shoulder. "You don't understand, son. They were usin' the power. With the Gutbucket behind it. You knows how it made you feel. If you hadn't found your way to your own power, to stop it, you would have gone lower and lower until you just laid down and died. Or worse, you would have gone on out there to them."

"Couldn't you have stopped them?"

"Yep," Progress answered, an amused look on his face. "I s'pect I could have. But I needed you to find your way to your own power. I figured with Nadine and you at risk, you'd find your way to it. And you did."

"But why didn't you *tell* me?" Slim said, half angry.

"If I had've, you wouldn't have found it inside you. I had to make you depend on you. If I was doin' it, I knew you wouldn't have tried on your own, knowin' I was there to back you up. But with Nadine in trouble, I knowed you'd rise up outta yourself and get it."

"Yeah," Slim said. "I guess maybe you're right. But listen, I wish you'd warn me about stuff."

"No, son." Progress smiled at him. "You keep on findin' your way through the changes when they come at you sudden like, then pretty soon you're not gonna need to have no warnin'."

Belizaire handed Slim a leather pouch with a long, looped drawstring.

"What's this?" Slim asked as he took it in his hand. It had a feeling to it, a power that he couldn't identify or understand.

"You keep it, cum sa? Dis to knock some de pain out your soul. It help you, eh? And it fo' later. You know when you need use it. Wear it roun' your neck, close your heart. De time to use it, she come." Belizaire turned to Progress. "You go home now, papa. I got tings to do, me, to take dis pain and killin' from de groun'. I be there whenever you need me." He turned and walked back into the house, leaving them alone on the porch.

They piled back into the pickup and drove away. Slim turned his eyes aside as they went past the wrecked black car. He didn't want to see.

"I don't want to go home," Nadine said. "Not right now. I know we have to deal with that *thing* sometime, but the hound'll keep it safe for a while longer. What do you say we go to Mitchell's, Daddy? Have something to eat and drink. Relax a little."

"Okay with me, Nadine. How 'bout you, Slim?"

Slim was preoccupied, thinking about what had just happened and wondering how he could manage to sneakily put his arm around Nadine. "Anywhere's okay with me," he said. "I could use some food. I feel pretty empty."

"That's the power," Progress said. "Usin' it will eat you up if you ain't careful to eat good."

"But I didn't hardly do anything."

"More than you think," Nadine said softly. "More than I can do."

"Nadine?" Slim whispered.

"Never mind," she said. "Come on, Daddy. Let's just go to Mitchell's."

She wouldn't talk any more on the way to town, but Slim was pleased and surprised when she grabbed his arm and put it around her small shoulders and then snuggled in close against him. Maybe he wasn't as much of a joke to her as he had been.

10

Not only are the blues viewed as having physical
attributes, which allow them to walk and run,
talk to and shake the victim, but they can also
predict the future and cause emotional reactions.
They can even enslave the sufferer . . .
—Daphne Duval Harrison, *Black Pearls*

The Blues Ain't Nothin'

I'm gonna build myself a raft, and float that river down,
I'll build myself a shack in some old Tejas town, Mmmm,
*   Mmmm,*
'Cause the blues ain't nothin', no the blues ain't nothin',
But a good man feelin' down.

Goin' down on the levee, gonna take a rockin' chair,
If my lovin' gal don't change, I rock away from there,
*   Mmmm, Mmmm,*
'Cause the blues ain't nothin', no the blues ain't nothin',
But a good man feelin' down.

Why'd you leave me blue, oh why did you leave me blue,
All I can do is sit and cry and cry for you, Mmmm, Mmmm,

'Cause the blues ain't nothin', no the blues ain't nothin'
But a good man feelin' down.

It was a slow day at Mitchell's. The waitress moved languidly to take and fill their orders. They got a pitcher of beer and all three ordered the chili and corn bread, bottomless-bowl style. The chili was full-bodied, spicy and satisfying, the corn bread light, but tight, yellow and solid. Slim could taste why it was the specialty of the house.

"Progress," he said. "I can feel it now—the power I mean. But I didn't know what I was doing. How do I make it work? How do I control it?"

Progress kept on eating and thinking. Slim waited for him to answer, which he did, after a few minutes and chews. "Well, son," he said. "Onliest way I can tell you, is by talkin' blues, 'cause that's what it is, you see? It's about upholdin' values and havin' fun. The power's there for you, for anyone. But there's lots of things people don't want to hear, and the last thing they want to hear is that power and freedom comes from discipline. That's somethin' you got to have. I guess players got it 'cause we got to work so hard to learn to play and keep it goin', and 'cause we gots to work into the structure of the music. But you gots to give it latitude, too. Latitude's your wings. That's important. You be feelin' slow, or fast, or in between, and you want to lay back, but blues players don't slow down, they stretch time. They lay back so much they come sneakin' up on you.

"I'm talkin' an attitude now, not chops. Chops is fine, but chops is just chops, just tricks. You want the real power. It's like bein' a singer. You might be a great singer, but if you don't have a great song, what are you gonna do? It's the same with players, and with the power. If you don't have a great song to play a solo with, a good heart to base the power on, a base or foundation to do somethin' melodically, chops don't mean nothin'."

"I don't understand," Slim said. "I don't get what you mean."

"It's what I'm tellin' you son. To use the power to fight, or enhance or enchant, you got to harmonize with the situation, work with what's there. Songs and people are weird things. If you pick everything off of 'em, all you got left is the bare bones, then you got to follow that. If you're a painter, then you start out with an empty canvas. If you're a player, your canvas is silence. Now if you fucks around with that—if you're a player you fucks around with silence. And you leave some spaces, you leave some movement. Maybe it ain't quick or flashy, but it works better and it's a lot harder than just knockin' off few quick licks. Savor each note before you go on to the next, and come up for air, too. Don't forget to breathe and play the spaces as well as the notes. That silence is a condition of the sound, just like sleepin' is a condition of life. You understand?"

"I think so," Slim said. "Sort of, coming at it sideways. I just don't know if I can do it."

"You already has, son. Look here, you gots to remember no matter where you is, that you're on stage and you gots to give it everything. Don't forget what you're doin' there. If you wants to show the peoples what playin' is all about, you get on it and *show* 'em. When you put your hand in the air you better mean it. You don't get out there and act like no weasel, you stick that arm in the air and you make that guitar do its thing.

"You see, son, people ain't looking for the meaning of life. What they want is an experience of bein' *alive*. If you wants to use the power good, if you wants to help the peoples, what you gots to show 'em is a way to live in the world, to live with people. A lump in the throat is worth two on the head. You gots to sing like you don't need the money and dance like ain't nobody watchin'. You do that, and the day will come when you trust *you* more than you do now. It's a choice. You can be one of two things. You can look like one, or you can *be* one."

Slim started on his second bowl of chili and his third beer. He thought about what Progress had just said. It did make sense, if you thought of the blues as power. Like his own blues, though, there was a connection missing, and he had to ask. "What about love, Progress? Where does love fit in?"

He'd come to think that, no matter how hard he loved, he didn't know how to love, and that that was what was missing, what was holding him back.

"Oh, son," Progress said. "Come on and wake up, the early bird get the pancakes. Love's what's there, the heart and soul of it. Love's the only thing in the world matters scratch. Everything else grows out of that."

Progress looked sad, and Slim wondered if he was thinking about his wife.

"Let me tell you how to love," the old man said. "Because there's only one way in the world to do it right. See, when you love someone, you gots to love that person like every moment's the last time you'll see 'em 'cause if you don't, if you don't, and somethin' happens to 'em and they die, you'll think, 'I didn't hug 'em, I didn't tell 'em I loved 'em,' or you'll think, 'We argued and out last words was angry.' And son, if that happens, it'll tear your heart out the rest of your life. That's why you gots to make the things you do and say count forever. You gots to dust your blues and make your love come down, every minute, every day. 'Cause that's a mighty power, too. Maybe the mightiest. But it's a power you cain't use, cain't hold on to. It's a power you got to constantly give away. You see? The onliest thing in life that's free is love. Everything else, you can earn or steal."

Slim shook his head. "That's almost too deep to get under," he said. "I hope I can love that way. I wish I could. What about you though? Why didn't you ever get married again?"

Nadine punched him in the gut. "Slim!" she said, looking at him angrily. Then, rather than say anything else, she got up and headed to the bathroom.

Progress chuckled through a mouthful of corn bread. "Don't mind her," he said. "Nadine's a double-barreled woman. Just about the time you think the smoke's cleared, she'll open up and let you have the full load." He sighed and looked at Slim with sadness in his eyes, sadness and hurt. "She don't like to talk about her mama much. Thinks I don't either. But don't you worry none about her. I know she's a hard woman, she can get way down on a man. But that's just her way, you see. She's all the time testin' a man, seein' if he lives up to it. Was I you, I'd just lay back and mole when she's jivin', 'less you can think of a good answer. But when it's time to move, then you jump up and stand out and take care of your business. You're makin' her love come down, don't give up just cause it's hard."

He paused reflectively. "Far as me and her mama, truth is, I just couldn't find no better woman. There was lots before her. I'd be lyin' if I said there wasn't. But emotionally, sexually, in every way, there just couldn't be no one after her. Oh, I have me a woman now and again, but it's just feedin' the fire. It ain't marryin'. It's one thing to spend a night or two with someone soft and friendly, but it's a whole other gig to spend a life."

Progress looked around suspiciously. Nadine was still in the bathroom, so he moved his chair close up to Slim's.

"I'll tell you a secret," he said, smiling. "Big secret. Maybe it'll help you. Probably it won't. Most folks it don't. See, the thing is, when it comes to men and women—anybody, I guess—peoples behave the way other folks expect 'em to. You gets together with a nice lady, see, and you expect her to act in a certain way. And she's expectin' you to act in a certain way. So's, with each of you doin' so much expectin', you naturally try to live up to each other's expectations, good *or* bad. So what I figure is, what you got to do is to always expect the best from people. Then they'll try to give the best, maybe. It's a hard way to live, I ain't sayin' it ain't. It's livin' on faith, is what it is, but if we expect a person to act a certain way, then we moves 'em towards makin' that the easiest way for 'em to act. So if we act in faith that the other person gonna give us their best, that's just what they gots to do, seems like. And by actin' in that faith, their expectations of *you* will change for the best. That make any sense to you?"

"Yeah, it does," Slim said. "It makes a lot of sense." Slim had always expected the best, he thought. But if he was brutally honest with himself, he always expected the women to treat him cruelly and abandon him. Now he wondered if that expectation, and the way he, himself, acted because of it, was what caused the women to act the way they did. They were reflecting his pattern.

"Good," Progress said, shifting his chair back to its place in front of his plate. "Hush up, now. Here comes Nadine back." Then he sniffed. "You smell anything?"

Now Slim became aware of it. "Something burning. Bad smell. Almost like—"

Nadine pulled out her chair to sit down, and screamed. There was something on it, burning.

Slim lurched up, grabbing for the thing, to get it the hell out of her way. But Progress moved faster, blocking him off. "Don' touch it!"

Then Slim realized what it was: the flaming Glory Hand. Right there by their table, on her chair. It had been out of sight until she pulled the chair out.

A stout, tough man armed with a beltful of knives and cleavers forged across to them. Slim was alarmed, but Progress wasn't. "What's this?" the man demanded.

"A Glory Hand," Nadine said, shaken and disgusted.

"I know that, girl! What's it doing here?"

"Mitchell, it's after Slim Chance, here," Progress said. "Showed up twice at my house. Once I threw it in the river, once I boxed it and put a hound to guard it. I sure don' know how they got it here. Nadine was sittin' right there not a moment ago."

Mitchell nodded. "Well, it ain't going to bother you no more," he said gruffly. He hauled a cleaver from his belt and spiked the hand with it, using precisely enough force to catch it without cutting it in half. The flames doused the moment the blade touched it. He lifted it high. "Disinfect this chair," he barked at the waitress. "Bring 'Dine a new one." He marched off, bearing the hand, as the waitress hastened to exchange chairs.

"He's mad," Progress said with a certain satisfaction. "There won't be nobody sneaking nothin' like that in here again. Nobody does a thing like that to him twice."

Slim, though shaken, tried to make light of it. "Sure made Nadine sound off, though!"

Nadine sat down, glaring at Slim. He only smiled at her. She looked at Progress, then back at Slim. The confusion was clear in her eyes as she looked down to dip her corn bread in her chili.

Progress cleared his throat, and he and Slim laughed, which made Nadine glare at them again. Slim tried to concentrate on his chili and beer, but Progress wasn't finished.

"Slim," he said, just as if nothing had happened. The gold teeth were gleaming now. "What you like to drive? We gots to get you a vehicle."

"Progress, I can't let you keep buyin' me things. It isn't right."

"Daddy," Nadine interrupted. "Let him be. If he doesn't want it, he doesn't."

"Oh, bullshit, Nadine." He turned to Slim and looked him straight in the eye. "Look here, son," he said. "I gots more money than I can spend. You come into this here world with nothin'. How you think you get along? You gots to have a vehicle. After this here trouble is done and you start workin' gigs, then you pay me back as you can. Now what you like to drive?"

Slim considered a moment. In his whole life no one had ever been generous to him before, and he didn't know how to handle it, or even how to accept it. But he knew that he felt good for someone believing in him enough to extend the generosity.

"I guess I pretty much like vans," he said. "They're all I've owned the last twenty years. I can fix 'em up nice and stuff."

"Well, then," Progress said. "If we're all finished eatin', let's go down Sixth Street and see can't we find somethin' you like. What you say?"

Slim though about protesting again, uncomfortable with the gift giving, but Nadine shook her head.

"Don't bother to argue," she said. "Daddy does just what he wants. And he's right, so just sit back and enjoy it, because it's going to happen anyway."

"Okay, okay," Slim said, holding his hands up in surrender. "I'll go."

11

*As a poetic vehicle astonishingly free of the excess
moral baggage of "civilization," the blues provides
us with exemplary criteria, requiring total candor,
a willingness to assume risks, an unfettered
expression of the inner personality, an
unreserved fidelity to one's deepest aspirations, an
enthusiastic readiness for inspiration at all times.
By the same token, the blues is absolutely
incompatible with puritanism . . . piety
dogmatism, smugness, classicism, artifice, fascism,
masochism . . .*
—Paul Garon, *Blues and the Poetic Spirit*

It was another day with breakfast. Nadine was the best cook Slim had ever known, but he was kind of surprised at the menu. Today's breakfast consisted of refried beans, potato and egg and cheese burritos, and chiles rellenos. It wasn't the kind, or the amount, of breakfast he was accustomed to, but as long as Nadine cooked it, he was sure he could adapt.

For a moment he reflected on the prior meal, when the Glory Hand had shown up again, and he had almost grabbed it. Someone must have dropped it in the chair while Slim was in animated conversation with Progress, and used magic to light it. He was sure it wouldn't return again, because Mitchell had clearly intended to destroy it. But it had been one close call. When they returned home, they had found the hound dog lying in a far corner, and the box with the hand gone. They dog had been beaten unconscious, but would survive. Obviously he had tried to defend the house, but couldn't stand up against a metal pipe.

"Chillen," Progress said, once the eating was done and the table was cleared. "Today we splits up again. You got the van now, Slim, so that should be no problem. We've still got to get Cannon's Jug Stompers, Willy G., Sonny Early, Spider John Koerner, and Earthman Jack. I can get those folks, they should be easy."

"What do *we* do, Daddy?" Nadine asked. "Who do we get?"

Progress seemed very reluctant to answer and, when he did, he didn't look at them. "I want you two," he said quietly, "to go get Heap of Bears."

Nadine stiffened and whipped her head around to look at Progress. There was a look of astonished rage on her face. Her eyes were narrowed, the pupils almost pinpoints. "*What!*" She nearly screamed it. "You can't mean that, not *him.*"

"Nadine," Progress said sadly. "We needs him for this. I thought maybe we could get by without him, but when they got that Glory Hand into Mitchell's without none of us noticin', I knew we had to step up the power. And it's time you made your peace with it. We've all three got to go to Elijigbo's tomorrow. You know how he and his people are. You gots to get this out of your system."

Nadine sighed. "I'll go," she said. "But don't expect anything. You know how I feel."

She stood and stalked out the door, without saying a word or letting any one else, slamming the door behind her. Slim was puzzled. "Who's Heap of Bears?" he asked. "And why's Nadine so pissed about it?"

"Well, son," Progress said, "you know how hard Nadine is on men. Or maybe you don't, she's been easy on you. But she's a total bitch sometimes. I've seen her cut a man down to nothin' and leave him bleedin' on the floor without a thought. Heap of Bears is the man made her that way. He was a cousin of her mama's, from the Indian Nations. A Shaman, medicine man. He come to stay with us when Nadine was about sixteen. He wanted to get to know her mama. Nadine, she fell real hard for him, and he seemed to take to her, too. They was together constantly. I s'pect he was her first lover. One day he just up and left, went back to the Cheyenne to finished his training. Embarada, that was my wife's name, she tried to explain to Nadine that since he was a Shaman, he couldn't marry. And even if he could, the rules the tribe has to live with are hard. He could never marry blood kin on his mother's side, which Nadine was. But Nadine, she took it hard. That was when she moved out on her own and started singin'. She never had much to do with any man after that. Until now, with you."

Slim was surprised. He would have expected Nadine to be sought after, the kind of woman who would enjoy her pleasures, whether she respected the man or not. But for him to be the first man she'd been involved with since she'd been sixteen, that's not what he would have suspected. Nor was he entirely sure that was what he wanted.

"A few years ago," Progress continued, "Heap of Bears moved back to Tejas. Nadine 'bout went crazy. Wanted to track him down and kill him. Now, I'm sendin' her right to him."

"But won't she—?"

Progress shook his head. "No. Her hate's gone too far and too old for nothin' but pain. But you listen, son. She's gonna need you. No matter what she says or does, you hold on tight to her, hold on tight to your love for her. I know how you feel it. I can see it in your eyes every time you look at her. I can hear your heart achin' with it when she smiles at you or holds your hand. Now, you're the first man she's ever let herself down with, and I wants you two to be together. I know I'm only a foolish old man, but you're right for each other. So you hold on to it all, today. She'll need you."

"Okay, Progress. I'll try my best."

"I knows you will, son. I knows you will. You best get movin' now. I knows Nadine, and I'd bet she's sittin' out in that van waitin' for you."

Nadine *had* been waiting in the van, an evil look on her face. Other than succinct directions, she hadn't said a word as Slim drove. She just turned on the stereo, lit a joint, drank a soda and rode. Slim wanted to talk to her, wanted to say something, anything. But he couldn't think of anything to say that he didn't think would make things worse; or bring her anger down on him. She seemed to him, at that moment, so hurt, so small. He was used to her strength and spirit. He didn't like seeing her like this. It bothered him a lot.

They drove in comparative silence for three hours. The van was comfortable and had a good-size motor that made driving a pleasure. But Slim was nervous and uncomfortable because he knew Nadine hurt and he didn't know what to do, what to expect. He knew it was at least partly his fault, because the Glory Hand was after him, and its appearance had made Progress decide that they had to enlist this Heap of Bears character.

Finally, she pointed down a dirt road and he turned on to it. They went a mile or so through the scrub and mesquite and pulled up in front of a grouping of wickiups and hogans.

They got out of the van and Nadine walked around to Slim. She looked at him oddly, her eyes soft and deep green. Then she pressed him up against the side of the van and kissed him, hard, molding her body to his. Slim's brain almost exploded as he put his arms around her and returned the kiss. When she released him, he nearly fell down from the sudden weakness in his knees. Talk of mercurial changes! He had thought she was mad at him all this time. If so, she had a funny way of showing it. And maybe she *was* mad, and doing this to set him up for a hard fall. If so, her effort was wasted; he had already fallen. For her.

"Come on," she said, taking his hand. He followed, in a daze, trying to keep his head. They walked through the clean, bare dirt compound to the largest, most heavily decorated tipi, through the tented door to the dim light of the interior. Inside, it was furnished with corn husks, animal skins and feathers. There were sleeping benches against the wall, and branch constructions whose function wasn't clear. A half-naked man sat, eyes closed and peaceful, before a smoldering fire pit in the center of the floor. He heard Nadine gasp and felt her hand tighten almost painfully on his. The man's face and body had been cicatrized: he had been cut, and flesh had drawn together around the wounds, rendering him into something strange. The pain of it must have been unbearable by any but the most truly dedicated disciple of the ritual. The scars stood out as dark black patterns against his bronze flesh.

"Heap of Bears," Nadine said, almost whispered.

The man looked up at her. There was a faraway pain in his eyes. He didn't smile.

"Welcome to my home," he said. "Sit."

They sat together on a buffalo skin, across the fire pit from Heap of Bears. The man studied them closely as they sat. Nadine put her arm through the crook of Slim's elbow and held tightly to him. He tried very hard to be strong, and to make Nadine feel his love for her.

"It has been many years, Little Wing," Heap of Bears said, and Slim felt her body tighten at the sound of the name he called her. This man had not lost all of his power over her. "Are you well?"

"I'm okay," Nadine replied curtly, sarcastically.

"Who is this man you bring to my tipi?"

Nadine's hand tightened on his arm. Her short nails dug into his skin. "This is Slim," she said. "My lover."

Slim almost jumped. Then he remembered what Progress had said. *No matter what, hang on tight.*

"Is he a good man?" Heap of Bears asked.

"He's trying to be."

"You are angry with me?"

Slim could feel Nadine tremble. "Shouldn't I be?" she asked. "I loved you. You left me."

"No—you do not remember right. And there are things you do not know."

"What don't I know?" Nadine's voice was venomous.

"Little Wing, you were so young. I know that you thought you loved me. But I could not love you. You were not the woman for me. No woman is the woman for me."

Nadine pulled Slim's arm around her and pressed his hand against her small breast. He could feel her heart beating wildly and, at the moment, he would gratefully and gladly have died for her.

"Then why?" she asked.

"When I came to renew my kinship with your mother, my cousin, she asked me to initiate you into womanhood. It is our way, you see, for a relative, especially a Shaman, to initiate kin. I enjoyed you, and I cherished you, but I was not, and am not, allowed to love, not in that manner."

"My mother asked you to fuck me?"

Heap of Bears grimaced. "Do not be crude, Little Wing. There was no intention to harm you. And, truly, would you still want me, now, with the Shaman's marks covering my body?"

"I don't know," Nadine said, pressing Slim's hand more closely to her breast. "I was never given a chance to find out what I wanted. How could my mother do that to me?"

"It is the way our people live." Heap of Bears shrugged. "I could not refuse your mother's request to teach you love and the pains of womanhood. She was Cheyenne. I am Cheyenne, and Shaman. She wanted you to know."

Slim felt Nadine relax suddenly. "Yeah, well, fuck it," she said. "Who needs it. Let's go, Slim."

To his surprise and confusion, with his arm around Nadine, with her nipple burning into his palm, he said, "No. We came here for a reason. Maybe you hate him. I can understand that. But we gotta do what Progress wants us to."

"Shit," Nadine said. "You're right."

The Shaman's gaze played across Slim with disturbing awareness. It was apparent that this man could jerk Nadine around emotionally in much the way she jerked Slim around, but he was no jerk. He made her look like a petulant child. "Your man has strength and courage, Little Wing."

"I guess he does," she said, looking at Slim with a new softness in her eyes. There seemed to be a force beyond their control, one that everyone but them conspired with, drawing them together.

Nadine told Heap of Bears the story that they were both getting tired of telling, a story that grew with each recitation.

Heap of Bears didn't react to it. Instead, he said, "Will you make peace with me, Little Wing? Will you and your man smoke the pipe?"

"Oh, I guess," Nadine said. "The hate hasn't done me any good."

Heap of Bears stood and took a long stone pipe from a feather-and-corn-bedecked rack against the wall. It was intricately carved with the interlocked heads of eagles, painted, and already filled with a rough, musky-smelling tobacco. He plucked a small glowing coal from the fire and laid it in the bowl of the pipe. He then held the pipe up to the North, the South, the East and the West, letting the smoke drift in all four directions, toward the differently colored stones that were set in the floor at each compass point. Then Heap of Bears drew in a deep lungful of the sweet smoke and handed the pipe to Nadine.

Nadine held the pipe in her hands for a few moments as the smoke curled up into her face and hair, limning her with a blue haze. She looked at the pipe, and at Heap of Bears. The she lifted it to her lips and drew in the smoke. She exhaled slowly, softly, and passed the pipe to Slim.

He held the pipe gently in his hands. He could felt the power in the stone. It almost seemed to vibrate, and he knew the pipe was a serious matter. He had held it, thinking, for a while when he felt Nadine elbow him in the ribs. He lifted it and sucked in the smoke. It tasted like no tobacco he had ever smoked, and felt as if he'd drawn much more than simple smoke into his lungs. He coughed and handed the pipe back to Heap of Bears, who lifted it once again to the four directions, then placed it, still burning, back into its rack.

"Does you father know what he asks of me?" Heap of Bears said. "I am a healer, a man of medicine."

Slim felt full of power and decided to reply to Heap of Bears instead of waiting for Nadine to answer.

"This *is* a healing," he said. "Not a person, maybe, but the music. It's just that to do the healing, we're going to have to fight."

"I see," the Shaman said. "That is a good thing. I will come, then." He looked closely at Nadine. "Can there now be peace between us, Little Wing? Can we now let the past remain in the past?"

Nadine stood up and brushed her pants off. "I suppose," she said. "But don't expect to be friends. I don't need friends like you."

"The peace alone is sufficient," Heap of Bears said. "As long as the hate does not live between us, I am happy."

"Yeah, sure," she said.

"But for it to be complete, so that your power can grow to repel the evil behind the severed hand, you must in turn love another." His eyes seemed to intensify as they touched her. "In deed as well as in word."

Slim realized then that her words had not fooled the Shaman, and that Heap of Bears had taken it in stride with amusement rather than annoyance.

Nadine nodded and grabbed Slim's hand. He stood up, unsure of what to say or do. He wished Nadine had been able to accept the man's peace with better grace. It was apparent that she had done what she had to do, grudgingly, and thereby gained only a fraction of what was available.

"Let's go," Nadine said. "I don't want to be here any more."

Slim walked with her, out the door, back to the van. "Where to now?" he asked. "Back home?"

"No, I don't want to go home right now. Just drive back to town and we'll figure it out then. I have to think."

"Oh, Nadine," Slim said. "If you didn't drive me to tears, we'd never go anywhere at all."

She laughed, her mood yielding to his humor. "Damn it, Slim, drive." She pointed down the road. "Just go that way."

"That's what I like," he replied. "A woman with a good sense of direction."

"Slim," she said. "You're cute. About cute enough to keep in a trunk and bring out only on Sundays." She sighed. "I wish loving you was as easy as you are."

"*Me?*" he said. "I'm not easy. I just—I just love you." He'd said it, finally, and the lump in his throat went all the way down to his balls. Maybe seeing her human weakness in the presence of the man who had taught her love and loss had emboldened him. And he was afraid of what she might say in reply. But Nadine remained quiet. She just smiled and sat back as they drove once more in silence.

Slim knew that what she'd said to Heap of Bears, about his being her lover, had been said to try to hurt the man. But he wondered if she knew that, in a way, it had hurt Slim, too, a little. It wasn't that he minded being used in that way, but that he wanted so badly for it to be true. He'd never wanted *any* woman as much as he wanted Nadine, far beyond the merely physical. Every time she touched him it was like a fire on his skin and a storm in his heart, like a hard wind blowing him away.

He'd looked for love all of his life. He'd looked in all the wrong women at all the wrong times. Now that he'd found it in himself, he didn't know just what to do with it. The way Nadine acted, he was sure she felt *something* for him. But she was so sharp, sometimes, as if she could zero in on his worst weaknesses and strike directly at them. He understood now, though, why she might be so hard on men. But everyone had said she was treating him differently. He wasn't sure he understood that at all.

It was, in all respects, a long, thoughtful drive back into town. Nadine told him to pull off the freeway and get on River Road. After they'd gone a few miles, she directed him onto a side road and then told him to drive into a field. They ended up in a tree-hidden copse, overlooking a slow, quiet creek. She turned in the seat and stood up.

"Let's go in the back," she said, turning the stereo up.

Slim followed her into the back of the van. He didn't dare even conjecture what was on her mind. She lay down on the padded, carpeted floor and pulled him down beside her.

"Nadine—" he started.

But she put her finger to his mouth. "It's time."

She pulled him close, kissed him, her tongue playing in his mouth. He felt her hand unbuttoning his jeans. He reached under her blouse for her breast, felt it hot in his hand. When he felt her hand holding and caressing his dick, he thought he would die on the spot and couldn't stop his hips from pressing into her.

They quickly, instinctively undressed each other, and their lovemaking was hard and passionate. The smell and taste of her made Slim wild, and they smelled and tasted each other everywhere, explored every inch of each other's skin from head to toe.

When it was over, he licked the sweat from her breasts and belly, marveled at the smooth texture of her caramel skin, gazed into her eyes and held her tightly against him, not wanting to lose the moment, in fear it would never come again.

"I'm sorry," she said.

"Sorry? What in the world for?"

"I should have waited for you to start this," she said. "I promised myself I would."

"You shit and fall back in it," Slim said. "This was perfect. You think I give a damn who starts anything? If we'd waited for me, we might never have gotten here. I've been wanting this since the first time I saw you. Since I saw your picture. Sorry? No, Nadine. Thank you. Thank you for this."

"Thank you, too," she said, smiling and caressing his cheek. "If it's worth anything, and I guess it is, I think Daddy's right about you."

"Right?" Slim asked. "Right about what?"

"He told me from the start that you were the right man for me. You're still kind of a fool, sorry. But I do think he was right. I don't know why. I guess I don't care. Something inside me keeps going right to you. Can I tell you something?"

"You can tell me anything, Nadine."

"Um, you know about Heap of Bears, now. Does it make a difference?"

"No," Slim said quickly. "Not in loving you. In trying to understand you, yes, but not in loving you."

"Well," she said shyly. "I want you to know that, until now, there haven't been any other men. I mean, I haven't made love with anyone since I was sixteen. Not until you."

Slim pulled her closer. How could he answer that except with his body and his heart? While they'd been talking, they'd also been playing, and Slim had risen to the occasion. Nadine turned around, and they loved each other with their hands and mouths until the inevitable climax rolled them away again.

They lay quietly in each other's arms, hands playing idly with exhausted body parts, feeling the slipperiness of sweat on delightful skin.

"We'd better get going," Nadine said abruptly, sitting up and grabbing her clothes.

"Where to?" Slim asked, also dressing himself. "I don't feel like going home just yet. I want you to myself for a little while longer."

"Okay. You want to go to Mitchell's and then go out dancing or something?"

"Sure," he said. "I'd love to dance with *you.*"

12

They both had "Specialburgers" at Mitchell's, and Slim began to wonder if Nadine was picking up his eating habits. Then thought that that was wholly ridiculous idea. But her hand in his, walking out of the restaurant, was far from ridiculous. His body was still burning sublimely from their lovemaking, his mind and heart in delicious turmoil. He was almost afraid that his whole body glowed with it, making it obvious to everyone they encountered. Then he realized that it wasn't fear he felt, but pride. Let the whole world know!

They drove to Forty-fifth and Canyon, to a little club that Nadine chose. He could hear the music from the parking lot, a twangy, swampy sound, concentrated around a singer that growled like Howlin' Wolf. The sign on the door said the band called itself Omar and the Howlers. Slim liked it. It had a simple, clean sound, unaffected by the power. It was clearly entertainment, dance music, and for the lack of added meaning, Slim was relieved.

Nadine changed to a black miniskirt and a thin, black blouse that flowed in the most delightful way when her breasts bounced beneath it.

"You always carry a change of clothes?" he asked when she changed.

"Sometimes," she said. "I did today."

"Well, you look beautiful."

"Thanks."

They walked hand in hand into the club. It was a surprise on the inside, perhaps the cleanest nightclub he'd ever seen. They walked through a short hallway into the bar area. Guitars were hung in a row all around the walls, just below the ceiling. The collection represented more instrumental wealth than Slim could imagine, and though he failed to recognize the make of most of them, he was envious and coveted them all. The bar was circular, in the middle of the club. To the back of the bar was a small sunken area filled with pool tables no one was using. To the front of the bar, in another sunken area, were tables, a small dance floor and a stage on which four musicians were calling the tunes.

They ordered a couple of beers, and then sat at a table near the stage, watching the dancers. Slim loved to dance, had always loved dancing, but he was shy and self-conscious about it till he'd gotten a fair amount of beer down. He was an energetic dancer, despite his size, but not a fancy dancer. Just the old step and slide and rock and hip shot. Sticking to the groove. There had been a few times, though, with a few ladies, when he'd known he was doing well enough that people were watching him. Though he'd never known for sure if it was admiration or amusement on the part of the watchers, and he hadn't wondered long on it, preferring to believe it was the former.

He looked at Nadine, trying to gauge how long he could stretch before she would want to dance. He was scared of it, with her, but she seemed to be in no hurry. Like him, she was drinking her beer and listening to Omar singing about hard times in a land of plenty.

"Nadine," he said/yelled.

"What?"

"I'm kind of shy about dancing," he said. "Is that okay?"

She laughed. "So am I."

"*You?*" he said incredulously. "But on stage you dance so good."

"Sure, but that's on stage. Part of the act, you know what I mean. This is real life. It's different."

"I'll be damned," Slim said to himself. It was nearly impossible to carry on a conversation, so they just listened and had two more beers. After the band had taken a break, to be replaced by what evidently passed for Top 40 in this world, played loudly over a bad sound system, he thought he was about ready.

"You wanna dance?" he said as the band returned. Nadine shook her head yes. He stood and took her hand as they walked out onto the dance floor. Sometimes it was easier to dance than others. If his fingers itched to hold a guitar and play a better lead than the one coming from the stage, it was very hard for him to dance. But Omar and the Howlers were laying it down solid, so moving came as easily as listening. For a moment, they were the only couple on the floor, the only couple dancing. But soon other people began to dance, moving to the music. Slim and Nadine out-danced them all. Even the band watched them with some admiration. They had their own steps, their own style but somehow, together, they made a perfect couple.

The song ended and they barely had time to walk over to their table for a quick drink before the music began again. Slim danced, but he watched Nadine dance even more closely. She closed her eyes, swayed and swirled and turned, dancing circles around him. He watched her breasts bounce and bob under the thin blouse, and saw, with great satisfaction, that other men, handsomer, more nicely dressed than he, thinner, watched her dance also. He felt they must envy him, and he loved the feeling.

The next one was a slow song and he and Nadine pressed closely together. He tightened his hips against her, though his pubic bone hurt from their earlier lovemaking, trying to convey his love and desire through his movement. The curve and softness of her nestled against him and made him feel better than he'd ever felt. She held him tighter and pushed against him, excited by the effect she was clearly having on him, his desire for her. Slim ground against her, his erection almost painful in its intensity, fired by the memory of their afternoon. Nadine, smiling, lifted up on her toes and rubbed against him feverishly, maliciously. Then she touched him softly on the back, low on his spine, and he exploded in orgasm, knees buckling and arms squeezing her tightly. All he could hear was her delighted laughter.

Nadine wouldn't let him stop dancing, even though he was sure his face was red through it all. For forty-five more minutes they danced, Nadine breaking out in giggle fits now and then, sometimes so severely she had to stop dancing to laugh. Slim thought he should be angry or embarrassed, but somehow it made him love her more that she should be so amused by getting him off the way she had. It made him feel almost young and foolish again.

Then, the music was stilled, the beers were drunk and they were sitting in the van. Nadine was still giggling.

"Oh, Slim," she said, "you should have seen your face. You were so surprised."

"Jeez, Nadine. Is sex always so—*public* around here, along with talking about my personal life?"

"I'm afraid so," she said. "Most folks around here, well, we just don't care. It's not everywhere. There are places you can and places you can't. I generally try not to go to the places you can't."

"But you said you didn't—that there weren't any other men."

"There aren't," she said. "That was true. But I like the people and the attitudes better where you can have that kind of freedom." She laughed again. "Listen, Slim, the only reason I didn't just reach down your pants and grab you is because I didn't think you could handle it. Didn't you see the other people on the dance floor or at the tables?"

He shook his head and smiled. "No, I only saw you."

"That's sweet," Nadine said. "I know this isn't your world, okay? But for a lot of us, sex is out in the open. No one cares. It's not loose. I mean people don't just do it with *anyone*. But when people are in love and joyful with each other, we just let it go. It makes us feel good, you understand?"

"No," Slim said, "not really. You mean—I don't know what you mean."

"It's like I said. There are some clubs around town where folks are free to do what they want as long as nobody gets hurt. If you wanted to drink one beer too many, someone would have stopped you. Or if you'd tried to start a fight, you'd soon have been surrounded by people determined not to let you. But if you and I want to discreetly fool around on the floor, no one cares as long as we're not in the way."

"I see," he said. "You know something? I honestly do like this world. It's strange, but it's strange my way. Is it all free like that?"

"I don't know," Nadine said. "I don't know what's different about your world to what it is here. From everything you've told me, though, your world isn't a very happy place."

"No, it's not. It's not at all."

"Tell me a little about it," she said. "What your world's like."

Slim sighed. Where did he even begin to describe his world? "It's dirty," he said. "The air, the water, the land, all polluted and dying. There are too many people, way too many people. Most of them mean. They hurt each other, kill each other. It's a mean place, full of violence and loneliness and fascism disguised as a democracy. People don't cooperate or care about one another. People, children, live on the streets, homeless, starving to death, while people who could help them walk by unseeing. I don't even want to talk about the stupidity, the ignorance and illiteracy, the wars."

"How did it get that way?"

"Damned if I know. Back in the sixties, it seemed like it was changing. There was a movement toward the good, toward freedom. But people like T-Bone crushed it and twisted it completely until all the most beautiful aspects of it were selling soap and cars and underarm deodorant. I guess the worst thing, to me at least, is that people of different races hate each other and victimize each other. None of it makes any sense to me, but it's there. People beat and abuse their children, and their children grow up to beat and abuse other children and each other. And women, well, women don't get treated any good at all in my world. It seems like they're everybody's victims. And the politicians and idiots call it a good world. It sucks."

"Isn't there anything good about it at all?" she asked.

"Mmm, I guess, yeah. Sunshine, when you can see it. Animals, the ones that are still left alive. What there is to enjoy of nature and beauty. And I love driving. The music's good, sometimes, too. The blues is alive, but scant. And we got rock and roll. That isn't here."

"What is it?" Nadine said, puzzled.

"That's hard to explain," Slim said. "It grew from the blues, but it got complicated and different. I'll sit down and play it for you when this Gutbucket gig is done, that's the only way I can explain it. It's blues, but it's played with a different rhythm and a different attitude. Who knows, maybe this world is ready for a little rock and roll."

"You think?"

"I don't know," Slim said resignedly. "Me, I like the blues a lot better. When rock and roll came along in my world, real blues sort of fell out. I don't want that to happen here. I love the blues too much."

"Don't let it happen, then. Just play it for me and we'll keep it our secret." She paused and took his hand. "Nothing else good in your world?" she asked.

"Probably is," Slim said. "But nothing I can't find here, and better. Besides, you're in this world, and that makes it far far more wonderful than mine."

"Thanks," she said. "Listen, let's get back to the house. You sleep with me from now on, okay?"

The flat statement nearly knocked him over, but he tried very hard not to let it show. "Okay," he said. A few moments passed in his avid gazing into her eyes. Then he said, "Nadine? Do you love me a little, maybe?"

"Maybe," she replied, smiling. "Ask me tomorrow or something. I don't know yet."

Slim wondered achingly when she *would* know. He wondered with all his heart and soul when she would know. It seemed, to him, that that was one of those little things it was important to have a definite opinion about. But, then, she must have one, he thought. She had made love to him.

13

*The hero is himself the spokesman and the
representation given (in this case in the songs)
brings before the audience . . . self-conscious
human beings, who know their own rights and
purposes, the power and the will belonging to
their specific nature, and who know how to state
them. They are artists who do not express with
unconscious naivete and naturalness the merely
external aspect of what they begin and what they
decide on . . . They make the very inner being
eternal, they prove the righteousness of their
action, and the pathos controlling them is subtly
asserted and definitely expressed in its universal
individuality.*
—G. W. F. Hegel, *On Tragedy*

Back in the pickup, once again on the road, the next day, Slim
sensed that Progress, and to a lesser extent Nadine, was very
nervous. The ever-present gold smile had vanished, and the
mood was serious, even afraid. It made Slim jumpy. Nadine's hand in
his didn't even calm his anxiety, since he could feel, in the flesh-to-
flesh touch, how tense she was. Finally, near to town, he could bear it
no longer.

"Okay, Progress," he said. "Who's the guy we're going to see—what's his name?"

"Elijigbo," Progress answered simply.

"Why's going to see this Elijigbo makin' everybody so uptight?"

Progress whooped, and his hands relaxed minimally on the steering wheel. "That's a good question," he said. "I don't know if anyone knows the answer to it. But I'll tells you what I do know. Elijigbo, he's the leader of a community, a town. It's separate, but in town. A religious community. They came here about forty years ago, nobody knowed from where, and set it up. It's a big place, all walled around. Peoples can go in, but they gots to follow the rules inside. And Eli, he's 'bout the most powerful man I know of. I don't understands it all, but it has to do with a whole mess of Gods they believe in. And knowin' Eli like I do, I guess I half believe in it my own self. They do got hold of *somethin'*."

"Don't the Christians get on their shit?" Slim asked.

"Christians?" Progress looked curious. "What are those?"

"A religion, in my world," Slim said. "One of the biggest, maybe the worst. For sure the richest and most powerful."

"I dunno," Progress said. "We got nothin' like that 'round here. We gots a lot of religions, but no one that's bigger or more powerful than the others. Folks just pretty much leaves other folks alone to believe what they wants to."

"What about you?" Slim said. "What do you believe?"

"Me? I believes in women, and I believes in the blues."

Slim laughed, truly delighted. "Me, too," he said. "That sounds good to me."

"Well, son, I don't want to make it sound all simple. I mean, there's things you does because you knows they're right. No one nowhere else gots to tell you. Way I figure it, you can spend your life tryin' to understand women and the blues, the two of 'em just naturally goin' together like they do. And if you gets even halfway there, then you're doin' real fine in this here world. Right, Nadine?"

Nadine shook her head. "Don't ask me, Daddy. I'm too busy just trying to understand myself and what's been happening."

"I understand it," Slim said happily. "I've spent my whole life trying to understand women and trying to figure the blues out."

"It ain't somethin' you can figure," Progress said. "Not really. You gots to live it, and the understandin' comes with the livin'. You jumps in, and you gets hurt, and you jumps right back again. The jumps get longer and harder, and if you're doin' it right, lookin' around, pickin' up any little understandin', they get further apart. Sooner or later, you still jumps, but you learns to land. Then the jumps get mighty interestin', with finer scenery on the way.

"But the jumpin's all there is to life. We jumps to women and we jumps to creation. Not everybody, I guess. Some folks thinks they need different things, so they jumps to those. And I guess women have things their own selves that they jumps to. Not so different maybe. I think people like you and me and Nadine, we needs a partner, a woman or a man, someone who opens us up and breaks out all those good things we got inside us tryin' to get out.

"In the end, you know, you gots to believe in yourself, before you believes in anything else. Believin' in somethin' else ain't gonna change the situation of your life. You does that by keepin' on jumpin' and gettin' hurt. You see where you lands and you walk on ahead from it. It's a hard road, I know, but you learns to take it slow and swerve 'round most of the bad bumps."

Nadine let Slim's hand loose and laid her own on his leg, awfully close to where he had often suspected his brains were located. "Oh, Daddy," she said. "You always say everything's a road. I keep thinking I'm going to wake up one of these days with tire tracks all up and down my ass. It's not that easy."

"Sure it is, Nadine. Life's easy unless you makes a choice for it to be hard. Look at you and Slim gettin' together. Is that makin' it hard or makin' it easy?"

"Both," Nadine said, moving her hand to the heart of the matter. "I don't know yet. It's a lot of changes."

"What about you, Slim?"

Slim looked at Nadine, a habit he had quickly gotten into lately. She smiled and her hand held him. He could see that, over the years, her touch would always reach deeply inside him. It made it hard to talk. "I don't know that it's easier," he said. "But I know it's better, that it's what I've wanted all my life." He hesitated. "Why is it that everyone I meet wants to discuss my personal life? Why does everyone ask such deep questions around here?"

Progress laughed heartily, his teeth shining in the sun. "Not everyone," he said. "The people you've been meetin' are people with power. You'll find that people like that go right to the center of things. No bullshit, no foolin' around. They ask the questions to judge your heart. They gots to know what kind of man you is. They don't have no time for small talk and foolin'. Their lives are important to 'em, so they only talk about the important things. You handle it, don't you?"

"Yeah," Slim said. "I guess so. It's embarrassing, though, for everyone to seem to know everything that's going on. It makes me uncomfortable."

"Me, too," Nadine said to Slim, "and I'm used to it."

"Well, chillen," Progress said, "we're here."

They drove past Two Dude's Holistic Auto Repair and pulled into the parking lot of a strange nightclub called Fluorescent City. It was painted in wild rhythmic colors, as were the roof-high adobe walls that stretched out on either side of it. If Slim was right, they were on the west side of town, about where, on his world, the Westgate Mall had been. He wasn't sure, because he'd never been there. But he knew it was a very large piece of land.

They got out of the truck and walked through the open door of the club. It was dark inside and filled with the smell of freshly baked bread that was stacked on racks against one painted wall. On other racks on other walls were woven baskets, pots of red clay and small statues and paintings. A very dark black woman, dressed in shiny white, stood behind the bar.

"Brother Progress," she said. "Welcome."

"Hello, Ayisha," Progress replied, with a friendliness that made it clear he was far from an infrequent visitor. "Is Eli around?"

"Why sure. He's out and about the Torriero. Go on through, he'll find you. You know how it goes."

They walked to the back of the club and through another door. Slim felt, on passing through, that he'd walked into yet another world. White adobe houses with thatched roofs lined the streets. People bustled everywhere, dressed in white and active, yet without giving the impression of hurrying. There were people walking, carving wood, doing laundry in large iron pots wreathed in steam, working on houses, painting, cooking over open fires, tending goats or chickens, working in small, front-yard gardens. There were the smells of meat cooking in rich spices, bread baking, beans boiling and flowers. "This is the Torriero," Progress said quietly. "The club is the only entrance. They call their religion Candomble. One of the rules is that you cain't just go in and see who you want. Eli says you gots to walk around the Torriero awhile, visitin' and thinkin'."

They passed several dark old men throwing bones on the dirt ground. Slim stared at the religious murals that seemed to be lovingly painted on every house. The murals depicted men and women dressed in white, dancing and singing. Nearly transparent, brightly colored, often humorous creatures who appeared nearly human rode on their shoulders and backs, melded with their bodies. The creatures, Slim could see, were painted to invoke visions of water or lightning, Earth or wind or sex. Their Gods, Slim assumed, right out in the open, where the people would live with constant reminders of their presence.

The sounds of music and singing were constant in the Torriero. Rhythms that matched and complemented the tasks that each person was performing. Wildly different songs that blended, somehow, into a pleasant, if odd, harmony. These people were happy, Slim thought, and peaceful. Whether it was the religious beliefs, or simply the coherence and cooperation of the community didn't matter. It was there, solid, and Slim felt good being in the midst of it.

A young, beautiful woman danced up to them. She was, like the rest of the people in the Torriero, dressed in white, wearing a white turban and red and white beads around her neck. Her dancing motions never slowing or ceasing, she reached into the woven basket she carried and began sprinkling them with fresh, sweet-smelling, multi-colored flower petals. When she'd covered them to her satisfaction, she danced off with the small group of curious children who had been following them.

"What was that all about?" Slim asked, brushing himself off.

"It's the Candomble way of purifying us," Progress replied. "We should run into Eli pretty soon. They don't send someone around to purify you until it's nearly time to get down to business."

They continued walking aimlessly along the dirt roads of the Torriero, greeting people, listening to this or that one singing or playing, watching dancers, enjoying the savory smells of the cooking, sampling the bits that were offered. Shortly, a man approached them.

"Come with me," he said.

They followed him onto a narrow, tree- and plant-lined path to a large building sitting isolated, almost hidden in the foliage, then went inside. The interior was one large room, like a warehouse. The furnishings consisted solely of a large table and its accompanying chairs, and a stage against one wall, set up with band instruments, ready to use. It was dark inside.

The man said, "Sit down," and then he left.

They sat at the table and waited. Soon, from the rear of the building, a man approached them. They heard his bare feet slapping on the polished wooden floor before they saw him. When he came into sight, they saw he was also dressed in white, a long white robe, and there were multicolored beads around his neck. Many strands of them. His face was ebony and unlined, his age undeterminable. He moved with unusual grace, arms and legs swinging easily, loosely, feet planted solidly on the ground, lifting off naturally. He smiled when he saw them.

"Progress," he said happily. His voice was deep, rumbling. "A pleasure to see you again. And you, too, Nadine." He looked a Slim a few moments, and Slim could feel power exuding from Elijigbo's body. "And you, too, young man," he continued. "Welcome to the Torriero."

"Howdy, Eli," Progress said. "How you be?"

"Ah," Eli laughed. "I am wonderfully well. The Torriero prospers, the people are happy and in love. The Orishas are pleased, life is good. And you, my friend?"

"Well enough, I suppose," Progress replied. "I guess it's foolish to ask, but do you already know the problem we've come here about?"

"I've heard some few things. What do you need from us?"

"Well, we're settin' up a blues festival for the thing. I was hoping you and your people would set it up for us. Road crew, security, all the regular stuff."

"My people would be happy to do the festival work," Elijigbo said. "Is that all you need?"

Progress looked almost scared. "No," he said. "I was hopin' you'd be willin' to play with us, you and your drummers."

"Why me?"

"Eli," Progress said. "I need you. I need your power behind us. I need it for this boy here, Slim, and I need it for the Gutbucket."

Something in what Progress had said, in what other people had said and done, made Slim begin to believe that he was intended to play a larger part in this business than he had first thought. It seemed, ridiculous as it sounded to him, that he was a pivot, around which the whole resolution of the problem revolved. But how could that be? He was just himself, nobody important.

Elijigbo looked at him, as if sensing his thought. Slim could feel the man's eyes piercing his soul and mind.

"What about you, Slim? You got anything to say for yourself?"

"Eli!" Nadine protested.

"Now, Nadine," Elijigbo said. "You hush. This man has a right to speak for himself. That hand is only the beginning of what he has to face, and not the worst."

Something worse than the Glory Hand? Elijigbo saw the scared look Slim flashed at Nadine, knew he was hopelessly in love with her.

"Nadine," he said, "is this man your lover?"

"Yes," she answered.

"You be careful with him, you hear me?"

Nadine was startled by the fierce look in Elijigbo's eyes. There was only a puzzled look in her own, one reflected in Slim's as she looked at him and took his hand. She could feel the instant rush of total love and relief that passed through Slim's body as she touched him. But she and Slim were left with the impression that Elijigbo knew more than he was telling them.

"Go ahead," she said, "Eli's a friend. Speak your mind." She paused. "I'd like to hear, too."

Slim looked at Progress.

"Don't be lookin' at me, son," Progress said. "There's been entirely too much lookin' around at this table as it is."

"Come along," Elijigbo said. "What do you think?"

Slim bowed his head. He felt, at that moment, that he had reached a point at which he had to fail or be brave. He had to prove himself to

Elijigbo, to Progress, and most of all to Nadine. If he didn't do it now, he might never have the courage for it. He squeezed Nadine's hand and looked up at her, trying to communicate all the love he felt through his eyes. "I don't know," he said to Elijigbo. "I guess, right now, I'd rather play than talk."

Nadine started to say something, but Elijigbo stopped her with a look.

"Slim," he said. "You aren't nearly as stupid as you look. Stand on up and go over and pick out a guitar you like. I think we can arrange something for you. Just let me go get some of the boys and break out the jammin' jar. I'll be back in a few minutes. That'll give you a chance to warm up."

Elijigbo walked away from the table, back out the way he'd come. Slim stood up and his knees only shook a little as he walked over to the stage. He saw a maple-necked strat and he knew that was the guitar he'd use. Progress laid a hand on his shoulder.

"Don't worry," Progress said. "I'll be up there playin' with you."

Slim turned to him. "No, Progress. I want to do this on my own. You sit this one out."

"Okay, son. If that's what you feel, then that's what's right. I don't think you got anythin' to worry about, but I'd say Eli's decision is gonna rest on is you any good."

Slim smiled. "No pressure, right? I had a feeling it'd be this way. But I can handle it. I have to show Nadine I can play."

Slim looked over at her. There was a strange look on her face, half scared, half admiring. Slim knew that he could blow it badly, but he felt good, all the same.

"I understand," Progress said. "Just jump, son. You'll do fine."

Progress walked back over to the table and sat near Nadine. They whispered to each other, but Slim couldn't pay attention as he plugged into an amplifier and began to warm his fingers up, scaling the neck to get used to the strange guitar. He had to play something that was familiar to him, but something that was new, and would impress everybody else. He thought he had a trick or two up his sleeve. Maybe this world, this blues, hadn't developed the boogie, yet. He hadn't heard any of it. He'd show Elijigbo and his boys how to boogie, and he'd play his ass off to prove himself. He started running through the particular scales, reminding himself of some of the odd positions he could play in for the three-chord boogie. He was comfortable with the scales, and he knew a few good tricks he could pull out. Finger-tapping and such.

Elijigbo came back, followed by three other men. They reached the stage and Eli handed Slim a small jar filled with a clear liquid.

"Take a drink from the jammin' jar, Slim. Relax yourself a little."

Slim took a drink and passed the jar on. He was unprepared for the liquid fire that coursed down his throat, but it did immediately relax him, loosen him up. It made him feel good. The other men also took drinks, larger than Slim's. Then Eli took up a bass guitar, and the other men sat behind the drums or picked up their own guitars.

"All right," Elijigbo said. "Everything's turned on and we're ready. What are you going to do with it?"

"Something new," Slim said. "I hope it's new, anyway. Called the boogie. It's a I-III-IV, A, C and D. Let me show you."

Slim showed Eli the three-position repetitive bass line. He decided to put a twist in it by having him play it using alternating octave notes. That would add a sense of lightness and liveliness to it. He told the drummer to just follow the bass. If he was a good drummer, he already knew how to find the groove in it. To the rhythm players, he showed how to lay back on the A, and how to stand forward on the single hit, rolling C and D, to get the right emphasis.

The band started to have fun with a thing that was obviously new to them. The beat solidified and Slim jumped in, playing the single-string, double-octave lead line that intro'd the song. He moled for thirty-six bars, and then he moved to the A scale and started playing his lead on the lower strings, slow at first. As he moved down to the higher strings, he sped his playing up and tried to grab the melody.

He was stiff at first, taking no risks, not going outside the standard box pattern riffs and following chords. But, soon, the music caught him up and he began playing wildly all over the neck. He didn't think about what he was playing, he just let his fingers and his heart go free. The boogie had always been his favorite music, but he'd never thought of it as a love song. Somehow, though, it was working that way. Whether it was Nadine, or this world, or just the right time, he finally had a little of the feeling he'd been missing. There was no sense of wrongness, as there had been at Nadine's gig. Everything was copacetic: completely satisfactory.

He looked at the other men on the stage. Their eyes were closed, as if they were in a trance. Maybe it was, in a way, he thought, continuing with his own playing. He started fingertapping wildly, hammering down on the frets, all over the neck. It seemed that no matter where he played, it fit. He went into a double-string fingertapped run from the twelfth fret down to the third that sounded like a classical guitar riff.

He was mad, he was crazy, he was in love. He was having more sheer fun playing than he'd ever had in his life. He went on jamming for what seemed like hours, but when the song finally ended on Elijigbo's signal, it felt all too soon. He was drained, but exhilarated.

Elijigbo put his bass down. There was a serious, concerned look on his face. "Slim," he said. "I have to go and think about what just happened. You tell Progress that my people and I will give any help that's asked of us." He laughed, and it was comforting, mischievous laugh. "I don't think I'd want to miss what's going to happen at that festival." He and the men who'd come with him walked silently out of the building.

Slim reluctantly put the little guitar back on its stand and walked over to the table, waiting for the judgment. Nadine stood, walked over to him and kissed him, holding him tightly against her. If love-making could be contained in a kiss, Slim would have sworn it lived in that one. He had what he though of as an orgasm, taking place entirely in his mind and heart. Nadine broke the kiss, breathing heavily, and moved to stand by his side. He put his arm around her small shoulders and looked to Progress, waiting to hear what the old man would say.

Progress looked up at him curiously, then looked back down and shook his head.

"Son," he said. "I can see, now, I've underestimated you. That was—I don't know *what* that was. Never heard nothin' like it. Do you realize you almost called up the deep power all by yourself?"

"I didn't mean to," Slim said. "I didn't know I was doing anything. I was just playing for me and Nadine."

"I know you was, son. That's the way of the power. It just comes. But I gots to say, I didn't have no idea you had *that* much in you."

"*I* did," Nadine said proudly, patting Slim's head.

"Nadine, girl, this is the man you called a long-haired fool," Progress said. "Now you say you knew? Girl, you *lyin'*."

"I am not," she said. "I could tell. I just didn't think I liked him. I didn't like him having so much when I can hardly use what little I have."

"Girl," Progress said, his eyes narrowing. "That's your own fault. You scared of it, that's all. You got to forget that. You're a part of this, too. Separate what you do from who you is. You still gots to come home and eat spaghetti with your daddy, now and then. Get over it. You can't keep buttin' your head out on a stoopin' post."

"Listen, folks," Slim interrupted, made uncomfortable by the direction the talk was taking. "Can we postpone this and get out of here?"

"Yes, Daddy. Would you mind driving us home to get the van? I'd like to take Slim to my place and spend the night there. I bet he looks real good when he's cleaned up. Is that okay?"

"It's fine with me," Progress said. "Long as you be careful. We gots the people we need, so there ain't much doin' till the festival's set up. You two go on and enjoy yourselves. But watch out, you hear? We ain't seen the last of the Vipers yet. Not by a long shot."

14

Human freedom depends not only on the
destruction and restructuring of the economic
system, but on the restructuring of the mind. New
modes of poetic action, new networks of analogy,
new possibilities of expression all help formulate
the nature of the super session of reality, the
transformation of everyday life as it encumbers us
today, the unfolding and eventual triumph
of the marvelous.
—Paul Garon, *Blues and the Poetic Spirit*

My baby gets unruly, thinks she can stop a train,
Hold up her head, stop the lightning and the rain.
—Johnny Shines, "Black Panther"
(unreleased version)

Nadine's apartment was a surprise to Slim. It was neat and
clean and attractive, filled with books and plants and wonderfully odd things that caught the attention no matter
where one looked. One entire wall was taken up with a fancy stereo
cabinet and a large-screen TV. The rooms smelled healthy and alive as
Nadine hurried around, watering the neglected plants. As she wa-
tered, Slim was happy to see several wolf spiders crawl out from their
hiding places, as if in greeting. When one jumped on her, she reacted

only by inducing it to crawl onto her fingers and putting it back on the wall.

"This is where you live, huh?" What a lousy line for such a neat lady, Slim thought.

"Yes," Nadine replied. "I've lived here since I was eighteen. In fact," she said, "I own the building."

"Really? That's neat."

"Sounds good, doesn't it? Not so good, though, when you have to take care of it, too. But it is mine, free and clear. I only have to pay rent once a year when the taxes are due."

"Are you a mean, vicious landlord?" Slim asked, smiling.

"You bet," she said. "Why, if my tenants don't pay their rent within six months or so, out they go." She put the water pitcher she'd been using down, the job done. "Actually, I know all the people here. I only rent to musicians and their families. I've sung with most of them at one time or another. Good folks. They fall on hard times now and then, but we all help each other out, and they know I'll carry them until they get back up."

"What happens if we don't get the Gutbucket back?"

"We'll all be poor, then, I guess. And we'll lose the music. I don't want to talk about it, okay? You want to take a shower?"

"With you?" Slim asked.

She arched a brow. "You have a problem with that?"

"Let's go."

They undressed in the small bathroom, bumping butts and elbows, enjoying each moment of it. He didn't think he would ever get over the wonder of her naked body. The champagne-glass-sized breasts, the large nipples that stood out so high and proud, the small bulge her belly made that was just right to lay his head on, the way her ribs and hips stood out, the protruding hipbones that were so much fun to hang on to and wrap his hand around, the fine, curly hair between her legs, her small, kissable ass. Though he knew nobody was perfect, really perfect, for *him,* she was. And he truly hoped that, somehow, despite his fat and his age, she might feel a little of the same about him. He chided himself for being unable to accept her seeming love at face value, but that was the way he was, the way he had always been: unable to believe. She had given him her body, but he just wasn't sure about her heart.

Nadine adjusted the water and stepped into the shower. Slim followed and tried to slide past her, but she made sure to rub everything she had against him. She positioned him under the water and, grabbing the soap, began to lather his body, paying special attention to all the vital parts. He returned the favor, and they spent the time exploring each other's soapy bodies until the soap was washed away and the water turned cold.

They toweled each other off, then Nadine grabbed his dick and led him into the bedroom, into bed. "Time to stop teasing this thing," she murmured, laughing, "before it swells up any bigger. I don't like swelled heads." There was no foreplay after the shower, just passionate grasping and loving, arms and legs and lips locked, barely moving, trying to blend two bodies into one heart.

While Nadine lay sleeping, nestled into the crook of his arm, head resting on his chest, Slim lay awake, thinking.

He'd looked for this all his life. Apart from the problems he'd had with women, he was blessed, or cursed, depending on one's viewpoint, with an abnormally high sex drive, and tastes that some of his more prudish partners had described as kinky. It was difficult to find a woman that enjoyed all that he did, the way he did, but he had a feeling that Nadine would match him, and would also match the intense, almost obsessive way that he loved. And that scared him.

The family he'd grown up a part of didn't teach love. It didn't even teach normality or reality. He'd starved for love all his life. Now, having found it, he believed, he didn't know what to do. For a long time, he'd mistaken abuse for love, and so the meaner the women had been to him, the more loved he felt, even through the hurt and confusion. What little he *did* know about love, he'd learned from movies and television. Those weren't good examples, he knew, but they were all he'd had, growing up. So, for him, love was intense, sexual, constant, faithful and forever. It was frightening for him to realize, now, that he didn't actually know anything about love in the real world.

Nadine was so small and had hurt over Heap of Bears for so many years. He didn't want to hurt her the way women over the years had said they'd been hurt by Slim. He didn't know what he'd done but love them, but whatever it was he didn't want to do it to Nadine.

He'd been different, though, since he'd come to this world. He hadn't left his problems behind, but he'd somehow found ways to start overcoming them. Still, having Nadine believe in him, count on him, was pretty scary.

He remembered one woman, Nettie, when they were breaking up. "You're nothing but a ghost," she said. "There's nothing inside you. I never knew a man to be so intelligent and so stupid at the same time." And all the time she'd been betraying and abandoning him, he'd wanted to say, "But I *love* you! Doesn't that mean *anything?*" It hadn't, and he didn't understand when she'd thrown him out of his own home. Love was love, no matter what else went on. You didn't just dump somebody because times got hard. You didn't just give up. It wasn't right and it wasn't fair.

And sex. He'd never understand women's attitudes about sex. He could remember each time a woman hadn't wanted to make love to him because the house wasn't clean, or they were having problems, or any of a dozen other reasons he considered equally lame. He'd wanted to scream at them, "What the fuck does that have to do with making love?" But he knew they'd never answer. It was useless. All he could do was hope to find someone who loved the way he did. He thought it was Nadine.

He was surprised, as he lay there holding Nadine, to discover so much rage in himself. It was a rage that, while not directed toward any individual woman, was directed toward women in general, because of the cruel way they'd treated him. He remembered one woman saying, "A good man is hard to find." He'd answered her, cynically, "That's because women make it so hard to be good." He'd wondered sometimes in the past, if women were even capable of loving anyone but themselves, caring about anyone's feelings or survival but their own. Wondered why they all seemed so heartless, why they were always so needlessly cruel.

Now, though, he wasn't sure anymore. Here was Nadine next to him. She hadn't yet said she loved him, but he felt that she did. He felt loved by her, and she was only a little bit abusive, in a fun way. If someone as wonderful as she was could love him, how, then, could he keep holding on to that rage inside him? It could only get in the way of and hurt any good relationship he could build with Nadine. But how did he let go of it, let it out?

And what of the threat against him, as indicated by the pursuit of the black sedan and the several appearances of the horrible Glory Hand? There was an enemy who wanted to get rid of him somehow, either by killing him or by sending him back to his own world. At this point, the one was as bad as the other, because he'd as soon die as lose what he was finding here. It seemed they wanted to be rid of him because he had some key connection to the Gutbucket. He didn't know what that connection could be, but people like Heap of Bears and Elijigbo had hinted at it. They evidently saw something in him. He hoped, for the sake of Progress and Nadine and all the wonderful folk of this world, that they were right. He hoped he could stay here and survive and do whatever it was that needed to be done, justifying his presence here. He found so much here that he loved, he wanted to be worthy of it. To give something back.

As he slipped into sleep, he thought the only thing he could do, the only real choice he had, right now, was to hold on to Nadine, and hope his love for her, and hers for him, would help him work things out inside himself. So that whatever it was that he was here to do, would get done. So that he wouldn't mess it up, this time.

When they woke up, the next morning, they made love and Nadine made coffee. She slapped Slim on the ass while he was bent over getting his pants from the floor and, to his surprise, he liked it. It made him feel loved and appreciated. So he tickled her in return, making sure to take little side trips to visit her nipples. It wasn't long before the horseplay turned into loveplay, and they were both naked and in bed again.

"You want to get some breakfast?" Nadine said afterwards.

"I got my breakfast right here," Slim said, using his hand to indicate the exact portion he had in mind.

Nadine moaned and pushed his hand away. "Quit it, monster," she said with mock severity. "Come on, we're going to kill ourselves."

"Never heard of anybody dying from it yet," Slim replied. "Besides, Nadine, this is the way I am. Not just now, not when it's new. Always. I'm kind of abnormal."

"You're telling *me?*" she said. Then she saw a hurt look on his face, so she kissed him tenderly. "Okay, I know you carry your heart in your pants. To tell you the honest truth, I guess I do, too. But we just can't keep going. Save it up; let's go get some breakfast."

"Okay," said Slim, getting out of bed and getting dressed again. "Where do you want to go?"

Nadine laughed and caught herself half-in, half-out of the tight blouse she was putting on. She looked at him through an armhole and said, "Where do you think?"

"*Mitchell's,*" they both said in unison.

They stopped the van only once on the way. Nadine said she wanted to give him head right there on the street and Slim, in deep appreciation, was damned if he was going to say no. Right in the middle of town and everything. It took a while, since Slim's age and their previous activities were catching up with him, but it came to a satisfactory conclusion, just the same. And Nadine's sly, contented smile was worth any price in the world.

"Why always Mitchell's?" he asked. "Don't you ever go anywhere else?"

"No," Nadine replied. "Not if I can help it. Daddy raised me to like what he calls where-you-from-buddy restaurants. He says you can judge a restaurant by how many calendars it has hanging on the walls. It hasn't led me wrong yet, no matter where I've gone. But there aren't many more like that around. It's all chains and big business."

"Isn't that sort of what this whole thing is about, with the Gutbucket and all?" Slim asked.

"In a way. When Daddy grew up, restaurants and cafés and businesses were family, people you knew. If you asked him, he could take you to the town here in Tejas where the hamburger you like so much was invented. Or he could take you to the first Dairy Queen. Even when *I* was a kid, it was still pretty individual. But eventually, Pickens and people like him started moving in, sucking the heart out of things. There are still a few places around that are run by just folks. Daddy and I and people like us try to take our business there, but they still just get by while the chains make all the money. Really, all we have left is our music. We have to fight for that."

"What about the record companies?" Slim asked. "Aren't they chains, too?"

"Some are, some aren't. There are chains there, too. But there are a few that stay free. Cobra, Alligator, a few others. That's where Daddy and I do business. And Daddy isn't totally against chain businesses. He has one real big weakness. Stuckey's. He loves to go to Stuckey's. He calls it a museum of bad taste souvenir knickknacks. He loves the bacon-in-a-box, the ham-on-a-rope, the made-in-Mexico Indian trash, every cheap, horrible piece of crap ever invented to convince tourists they've actually been somewhere. He says anyone who runs a place like that, chain or not, can't be all bad. Ask him to show you his painted wooden plaque collection someday. I forbid him to ever hang any of them on his walls, or I wouldn't go out there. But any time he goes anywhere, he goes to Stuckeys, and if they have a plaque he doesn't already have, he brings it home. Other than that, we just don't go to the big businesses. It's the only way we've had to fight until now."

"But even if we get the Gutbucket back," Slim said, "won't Pickens just keep on trying to get us?"

"Not if we do it right," Nadine said. "Why do you think he's trying to get us? If we can get the Gutbucket, then we can destroy him, we can kill him. It won't solve the whole problem with the businesses, but it will eliminate the worst part of it."

"I don't want to kill people, Nadine. I don't like the idea of that." Slim fingered the gris-gris pouch around his neck. "I just don't have it in me."

"You think Daddy or I like it?" Nadine said angrily. "Sometimes you just don't have any choice. This isn't play. T-Bone's going to try to nullify you or kill us. That's the way it is. If you can't deal with it, you'd better say so now."

"No," Slim said. "I'll do whatever I have to do. I don't have to like it, though. I'm not even sure I buy it yet. What do *you* think about blues power?"

Nadine seemed to shiver for a moment, even in the hot summer air from the open window of the van. "I'm not the person to ask," she said quietly. "I've seen Daddy use it, and I've seen you use it—use it like no one else. And you played the pants off of anybody I've ever seen, by the way. But Daddy's right, I am scared of the power."

"You use it, though."

"I guess. Daddy says what I do is called enchantivating. I don't do it on purpose, it just happens." She sighed deeply, and her smile was wan and wistful. "All I ever wanted to do was sing. The rest of it doesn't have anything to do with me. It seems like cheating, somehow. I've seen you and Daddy do it, and it feels okay, but not for me. If I try to do it, it doesn't feel right, doesn't feel fair. That scares me. I'm sort of afraid that if I use it, I'll lose what I already have. I just want it to be *me* up there on that stage. Nothing else."

"But it *is* just you," Slim protested.

"That's what Daddy keeps telling me. But it doesn't *feel* like it. I want to know that it's *me* the people like, not the power."

Slim couldn't find an answer for that. It was a feeling he knew only too well.

They pulled into Mitchell's and, once inside, he noticed an insurance-agency calendar, an auto-parts-store calendar, two naked-women calendars, and four scenic-landscape calendars. Also on the walls were photos of the players and singers Slim assumed had eaten there, the Tejas Declaration of Independence, and a waterfall lithograph. Small, black and white hexagonal tiles covered the floor.

He experienced a sensation of reassurance, and in a moment he placed it: he *knew* there would be no foul Glory Hand turning up here again. That made it safe in a special way.

The only other people there were two old men, one black and one white, with faces which looked as if they had enjoyed long and satisfying usage. Carrying their arms folded behind them, they greeted each other with a light feminine touching of fingertips which spoke of the duration of their friendship. It made Slim happy and he was still smiling when he sat at a table with Nadine.

"You know," he said. "I asked Progress what he believed in, but I haven't asked you. How about it?"

Nadine shrugged. "You met Mother Phillips," she said. "That's part of it. Mostly, what I believe is something my mama used to tell me. She said that in the beginning of the world, after the people had emerged from the underground world, Spider Grandmother gave them two rules only. She told them not to hurt each other, and to try to understand things. So that's what I believe. I haven't found anything yet that it didn't cover."

"I like that," Slim said. "I like that a lot. You miss your mom, don't you?"

"Yes. Yes, I do. She was my friend. She and Daddy taught me what love was supposed to be like. And they never said do this or do that. They encouraged me to make my own decisions, all the way back when I was a little girl. They let me find my own ways to think. And Mama taught me about nature, what was there and why, how to find it and how to treat it."

"What about what Heap of Bears said?" Slim asked.

"That—that hurt at first. Like a betrayal. Now, well, it sounds like something Mama *would* do. I don't think she would ever mean me harm. She just didn't know I would fall so hard or get so carried away."

The waitress came and they ordered: cheeseburger, fries and a bowl of chili for Slim; ham, eggs and hash browns for Nadine.

"You have hamburgers for breakfast often?" she asked.

"Yeah," Slim said. "Whenever I can. I love hamburgers. I guess I'd eat 'em for every meal if I could. Or maybe not. I suppose I'd need a little variety now and then. Most people go crazy over steak or prime rib or whatever. But for me, a big meal is a chili-cheeseburger and a whole bunch of half-greasy fries and a big Coke. Man, that's good eating."

"You're crazy, Slim."

"Yeah, I know. You're not the first person to notice. It's just the way I am, I guess. I'm nearly forty and I haven't changed yet. I don't expect I will. Some people say it's my best quality."

The waitress brought their food and Slim spooned some chili onto his cheeseburger, then commenced dipping his fries into what was left in the bowl. He looked up between bites and saw Nadine watching him.

"What?" he said.

"You haven't been very happy, have you?" she asked.

"No," he replied. "It's hard to explain. I don't think I've ever been happy until now. My life seemed somehow to move from crisis to crisis, broken heart to broken heart. I think maybe I hold on to the crises as all I had. Maybe they gave me significance or something. It's like, after so many broken hearts, I lost belief in the world. So without the tragedy I had nothing. The thing that's sad, or that I find sad, is that all I ever wanted was to find someone who loved me no matter what."

Nadine's beautiful caramel skin turned a shade darker, and Slim thought she might be blushing. Then she looked him in the eye.

"*I love you,*" she said.

Slim was speechless. *She'd said it.* Finally. He thought that it must have taken some courage and thought for her to say it to him. He was so affected by the simple declaration, he could hardly look at her.

"Thanks, Nadine," he said. "That means a lot."

"Why are you so scared, Slim?"

As always, she seemed to go right to the weakness in him. "I've been hurt too much," he said. "I've loved too hard and been let down too many times. And I'm terrified that this whole thing might just be a dream. I mean, let's face it, people just don't get blown into other worlds, especially when that other world is so close to what they'd like it to be. In my world, people used to say, 'Watch what you wish for, you might get it.' Well, I got it, and now I'm waiting for the catch in it."

"What if there isn't any catch?" Nadine asked.

"There has to be. Everything has a catch. Everything's got a hook. It's like a song. It's no good without the hook. So I know it has to be here, waiting to get me."

"Look," Nadine said. "I love you. That's not an easy thing for me, but I do. And Daddy loves you, too, in his own way. There's no hook in that. Maybe it's in *you.* You're having to go through an awful lot of hard changes. You're having to grow and adapt. Maybe that's the catch, for you to let go of your hurt and anger and grow up, get rid of your stupidity and clumsiness. You're a nice guy. Maybe the catch is that you just have to admit it to yourself and go on from there."

"Yeah, maybe," Slim said, now uncomfortable. "I don't know. I'm just going along with everything, trying to do my best. I don't know yet if I can believe in all of it. It's too good to be true. It's almost as if I need that Glory Hand, to threaten me and scare me, to prove that this world has some bad things too. Otherwise it would be impossible to believe in it."

Nadine took his hand across the table. "Look, Slim," she said. "Believe in me, in you and me. That's real. If you can't get beyond that, it's okay, but believe in that."

There was no answer but for Slim to nod his head and smile.

15

Among all the forces capable of bewitching spirit,
forces which it must both submit to and revolt
against—poetry, painting, spectacles, war, misery,
debauchery, revolution, life and its inseparable
companion, death—is it possible to refuse music a
place among them, perhaps a very important
place?
—Paul Nouge, *Music Is Dangerous*

Breakfast was done before Slim was ready. The night, and the morning with Nadine had been the best times of his life, and he was greedy for more. It had been a long time since he had talked so much to anyone, so honestly. Nadine seemed to draw the honesty out of him, made him want, *need* to tell her all those things that he would normally have kept hidden inside. It was lucky he wasn't a spy, he thought, because the simple torture of her sweet touch would compel him to tell all.

And it had been a long time since he had slept with anyone. Nadine somehow knew the exactly perfect way he needed to sleep, cupped belly to back, dick to butt, and hand stretched over, holding her breast. That position made him feel secure and peaceful, and it was only those times he had slept with someone, in that position, that he'd gotten a full night's refreshing sleep. Otherwise, he slept and woke intermittently throughout the night, always insecure and anxious, depressed or manic or just exhausted.

His feelings for Nadine went far beyond anything he had any experience of. He could feel that there was an essential truth in his feelings, in their feelings for one another. He wondered how it was possible for two people to fall so far in love, so fast. Was it just their hunger and readiness that had caused it? Or were there hidden forces that had been connecting and intertwining their lives? Slim wondered if he cared. Both of them had been looking for a way out of loneliness, a way out of the walls they'd built around themselves.

Trying to stretch time he asked Nadine, "What are we gonna do today, baby?"

"What do you want to do?"

"Spend the day in bed?"

"Okay," Nadine said. "Let's go, then."

They stood and, after paying the tab, walked outside. It was, for summer, a beautiful day. The sun was hot, but not excessively so, and there was a slight breeze from the northwest. If Slim hadn't been so consumed by his thoughts and enjoyment of Nadine, he might have paid more attention to the several black cars parked variously in the street and parking lot surrounding Mitchell's. He might have noticed the black-suited men that were rapidly approaching them from all around. As it was, he wasn't aware there was anything wrong until the first of the suited men grabbed Nadine and jerked her away from him.

He turned and reached for her, but someone grabbed his arms. He twisted and turned but his captor's grasp was as tight as steel. He saw Nadine kick and punch the man who held her down to the pavement. But even as he went down in pain, four more men in black replaced him and, though Nadine fought viciously, valiantly, accounting for at least three of the men being injured, there were just too many of them for her.

Slim tried to slip the hold he was in, and had almost succeeded, when something very swift and very hard slammed into the back of his head. Though he tried to retain his consciousness, everything quickly went dark, matching the pavement he was soon lying on.

When he woke, he stumble-ran to the van and got in. He fumbled with the keys, started the motor, and was ready to haul ass chasing Nadine. Then he realized he had no idea where to go, where the men would have taken her. He wanted very badly to cry, but instead, he forced himself to be reasonably calm and to begin driving to Progress' house. He dreaded telling the gold-toothed old man that he'd lost Nadine, that the men in black had kidnapped her. If he just hadn't been so fascinated by her, so wrapped up in the love that was growing between them. If he'd just paid more attention, if he hadn't been stupid enough to relax, to think they had it made once everything was set up. If only he'd fought harder, had more courage. If only, if only. There were a thousand if-only's he could think about, but it all came down to one simple fact in Slim's mind. It was, he was sure, his fault.

There was a desperate, empty feeling inside him. And, for the first time, he realized that he could kill, happily and without conscience. He'd never considered it before. He'd spent some years studying martial arts in his youth, and his instructor had told him he would have to consider killing in self-defense. But Slim had always been the one in any crowd to advocate peaceful solutions to any problem. He'd been the one to walk away from arguments, to leave any bar where violence was brewing, to back down at his own cost rather than allow himself to be drawn into fighting.

But now, if T-Bone had hurt Nadine, Slim would gleefully fold, spindle and mutilate the man without a second thought. Would that make him cruel or coldhearted? He didn't think so. He thought, perhaps, it only made him human.

Two forces warred inside his soul. There was a childish, irrational urge to commit himself to some grand, futile gesture, ending in his death, most likely, trying to heroically rescue Nadine. There was that within him that was drawn to that death, that within him which believed it would prove the truth and purity of his love. Opposed to that was the part of Slim that knew death would accomplish nothing, that he'd rather live with Nadine than die for her. And, as they had all his sad life, his grand gesture would likely do more harm than good. It would be misunderstood, as had been all the grand gestures he had made. People would see only the stupid futility in it, not the love and need behind it. Besides, he thought, pulling into the driveway, Progress would know what to do.

Progress was sitting in the yard, picking at an old battered guitar when Slim walked up to him. His eyes widened and he put down the guitar, stood up and grabbed Slim's arm.

"What happened, son?" he said. "You knows you got blood all over you?"

"Blood?" Slim said weakly. He rubbed his hand on the back of his head. His fingers came away sticky red. There must have been a sick look on his face because Progress led him inside the house and sat him down at the table.

"Let's get you cleaned up," Progress said, going into the kitchen for a washrag. "You tell me what's happened."

"They got Nadine," Slim said, wincing as Progress washed his head gently. "It was my fault, all my fault. I wasn't paying attention. We were coming out of Mitchell's and all of a sudden they were all around us. Nadine fought. Man, she fought good!" he said proudly. "There were just too many for her, though. They were holding on to me. I tried to get loose, to help her, but one of 'em bashed me on the head, knocked me out. Oh, man, Progress. It's all my fault!"

Progress folded the bloodstained washrag and threw it back into the sink. "You hush, now," he said. "I gots to say, yes, you should have been payin' more attention. But so should Nadine have. It ain't your fault, get it through your head. You fought and you tried. Your heart was in it. I can see by this lump and cut on your head that you wasn't in no shape to be movin' around or goin' after 'em much. So you just gets the idea of fault out of you. It won't do you no good. You puts the blame right where it belongs, on T-Bone. You keep on blamin' your own self, you won't be no good at all gettin' Nadine back."

"How do we do that, Progress?"

"I got me some ideas. Lot of it goin' to be up to you. Right now, we needs Belizaire and a gun."

"Why," Slim asked, "do we need a gun? I don't like guns."

"There's liable to be some mighty nasty folks shootin' at us, son. Can you handle a gun?"

"I can shoot," Slim said thoughtfully. "I mean, I can handle a gun for like target shooting and stuff. But I don't think I could do much of anything about someone shooting *at* me. I don't like guns, so I never learned much about them."

"Don't like 'em much my own self," Progress said. "But Belizaire, he can shoot the grease out of a biscuit and never break the crust. He's got that and he's got the gris-gris. Might be we could use somebody that can shoot if need be."

"I guess you're right," Slim said.

"You knows I am, son. Now, why don't you take you a shower while I call up Belizaire. Then we'll go out on the porch and listen to the wind walk and talk for a while."

The dry heat of the day felt good, and Slim's head had almost stopped pounding by the time Belizaire drove up in his rusty old truck. He looked as if he was still wearing the same clothes, with the same food stains on the stomach of his overalls, but now he was carrying a long, heavy-looking rifle.

When he saw Progress, he held the rifle up, shaking it as if it weighed nothing. "Dis be a bad business, papa," he said grimly. "Me, I don't be using no gun 'less death, she be at the door."

"That's where it be," Progress said. "You bring the bones?"

"Yeah. Me, I brung dem."

"Bones?" Slim asked. "What bones?"

Belizaire reached into his pocket. Then he walked around, bouncing, snapping his wrists, making sharp, rapid clacks with four things that looked like big ivory dominoes.

"Dese de bones," he said. He showed Slim how to hold the bones, one on each side of the middle fingers. Then he flung out his his wrist and sounded a pop like the crack of a whip. "Try dem in your hands, you," he said, handing them to Slim.

The bones were smooth, like old jade. Slim carefully inserted them between his fingers and snapped his wrist. Only a small, weak *clack-clack* was produced.

"You don't got it," Belizaire said. "Dese bones, dey carved from a buffalo steer's leg. You got to have de right bone, or da sound, she muffle. And de steer got to be big for da good ringing bones. I work at dis forty years, me. And just now getting good. Dat's why only ole, ole men play da good bones."

"Where'd you learn them?" Slim asked,

"Old man, he work on da zeppelin. He's got nuttin', him, but he loves da music, so he play da bones. He one day show me da carvin' and da playin'. Now, people axe me, 'Play da bones.' But da bones, I use dem only for da gris-gris."

"So what are we gonna do with 'em?" Slim asked.

"Belizaire's gonna help you find Nadine," Progress said.

"How are we gonna do that?"

"I'm goin' play de bones, me. And you goin' sing a finding song. You hooked up close wit' Nadine. You da only one can find her. You sing de right song, then you know what to do."

"But *how?*"

"The power, son. You gots it, now you're gonna learn how to use it. Just sing," Progress said. "Find the right song in you and wrap it around Nadine. You'll know."

Belizaire started playing the bones, clacking slowly, barely in a rhythm, waiting. Slim tried to think of a song that would connect him with Nadine. He thought, first, of "The Miss Meal Blues," since Nadine was connected in his mind, somehow, with food. But that didn't feel right. He listened more carefully to the clacking, snapping of the bones, his eyes closed. The clacking seemed to evolve into a pattern, a rhythm that pulled a strange and obscure old jug-band song from inside him. "Fishin' in the Dark." It wasn't the kind of song he'd have thought of with Nadine. But, if he stopped to analyze it, which he did, maybe it was right. Blues songs always meant more than the simple words; there was always an undercurrent of expression. Fishing, in the blues, was a euphemism for sex, and fishing, itself, was a kind of finding or searching.

As the bones continued clacking, holding the rhythm, Slim began to sing without thinking of anything but Nadine,

> *"Now look here, when I go fishin', that's no crime,*
> *When I'm fishin', I'm fishin' after somethin' of mine,*
> *Aw, fishin' in the dark,*
> *Fishin' in the dark'*
> *Aw fishin' in the dark,*
> *Honey, that's my birthmark.*
>
> *Goin' down to the river, jump in the spring,*
> *I catch the first fish, it don't mean a thing,*
> *Aw, fishin in the dark . . ."*

As he sang, Slim felt a connection growing, or the connection already there solidifying and changing. It was like a hunger, a craving.

He could *feel* Nadine, alive and hidden and hurting. There was a hook in his heart pulling him to her. He didn't know where she was, but he knew, beyond any doubt, that he could find her. He could also sense machinery around her—powerful, dangerous machinery. And when he felt that, he knew that, even if Pickens wasn't personally on the scene, it was his power that held her.

Progress had told him that the man was basically a coward, always hiding in his office while other people did his dirty work. That was why they were having the festival. Progress thought it was the only way to draw T-Bone out personally. "He has all the Vipers he needs," Progress had said. "We could fight 'em for years without touchin' T-Bone." Slim felt Nadine in danger, felt her hurt and fear. He would find her, he determined. And somehow, he would hurt T-Bone. Hurt him bad. He waved his hands and the bones went silent.

"Let's go get her," he said.

They were on the industrial side of town. Dirty, brown and half-abandoned-looking, the old brick buildings exuded a sense of threat that even Stavin' Chain, bandaged and limping, riding in the back of the pickup, howled at. This was Pickens' territory, that was clear. Many, if not most, of the buildings were empty and old with living businesses, here and there scattered among the derelicts.

Their direction seemed aimless, but Slim knew Nadine was somewhere in the area. It was just a matter of being able to feel where she was and follow the pull. He began, again, to sing his finding song, his fishing song. He sang quietly to himself, trying to get a better sense of her. He worked hard to recall the feeling of her, the smell of her hair and skin, the taste of her lips, her breasts in his palms, the way her toes curled against his. He worked to recall the way her pubic bone bruised down on his, her teeth as she bit his neck or shoulder when she came, the sound of her moans and laughter. It was all part of finding her inside himself, and then letting that point out her presence.

They drove past an abandoned motel. Stavin' Chain started barking and, for just a moment, Slim thought they'd found it. The feeling of Nadine was there, but not quite right, as if she'd been and gone. Then, behind the motel, in the next block, he spotted a large brick building, its whitewash dim and years old. He could feel the building's existence like a stone in his shoe. There was a bitter, metallic taste in his mouth, a taste of power. He knew, without any doubt, that that was where they would find Nadine.

"It's that building there," he said, pointing.

Progress pulled up on a side street about half a block from their destination, where they could get a good view. Slim started to get out of the truck.

"Wait, you." Belizaire grabbed his arm. "Mo' better we wait, us. We see what she look like, dis building. See what de struggle is."

"That's a Tejas Public Service building," Progress said. "They generates electricity in there. Mighty powerful place to keep Nadine. Now, look there at the parking lot."

Slim looked. Four black cars sat low and shiny in the lot.

"That means we gots to face from four to twelve Vipers," Progress said. "Plus who's ever in the buildin' already."

"Is Pickens in there, you think?" Slim asked.

"I doubts it, son. Like I told you, he don't do his own dirty work. He's in his office, workin' with his money, or with other folk's money, more like. But you can bet he's got some strap bucklin' plan here. We gonna have to do some coonin' to solve this here problem."

Belizaire sniffed the air and pulled his gun closer. "I smell death, me," he said. "If Nadine, she in there, she in trouble, some. Dere too much power dere. It make my head buzz."

"So," Slim said. "What do we do now?" The power was pulling at him, drawing him to rush into the building to Nadine.

Progress looked at him, shrugged. "Darned if I knows what to do, son. I ain't never rescued me no one been kidnapped before."

"We gotta do *something*," Slim said, a little desperately. "Have a plan. We can't just walk right in there and get her."

"Dat a good plan, yes?" Belizaire laughed loudly, his stomach jiggling, shaking the truck. "Walk in dere and get her, us? Bon. Dat what we got to do, walk in dere open eyes."

Slim looked at the big man, and saw nothing but good-humored confidence on his face. "Okay," he said, shrugging and opening the pickup door. He got out, and Progress got slowly out the driver's side. He got Stavin' Chain out of the back and attached a leash to the hound's collar. Belizaire clambered out after Slim, cradling the long gun in the crook of one huge elbow. Then they started walking slowly toward the building.

It was an intimidating structure, even without the power they could feel emanating from within it. A solid box of dirty white bricks with only a front door and a few high, narrow windows to show any sign of life or habitation. The blood-red TPS insignia above the front door seemed to signify, beyond any doubt, that the building was owned by Pickens.

Slim could feel the power from within the building, an almost physical pressure, as the three of them walked toward it. But the harmful effects of the power seemed to flow around them, being absorbed, somehow, by Stavin' Chain. Slim looked down and saw the dog's hackles were up and stiff and his mouth was curled in a snarl. He'd seen hounds before, but this was the first time he had seen one look angry or mean, the way Stavin' Chain looked. Of course the dog had good reason, after the way T-Bone's minions had beaten him and taken the Glory Hand he guarded. He probably smelled some of the same brutes here.

They got close to the building and Slim could hear a low hum. It made his skin crawl and he could feel oppression and despair trying to infect him, creeping through his body, a sense of emotional and spiritual exhaustion. He knew that he had to resist it, but it was strong and so hard to fight.

They struggled their way to the front door and Belizaire reached into a pocket of his overalls and pulled out a gris-gris pouch. "I'm through the door first, me," he said. "I take good care of de people inside de front. Den we get into de back so no one sees."

Slim and Progress and Stavin' Chain stood to one side as Belizaire opened the door and tossed the opened pouch inside. They heard a muffled whumpf and sensed, more than saw, a flash of violet light. Belizaire counted off fifteen seconds, and they they walked inside.

The lobby offices were smoky. A dusty, mold smell suffused the air. Slim glanced around. The offices were crowded with gray, unhappy-looking people sitting at desks and standing behind counters, but they were frozen in place, stiff and unseeing. Belizaire's gris-gris had done its work well.

Progress tapped Slim's shoulder. "Where to, son?"

Slim looked around the offices at the steel doors set in the back wall. One stood out from the rest. He pointed to it. "Through there," he said.

They walked to the door and tried the knob. It opened easily, and they entered the back room. It was huge and dark and filled with noise. Generators were spaced in even rows in all directions, their humming and turning almost too loud to hear. Stavin' Chain whined and cowered, and they could all feel the blast of oppression that beat down on them from the screaming machines. Belizaire brought the rifle up and held it ready, on guard.

"You go first," Progress said, his attempt at quiet raised nearly to a scream. "You the only one knows which way through here."

If Slim thought about it, the vision, the feel of Nadine retreated from him. But if he simply followed his feet, the tug of power, as if he'd walked this way before, his feet led him. Visions whispered through his mind, as of things he had seen before. But sometimes the angle was different, as if he'd looked down on them from above.

The room was dry, too dry, shaped as if by spirits trying to duplicate the façade of humanity. The walls and floor were covered with sheets of black granite, worn by the passage of uncounted feet. On the floor, scattered, lay the twisted frames and shattered glass of huge lamps that had once hung from the high ceiling. All scraped along the walls was the detritus of what looked like years of trashy neglect. There were oily spills on the floor. Some had soaked in, some was fresh and glistening. There was also evidence, unrepaired, of fires in the generating plant's history.

It was like passing through a cavern that had been transformed into a vast dwelling place for the huge machines that sat spaced and hulking on the floor. The struts and rods and boards of freestanding catwalks were indistinguishable from crowds of stalactites in the darkness.

And through it all, Slim saw nothing but the signs of ruin and decay, held together by artificial power and will. He felt the oppressiveness, as though a heavy weight of futility were being hammered into his mind. He thought he saw or heard rats or lizards, and he smelled the stench of rot. In the hot air, the hum of the generators filled his body with unpleasant vibration.

He moved forward to crouch in what he thought would be the shadow of one of the generators. Belizaire, with his gun, and Progress, leading Stavin' Chain, followed behind him. He closed his eyes and concentrated on feeling Nadine. It was strange for him to think about what he was doing. Was he using magic, he wondered, or ESP, or what? The power of the blues? The power of love? Whatever it was, in this world, it seemed to work, and work well, so far. He could feel Nadine's existence, her breath and her life, straight ahead of him. With his eyes closed, looking into darkness, Nadine's location showed as a dim blue glow that he started moving toward.

As he crept forward, so did the strange, unwanted thoughts in his mind. What if he were to die here? He'd done so little with his life and there were so many things he wanted to do. So much he hadn't experienced. He'd never thought of death as something imminent, inevitable; never imagined it as real. Death was something that had always been somewhere down the road. He couldn't conceive of his life ending without him making love to Nadine once more, without him knowing her, having the chance to know her. He couldn't imagine or tolerate the thought of dying without having the time to prove he could make a relationship work, to prove to himself he could be a good husband, a good man. It would be too unfair for him to die before he'd even begun to live.

His thoughts were interrupted by a loud *crack!* next to his ear, immediately followed by an even louder explosion from behind him. His eyes focused on his surroundings and he saw a man lying motionless on the floor, a few yards ahead. There was a pistol in his limp, outstretched hand. He looked back and saw a look of distaste and displeasure on Belizaire's face. The barrel of the long gun was smoking.

"He try to shoot you, him," Belizaire said, almost spitting the words. "He miss. I don't."

"Thanks," Slim said. He wanted to say more, would have said more, but the pull he felt from Nadine was too strong, turning him around, urging him forward. The machine power made it seem as if he were moving forward in a tunnel that led only to Nadine. His attention was narrowed down to a tight line, leading him, making him all but unaware of the surroundings. Dimly, he heard Progress begin to sing, and the sense of oppression they all felt began to slightly lessen.

He walked into what fell like a wall, and was stopped dead by it. Without thinking, caught up by the power, he tried to walk through it and couldn't, pressed so hard against it that it hurt. He could see nothing at all, but he reached out his hands and felt a solidity, a presence. It prevented him from going to Nadine and, as he looked through it, it blurred his vision. He thought he could sense shapes beyond the wall. And he knew Nadine was on the other side.

Progress and Stavin' Chain walked up beside him. Progress reached out and touched the wall. Stavin' Chain sniffed at it, then scratched at it with one forepaw. Belizaire walked up to it and kicked it.

"Dis be a *trick*," he said.

"What do you mean, a trick?" Slim asked.

"Just that," Progress said. "It's a trick. It ain't real. Not like you and me thinks of real. It's electricity."

"But that's impossible."

"Maybe yes, maybe no," Belizaire said. "No matter what maybe, dere she is, yes? But, me, I got somet'ing might could fix it." So saying, he pulled out another of the seemingly endless supply of gris-gris pouches he carried, making Slim wonder if he traveled loaded up with them all the time. Opening it, he poured a small pile of black and gray and silver powder onto the palm of his hand, then threw it hard against the barrier. Abruptly there was light, where before there had been only nothingness. They saw a thin wall, or shield of constantly moving light flashes, like a maelstrom of slow, spiraling lightning. It fought to break free of the power that held it, but it remained within the limits that had been set for it, swirling and circling and creating a barrier that, except for the gris-gris, had been unseen. But now, even though they could see it, they could find no way through it as it circled around the area they wanted to enter. Stavin' Chain sniffed at it, then flopped down on the floor and looked up at Progress.

"Let's all think about this," Progress said. "See can't we figger out a way to bust through. Son?" he said to Slim. "You think real hard. You gots you a better chance, what with your connection to Nadine and all."

Think? Sometimes it seemed like that was all anyone ever wanted him to do, all he ever did. He couldn't even begin to count the nights he had lain awake thinking, agonizing. Mostly about women, always about things that hurt or worried him. The times his heart had been broken, wondering why. The times he'd had to leave a home he loved, move, find work, start all over again, and again, and again.

There was a woman he'd met briefly in New Mexico, *his* world. He had no idea why thoughts of her were in his mind now, but he wasn't entirely in control of his thoughts, and it might be a clue or an idea so he let it run its course. She'd approached him shyly after a gig, asking questions about music and about how she could get into the business. She'd been short and he'd gotten the impressions that she'd been cute. She was dressed like a hippie, which always attracted him. She was quiet and sad and he'd talked with her a couple of minutes and then excused himself to walk away to the girl he'd been with at that time. Later, he felt more intensely guilty than at any other time in his life. He'd realized she'd been very sincere in her questioning, and he knew he should have taken the time to try to help her. But, at the same time, there'd been a chemistry, an attraction, both physical and emotional, that had somehow scared him, even though he'd known, at the time, that the feeling was mutual. And he'd known, later, that he should have been able to get past that attraction and given the woman the help and advice she'd needed, regardless of whether anything had developed. And the funny thing was, he'd been unable to get that woman, those two or three minutes in his life, out of his mind. It was another burden to add to the many he already thought about.

And now, there was Nadine. Caught and trapped and depending on *him.* He couldn't let her down as he'd let down so many of the other women he'd loved. But how could he think? What could he do? His mind was scattered, the power of the machines pressing down on him, tearing at him with sparked claws, confusing his mind. If there was something to fight, he would fight it. But he had to get *to* it first.

"Son," Progress said. "You look about as happy as a dead hog in the sun."

"I've been better," Slim replied. Then, another thought, another burden struck him. "Progress," he said. "How are you gonna do in this? You don't even have a weapon."

"Well, son," Progress said, his smile shining. "I'm gettin' too old to fight, but I ain't gonna run away. That's stupid, at my age, maybe. But stupidity don't kill you, it just makes you sweat. Don't you fret none, I gots a few tricks left in me still. Ain't nothin' ever went over my back that didn't come back under my belly. I guess I musta picked up some of my ole lady's attitude. She was always sayin' that if a man got handed a long life, why, chances are he'll die before it's over. Way I look at it, today's as good a day to die as any."

"Papa," Belizaire said. "You crazy man."

Slim laughed. "Where have I heard *that* before," he said. Abruptly, he was intensely aware of the noise of the generators and the sudden idea it gave him. He looked at the machines, seeing a large switch on each one.

"Progress," he said. "Let's shut off the generators, cut the power and see what happens."

Progress' golden smile beamed, even in the dark light. He nodded his head in agreement; then all three of them ran madly around the building, switching the monster machines off, one by one. As each grew still and silent, the chained lightning of the wall grew fractionally dimmer, weaker, slower. There was no way to shut off all the generators in the building, but after quite a few were silenced, the three met back at the wall where Stavin' Chain had waited.

There was only a weak, flickering glow left. Vision through the wall was nearly clear. Slim saw Nadine tied to a chair, looking straight at him, smiling and winking. She was surrounded by three men in black. Slim looked closely at them and noticed a strange thing. No matter how hard he tried, he couldn't quite make out their faces beyond a fuzzily detailed blur. They were just men in black, and there were only three of them. That made Slim more uneasy than if there had been a dozen. It was too few men, too easy.

He reached out to touch the wall, feeling an oily tingling as his fingers passed through. He turned to Belizaire.

"Can you shoot those men?" he asked, enraged by seeing Nadine in bondage.

"Naw," Belizaire said, shaking his head. "I can shoot, me, only if dey shoot first. I won't kill dem unless dey try to kill us."

Slim nodded in reluctant agreement. It wasn't what his emotions wanted, demanded, but he knew that it was right, had to be right. He'd never thought of rules applying to situations like this one. His teacher always taught him that if he was in fight, fight to kill because he wouldn't get into a fight until it had gone to that extreme. But now, he realized that there had to be rules or you'd just turn into the thing you were fighting, and there would be no honor in the victory. Was that why, he wondered, the good guys so often lost in the real world?

"I guess it's hand to hand, then," he said.

They backed off a little, and then all three passed through the wall together, running. The passage tingled and skewed their sense of direction but, otherwise, it did them no harm and had no effect. Once through, they ran straight for Nadine and the men in black.

Slim's study of the marital arts in his youth had taken him to proficiency. As he had gained weight and lost emotional strength, he had quit practicing but, even now, he could feel his body responding with retained knowledge and eagerness. So that when he ran up to the man he chose to fight, instead of fighting with his hands, as the man obviously expected, he lashed out with his foot, thrusting it solidly against the man's solar plexus, pushing him back.

Slim was enough out of practice and off balance that the force of the kick nearly knocked him over. When the man came back after him, he was still fighting to retain his balance. The man in black swung at him, and there was a glint in the man's hand. Slim stumbled backward as the knife snagged and cut the loose shirt over his belly.

Too close, he thought, stepping back a bit more. He looked quickly out the sides of his eyes. Belizaire and Progress were struggling with the other men in black. Nadine was squirming and fighting against the ropes that held her. Then his full attention had to return to the approaching man and the knife he held.

He knew he would likely have only one good chance against the knife. The man in black obviously knew how to use it, at least a lot better than Slim would have known. He tried to remember what his Sensei had taught him about weapons.

Study the weapon, how the opponent uses it, his motions.

Slim watched. The man swung his arm away from his body, extended it too far to be well in balance or to carry the optimum force that it could. Slim and the man in black circled one another, Slim keeping his distance, the man in black swinging the knife and blurrily smiling. He pushed his shoulder out and learned forward with each swing.

Most weapons, his Sensei had told him, *require some distance to be effective. A knife, a club, a sword, the way they are commonly used, need distance. So, to combat these weapons, you must get inside their range and attack the arm that holds them.*

That was the scary part for most people, moving right into the weapon, rather than away from it. *Take time,* Sensei had said. *Think, and when you are ready to fight, do not concentrate on the weapon. Watch your opponent's eyes and shoulders. They will tell you where he will strike next.*

Slim looked in the man's eyes. They were dark blobs, as black as the suit, but he thought he could see movement in them. He let the man move closer to him, a step at a time. The man's eyes flicked sideward and down and his shoulder pushed out as he swung the knife. Slim skipped easily out of distance, still studying. Then he stood in a good, solid stance. Not one of the traditional stances, which were mostly for learning, but his own stance, one which he'd found he could move smoothly and quickly from. He held his arms relaxed, slightly cocked, as the man moved closer to attack again.

Slim stood still, waiting. The black eyes twitched and he exploded into movement. His hands rose to the side of his head, then slashed downward. He hit the man's wrist hard, then held on. He pulled the man closer to him and took advantage of his motion to ram an elbow into the man's face. He pushed down on the man's arm and brought his knee up hard. He heard the man's bones break as he bent the arm over his rising knee. The knife fell to the floor.

Slim twisted on the single foot, stepped down, lowered his hands, then struck upward with his opened right hand. The fleshy base of his palm struck the point of the man's chin. He grunted and fell to the ground, unconscious.

Slim's heart was beating raggedly and his breath came hard. He was trembling. Not a violent man, he'd rarely been in fights. He picked up the knife and started toward Nadine, then stopped cold as he saw what was happening. Progress was lying flat on the ground. The other man in black was crouched over his body, knife raised high and ready to kill. Belizaire had finished off his own man and, even as Slim watched, the big man slammed the butt of the long rifle into the face of the man over Progress. Belizaire kicked the man in black's unconscious body off of Progress, but Progress just lay still.

"Get me loose!" Nadine yelled. She'd worked her gag off, and was now struggling mightily against her bonds. Slim rushed to cut the ropes. As soon as she was loose, she ran to Progress and started examining him. He was cut in two or three places, one deeply, if the amount of blood was any indication. And there was a quickly swelling cut and bruise on the side of his head, extending to his left eye.

"Nadine," Slim said, touching her shoulder. "Let's get out of here. We'll take him to the hospital."

"No," she replied harshly. "We *can't* take him to the hospital." She looked up, a pleading look in her eyes. "Belizaire?"

The gris-gris man bent down and picked Progress up as if his limp body weighed nothing. "Yes. Bon," he said. "We take papa to my home.

My woman and me, we take good care of him. But Slim is right, yes? Let's get out dis place. We cannot fight no more, us."

Belizaire carried Progress to the front of the building. Slim and Nadine followed tiredly. Nadine pulled Slim's arm around her shoulders and leaned against him as they walked.

It was nearly dark outside when they got to the pickup. Belizaire sat Progress gently in the middle of the seat. He got in and started the truck up. Slim got in the other side and, after helping Stavin' Chain get in the back, Nadine sat on Slim's lap. There was no pleasure in the contact, though he was happy that they had been able to get Nadine back. He was only afraid that the price might be the life of the old man he had come to love and admire.

"Papa be okay," Belizaire said as he drove. "He's not hurt so bad, him. I take care of him. But dis business, she's not finish, yes? You two must take care of it without papa."

"Yes," Nadine said. "We'll take care of our end. You just take care of Daddy. Slim and I'll do the rest."

We will? Slim thought, wondering how. He wondered all the way out to Progress' to get the van, and he wondered all the way back into town until they pulled up in front of Nadine's apartment building.

"Is this right, Nadine?" he asked.

"Yes," she said. "Belizaire's the best there is. If he says Daddy's going to be okay, he will be." She looked at him and love almost overcame the tiredness in her eyes. "Come on," she said, taking his hand. "I need to take a shower, bad. And it seems to me, you and I had some plans that were interrupted."

16

A correct, complete and detailed explanation of
music—that is, a full restatement, in terms of
concepts, of what music expresses . . . would also
be a sufficient restatement of the world in terms of
concepts, or completely in harmony with such a
restatement and explanation, and hence the true
philosophy.
—Schopenhauer, *The World as Will and Idea*

Wake Up Mama (E)

Wake up mama, come and dust my broom,
Say wake up pretty mama, come and dust my broom,
Spread out baby, give your daddy some lovin' room.

Wake up mama, get that jellyroll hot,
Said wake up sweet mama, get your jellyroll hot,
Your daddy wants, all the cookin' you got.

Wake up mama, white snake is at the door,
Said wake up mama, that ole snake is at the door,
Take all you got, and still come back for more.

I got the early mornin', moanin' blues again,
Yes I got the early mornin', moanin' blues again,
You know I can't do right, until I slip it in.

Wake up mama, hear that mornin' bell,
Say wake up mama, do you hear that mornin' bell,
You can trust your daddy, I will never fail.

Wake up mama, you cat scratchin' on me,
Said wake up mama, you cat scratchin' on me,
When that ole cat scratch, I just can't let it be.

Their night began in outrage and grew steadily more outrageous from there. Slim felt both more youthful and older than he was as he tried to keep up with Nadine's need for him. When she had finally exhausted herself enough to fall into a restless sleep in his arms, Slim was still awake and thinking.

She hadn't talked about what had happened. Refused to talk would be more accurate, and Slim wondered if it was more than just having been kidnapped. He didn't think she'd been raped. He'd had a couple of women friends who'd been raped and, almost invariably, they hadn't been able to stand being touched by a man for a long time, sometimes a very long time. Nadine had seemed to need him more, to need the sex almost desperately. But what, he wondered, would cause that kind of reaction?

As he thought about it, there was a tug on his power, on the place in his gut he had come to think of as the center of his burgeoning power. But he couldn't figure why thinking about it would cause the power to become active, even if only a little. He was puzzled, but he didn't yet know enough about anything to try to figure it out.

He passed it over and began wondering if he did, or would, miss his own world. He tried to think of all the things in his world that he thought were good: the animals; his cats; especially some of the scenery, though much of that was becoming overrun by people and destroyed by pollution; much of the music and the movies. He loved the movies a lot. He did have a certain reputation, a not inconsiderable fame and a place in history in his world, being one of the men who were said to have invented heavy metal. But he'd never been sure having a punk musician venerate his memory was exactly the kind of fame he wanted or appreciated. Still, he'd have to start over, here in Tejas. But he did have Progress to teach him, and if they managed to get out of this Gutbucket quest alive, he supposed a certain reputation would come from that. And this was a culture that had respect and opportunity as far as the blues were concerned. His damned reputation hadn't done him any good in *his* world, it hadn't gotten him any gigs once he was outside his area. Here, he could play the living blues, and have his reputation built on ability and talent.

And there was Nadine. There was always Nadine. She had to count as a major occurrence in this world's balance. There was, also, the seeming lack of racial conflict. That was a thing vitally important to Slim. The race hatred in his own world had caused him to suffer in ways most people would never think of or consider, looking at him as a white man. Walking through black neighborhoods to visit friends, and having the people look at him with suspicion and hostility. Even trying to make black friends, all the while knowing he would never be totally and truly trusted or accepted because he was white. For many, that made him the enemy. Or going to see the old-timers, trying to learn the heart of the blues, and being rebuffed because he was white and how could a white boy understand the blues. Trying to play in black clubs, often the only venues in some cities where you could play or hear the blues, and having the audience boo, or laugh at the white fool onstage. Here, in Tejas, his skin color didn't matter to anyone. It was what he did and was what counted, and that was nice.

He could find everything he loved in Tejas and, to tell the truth, he had grown dismally tired of his own world, of the United States and its repressive, restrictive laws and morality. In Tejas, there was *freedom.* It was under attack, certainly, but wasn't that true *everywhere?* And wasn't he right here on the front line, fighting for it? He could make a difference here.

He liked, also, the idea of living in a world that had a large and free Indian Nation. That had bothered him in his own world. He'd asked Progress about the Indian Nations. The old man had smiled and told him that, after the South had won the Civil War, the Indians had unified all the tribes and kicked ass on both armies, thrown them off the remaining Indian lands and held their territories against all comers. Slim had very nearly cheered to hear that. And when Progress told him that Tejas had made an alliance with the Indian Nations and gone on to kick ass on Mexico, he did cheer. He'd decided he would have to read a little history, but on the whole he liked the layout here.

As he thought more and more about it, tallying detail after detail, he could think of nothing in his own world, nothing he'd left behind, that he couldn't find in Tejas. It was, as farfetched as he knew the idea was, very nearly a perfect world. There was violence, to be sure, and a kind of evil. But those things would always exist and, at least, it was a type of evil he was familiar with. All in all, Slim felt that he was finally *home,* the way he thought of home, the home he'd never had. They said home was where your heart was, but Slim thought most people didn't truly understand that. But he did, and his heart was here, in Tejas, with Nadine.

Yet there were those who knew he was here, and knew why, and who sought to kill him or send him back to his own realm. He himself didn't know why he was here, precisely, but there did seem to be a purpose in it, and not just to find a woman to love. How he wished he knew what his enemies seemed to know: the true nature of his crossing and mission. It was, in part, their very determination to get rid of him that made him sure he belonged here.

But he knew that their effort had not ended. They seemed to have given up on the Glory Hand; maybe it was too hard to fashion a new one, once the old one had been destroyed. But they had abducted Nadine, without hurting her; obviously that had been a lure to bring him in to them. And they hadn't killed him when they could have, during that abduction, so maybe they had concluded that killing him wasn't the answer. Yet they could have captured him at the same time as they captured Nadine; why hadn't they? Surely death or capture would have dealt effectively with him, as far as they were concerned. Now as he reflected on it, it seemed to him that the man in black he had fought had not really been trying to kill him, or even to wound him, but to back him off. That first knife slash, that had sliced open his shirt without touching his belly—maybe that *hadn't* been his lucky break. At any other time, it would have caused him to back off, not risking another such narrow escape.

So maybe they didn't want to hurt him, physically. Yet they obviously wanted to be rid of him. What was their strategy? What made sense? There was a missing piece to this puzzle, and he needed to find it, lest it doom him.

Then he saw a possible answer. He had been told that the Glory Hand couldn't just be thrown at him; he had to *take* it. He had, however innocently, to ask for it, to invite it; only then did it have power over him. Power to banish him from this world. Maybe that was the case in other matters, too: they couldn't get rid of him unless he asked to be gotten rid of, funny as that sounded. Maybe if they killed him, another fat blues player would pop into this realm from somewhere else to take his place, gaining them nothing. So they had to do it gently, by their definitions, and not break the bubble. If he got scared, or thought it was the only way to save Nadine, so he was willing to take the Glory Hand or its equivalent, and be sent back to Texas, *then* they could send him. So they were trying one thing and another, without success so far.

So far. But they would keep trying, and now he had a growing foreboding that they would get more cunning as they zeroed in on him, until they found something that worked. He had escaped so far mostly by blind luck and the help of competent new friends. But if he had lost his fight with the man in black, and if Belizaire had lost, and they had been faced with the prospect of being helpless while the men in black tortured Nadine, made her scream in agony—

Slim shuddered. He had maybe come closer to losing everything than he thought—and it wasn't over yet, by a long shot. But what could he gain by being terrified of it? Better to put it mostly from his mind, but to be on guard. So as to be ready for whatever else they sent at him. Until he was able to do whatever it was that he was here to do.

He rolled onto his side, caressed Nadine's soft-nippled breast, then wrapped his arms around her and pulled her against him. The warmth of her skin, the smell of her freshly washed hair against his nose, her toes pressed against the tops of his feet, her breath on his neck, her breasts against his chest, the small sighing noises she made as she slept, all lulled him into a relaxation of mind and body so deep that it seemed like only seconds before he, too, slept.

When Slim woke in the morning, he found that his arms and legs had become entwined with Nadine's, and they had slept curled tightly into a ball. They were both sweaty and slick and the skin-to-skin contact felt wonderful. Without thinking, he shifted a few inches and slipped his dick inside her. She moaned and began moving slowly with him.

There was no urgency, no hunger, no sense of caring whether a climax was reached. Only an intense feeling of closeness, intimacy, and a pleasure that remained indefinable. It was, somehow, beyond lovemaking, beyond anything Slim had ever known. They moved softly together in a timeless rhythm, uncaring of anything but that single moment of shared existence. The orgasm that surprised and shattered them both had them gasping and shuddering and clutching at each other, suddenly wide awake and excruciatingly aware. Nadine bit into his shoulder and he thought it was the sweetest pain he'd ever felt.

"Wow," he whispered. "Nadine, you know, I'm starting to think maybe I've never really made love before."

"I know what you mean," she said. "Well, maybe I don't. Maybe it's because I *didn't* for so long—but this—this was so easy, so deep. I didn't have to do anything, just be."

Slim moaned, "I don't think I can move."

"*How* old did you say you were?"

"Almost forty."

"You don't act like a forty-year-old."

"I know," he said ruefully. "The secret of my success with women."

"Oh, come on, Slim."

"No, I'm serious, Nadine. Listen, I worked long and hard to learn how to make love well, how to treat a woman's body. Every woman I've ever been involved with has loved my abnormal sexual appetite. Oh, for a few, it's been too much of a good thing, too often, but I try hard to find women who would appreciate and enjoy me. Sometimes, though, I think maybe that's all I have. I mean, sure, I can make love wonderfully, I can turn women into jelly, but the rest of me's always kind of a flop.

"Everybody would tell you what a nice guy I am, how good I can fuck, but you can't screw all the time. And it's the rest of it I don't seem to have any talent for. As far as fucking, I have all the confidence in the world, but just being able to fuck don't make up for all the rest of it, you know?"

Nadine grabbed his arm. "Listen, you idiot," she said. "You're doing all right with me, so far. Did you ever *talk* about any of this with those other women you say you failed with, see if they could help you work it out?"

"No," Slim said. "Well, a couple of times, you know. But, see, there's stuff about life I just don't know. Stuff I'll *never* know, but other people take for granted. I need someone to tell me stuff sometimes. But when I've tried to talk about it, women just say that I'm trying to avoid responsibility, or if I cared, I'd know, or flat out call me a liar. They'll say they don't want to be my mother, and to get my shit together. It's beyond their imagination to understand how a person could go through life missing such big pieces of common knowledge."

Slim looked at her. Her eyes were caring, without anger, and she seemed truly concerned and interested. He held on to her breast for security. "My folks were drunks," he said. "That way—you just don't grow up with any sense of what normal life and behavior are. You don't know about the things you're supposed to do, you don't know about love. All you learn is how to repress your emotions, hide and try to avoid doing anything, good, bad or otherwise. You learn to distrust everything and everybody and just survive."

Tears were rolling down his cheeks, but he was unaware of them. "A life like that," he said, his voice breaking, "it cripples you, damn it. And it cripples you in ways nobody can see or understand. There's so much love and need and want inside you, but you don't know how to let your emotions out, not without 'em being twisted and turned on the way. And if you do, if you try really hard and do get 'em out to someone, it only takes having them trampled on a few times and all the walls go up again. You try to trust, and you get betrayed and abandoned and there's more walls. You say or do something unknowingly and the other person gets pissed off and you don't know why. You try to give help and advice and they see it as critical and patronizing instead of sincere, and they get angry again. You do something or you don't do something and they get pissed off. You don't understand why and they won't tell you because, damn it, *you're supposed to know.* But you don't, and then they abandon you and hate you and you *never* understand why. All you know is that once again you're a failure, but you don't know what you did to fail. After that happens a few times, you're a wreck. But you never give up because you can't live alone and survive. You know it's gonna turn out bad, that you're gonna get hurt and abandoned, but you need to love and be loved so badly that two months or two years of that love is worth any pain."

"Why are you telling me, now?" Nadine asked quietly.

Slim sighed. "Because I love you more than I ever have anybody," he said. "Maybe you won't be able to understand me, like everyone else, but I gotta try."

"I'm not everyone else," Nadine replied. "I'm me. I don't want to hear about everyone else. I—sort of understand. I can't promise I will, but as long as you'll talk to me about it, I'll try. Okay?"

"Okay," Slim mumbled. He was sucking on her nipple and felt safe. He continued for a few minutes, Nadine stroking his neck, then he lifted his head to look at her. "I want you to talk to me, too," he said. "The deal goes both ways. So talk, now. What happened to you when the Vipers had you? How come you were so weird when we got home, so desperate for sex?"

"You complaining?" she asked, smiling.

"No, never. But it was strange. So what happened?"

"Is this the talent portion of the show," she demanded, almost angrily, "when you jump to the wrong conclusions?"

"*Stash it,* Nadine. You want me to talk to *you* about stuff. Well, you gotta talk to me, too. Come on, be fair."

"Oh, Slim," she said, wrapping her arms around his neck and pulling him down to her breasts. "Okay. You know what the three-lock box is?"

"Yeah," he said. "A player's thing. Being together spiritually, mentally and physically. Giving it a hundred percent at the gig."

"Right. Daddy calls it being a blues outlaw with a six-string gun. Well," she sighed. "I lost it."

"What do you mean?"

"I—after they got me, I tried to use the power. Slim, I *couldn't*. Nothing happened. I sang my ass off, every song I could think of, but nothing happened."

"Did you—damn! I can't ever ask the right questions. I don't know enough to know if you did it wrong or did it right. I don't know what to think. For all I know, maybe it *did* work. Maybe that's what helped me to get to you."

"I don't know, Slim, but it was terrible. All these years Daddy's been telling me about the power, that I had it in me. All I had to do was let it out. But when I needed it, it wasn't *there* for me."

"Maybe it was all the machines."

"Did it stop *you*?" she said, looking at him seriously.

"Not from finding you, no. But we didn't use the power to get you. Belizaire used gris-gris, but most of it was physical."

"I guess so," Nadine said. "Maybe you're right. I don't know. But it bothers me."

"Why?"

"It's not because I want to use the power for gigs. You know, I told you that. That's got to be *me*."

"Then why is it bothering you so much?"

"I—for a few minutes, it made me hate you. I was furious at you. You come here and you just have all that power. And you can use it. But you're just you. He's *my* daddy; *I* should be the one to have it."

"But you don't even want the power," Slim said. He was starting to understand, but there was still a lot that remained a mystery to him.

"Right then, I did, I wanted the power. I didn't want you to come after me. I guess I didn't think you could do it, and I was afraid you'd get hurt. I wanted to get out on my own. But I was mad at you, too, and it made me feel bad. I mean, I knew you'd come after me." She looked down at him, her eyes wide. "Slim, how could I be so angry at you?"

He thought about it for a moment, trying to figure it out. "Maybe it wasn't *you*," he said, finally. "You know how their power makes people feel. So down and bad. Maybe it was because of that."

"I don't know. But anyway, that's why all the sex. I just wanted to sink into you, to become a part of you, and I didn't know any other way to do it. I felt so bad about hating you for something you couldn't help. It seemed to me like, somehow, if we could love enough, we could be a part of one another."

"We are," Slim said. "I mean, it's a surprise to me, but we really are."

Nadine shoved at his chest with her hands. "Come on, man," she said. "It's time to get up."

Slim stood and walked over to where his pants were lying on the floor. He thought of something else he wanted to say and turned around. Nadine was crouched on top of the bed and, before he could react, she leaped on him and knocked him to the ground. Then she straddled him and held him down.

"What the—?"

"I thought," she said, grinning, "that after eight hours of boredom, you might appreciate one moment of pure, abject terror."

"Right," Slim growled. "Just you let me up from here and I'll thank you."

"Nope. I've decided I'm not speaking to you."

"Well stop not doing it so loud," he said, almost laughing.

"Huh-uh. You're fair game."

"Hey," he said. "I may be fair, but I'm no game."

Nadine grabbed a vital organ. "I always thought this thing pointed the other direction," she said, wiggling it.

"Depends on which way it's going," Slim replied. But they both knew which way it was going to go.

17

Rhythm is one manifestation of the reign of law
throughout the universe.
—Victor Zuckerkandle, *Sound and Symbol*

Who Do You Love? (A-flat)
  (additional verses)

Crosstown shack and an uptown bus,
That kinda life don't give me enough,
Put me out in the sun and rain,
And when I die I'll come back again,
Got the mojo hand and the monkey's paw,
Eyeballs sittin' in alcohol,
Come on baby take a little walk
And tell me who do you love.
Took my darlin' by the hand,
And said ooh ooh darlin' I'll be your man.
Who do you love?
Who do you love?
Who do you love?
Tell me who, who do you love?

Well, the cat yowled up and the cat yowled down,
And a big black hearse rolled into town,
The man in back sat up and stared,
I ain't dyin' and I ain't scared,
Now who do you love?
Tell me who do you love?
Got a tombstone hand and a gravestone mind,
I lived long enough and I don't mind dyin'.
So who do you love?
Who do you love?
Who do you love?
Tell me who, who do you love?

Taking care of business was the business of the day. With Progress temporarily out of it, things fell on Slim and Nadine to keep up. Though it took them a while to get out of bed, get dressed and get out of the house, after a moderate delay they did so.

The first thing was to drive out to Progress' house. Slim picked up some clothes and his guitar, and then they headed back into town, to Charlie's. Orville, who was glad to see them, took charge of Slim's guitar. He would intonate it and make sure it was set up properly. Intonation was a process Slim had never quite understood. He knew the bridge pins had to be adjusted and such, but it was a mystery to him how a guitar could be in tune when it was open, and not in tune at the higher frets and octaves. But he could hear it was true when he played the guitar unintonated, and he had faith that Orville would make it right.

Nadine then told him to go into the front of the shop and pick out an amp. Slim tried to argue about it, but he was learning that arguing with Nadine was like swimming upstream in a flood. It couldn't be done, never, no how.

Normally, he would just have looked for a duplicate of the Fender Super Reverb he was used to and preferred. But, to his dismay, Fender didn't seem to exist in this world. And it seemed that, taking the power into account, he should be more than usually choosy about his amp. He started out deciding he would look only at tube-type amps, older models similar to the Super Reverb. He played through a few of them, checking them out, but none had the bite, the volume or the distortion he was used to. Then he noticed a dusty, ugly, orange crate of an amp sitting half-hidden in a corner. It was obvious that no one had looked at it or played with it in a long time. But it seemed to have a faint glow or shine about it, so he moved some other amps out of the way and rolled the orange monstrosity out to the center of the floor.

It was a simple construction of tubes, sheet metal, a reverb chamber, and unmarked, unnumbered dials. In fact, the only writing on it at all was the maker's name, wrought in blue chrome across the front of the speaker grille. A simple word; HILLS. But the sound that came from the speakers when Slim plugged in was the sweet dirty tone he was used to, the warm twisted sound he called his own. It was more, though, and as he played he could sense undertones and harmonics that seemed to vibrate deeply inside him, and when he played a thumb edge to get a pure high harmonic note, it screamed and rang with sustain, far longer than he'd ever been able to catch before. The amp, he knew, had its own power.

"This is *it*," he said, smiling, excited.

The blond kid, Wanger was his name, Slim remembered, looked slightly disturbed. "You sure you want *that* one?" he asked.

"Yeah, why? There something wrong with it?"

"Uhm, no. Not exactly. It's about twenty years old, but we reconditioned it, so it's in good shape."

"What, then," Slim said. The kid was fidgeting, and Slim wanted to know why.

Wanger looked over at Nadine. She only shrugged. Did she know something about it?

"Well, see," the boy mumbled. "We've sold that thing and had it returned ten or fifteen times so far. It sounds good and it works good, but people get freaked out by it or something. It's never anything they can explain, it just makes them uncomfortable to play it. A few of them—well, almost all of them, really—said it felt like the amp was *fighting* them."

"Feels okay to me," Slim said, ripping off a quick riff in B-flat. "Feels real good. Who knows, maybe it was just waiting for the right player."

"Maybe," Wanger said dubiously. "I won't be surprised to see you bring it back, though."

"Hah! No chance. This is exactly what I want. Throw in a thirty-foot cord and I'll take this sucker. If you can clean it up a little and have Orville tweak and match it, we'll pick it up when we come back for the guitar."

"Okay," Wanger said, shaking his head. "You got it, for what it's worth."

The next order of business was the trip to the Canadian River to see how Elijigbo's crew was doing setting up the festival site.

The site was crawling with activity. Crews were clearing brush and rocks from the audience area, smoothing it down and setting out trash cans. The stage had been constructed backing up to a hill, with the river behind it. The major activity centered around three cranes which were lifting a steel grid above the stage. Men and women were crawling on the grid, bolting it to columns which would support it, and attaching heavy cables to anchor and stabilize it.

Once the grid was secure, crews would attack electric winches to hoist up the lights and sound equipment which would be bolted to the grid. Then the whole construction would be roofed with heavy canvas so that, eventually, around thirty-two tons of steel, lights, speakers and wiring would be suspended above the stage.

Slim had always had a great respect for the road crews he'd worked with. It was hard work with few rewards. The men and women, the "roadies," who built the stage, hauled the instruments, went for food, strings, mikes and any other piece of "equipment" a player might want, loved the music and the work and the travel. Slim knew of more than a few who had been seriously injured or killed putting larger shows together. But roadies were quite often musicians themselves, working their way into the business, and those who weren't, were artists in their own right. A lousy sound or lighting man on the control boards could totally fuck up a show. And a good one could make a band look and sound better than it really was.

Slim and Nadine climbed up onto the stage. Slim jumped up and down on it and found it solid and acoustically sound. This crew knew what it was doing, that was clear. The stage wouldn't rumble or echo. Slim had played venues where the stage acted like a giant speaker box, muddying the sound with out-of-phase echo and bass. That was no problem here.

He walked to center stage and stared out. Slim had a habit of checking out empty stages and arenas. He was infinitely more comfortable with an audience in front of him. Empty platforms were uncomfortable and a little scary. They always made him wonder if he could pull the crowd, if he could grab hold of them and make them move to the groove. Non-players didn't understand. They couldn't comprehend how a person could be shy and nervous in real life, but at home onstage, totally comfortable. They couldn't imagine feeling that the sound coming his fingers, his guitar, was like an invisible tentacle that reached out to touch people in their hearts and gut. A non-player could never feel the joy of hitting that one right note that rang sweet and rich and lingered forever, or jumping to the rhythms of a jam that fell together naturally and only once, in a moment when everything was copacetic.

People always thought that when a player stood on stage, under the lights, with the beautiful darkness spread before him, that he couldn't see the audience. But that was a myth. He saw, selectively. Individuals would stand out; a beautiful woman with a certain look on her face; a man standing alone, rocking and dancing to the music, the kind of man who would never stand out in his own life, but whom, for a moment, the music had grabbed and lifted up. Yes, you saw the audience. And if you were any kind of player, you loved it.

When Slim played the blues, played it right and touched people, he often felt like an old-timer, playing for a roadhouse crowd of drinking, sweating, dancing people out to have a good time in the midst of misery. Blues had always been the joyful noise that had lifted people out of their troubles for a time. You could be poor, you could be sick, you could have lost your lover, but you could still have the blues and know you weren't alone. You could draw together in the sounds of the guitar with all the other people around you, and you could dance and sing, sweat and be happy. It was music from the heart, a music for the people.

Slim could play the blues and hear the deep heart lifting the sweet water to the top, founding and surrounding all the music he could think of. He could listen to a ten-year-old kid trying to find the blue notes, the flatted fifths, on a rough guitar with unskilled fingers, and he'd hear the heart and soul behind the attempt. And, here in this world, this *Tejas,* he thought he'd finally found his own heart.

Slim had never had many friends. He'd traveled through life alone, trusting that the women he loved would be his best friends. Which didn't help when he needed solace for a broken heart. He'd wondered many times if it was just because people didn't understand him, or because he made it impossible himself, unable to commit to any kind of friendship.

He looked over at Nadine, sitting in the passenger seat of the van as they drove back to town. It was as if she knew that he was deeply into his own mind. He wondered about Nadine, wondered if they'd be able to be good friends. Right now, they weren't beyond the first love and sex; they could see no further than the heart and flesh. Slim knew that that part of it didn't have to end, but it had to be built upon to last, and he wanted very much for part of that building to be their friendship.

Friendship had become nearly as important to Slim as love. Sex was sex, and as vital to him as breathing, but he needed someone to talk to as well. Nadine had said she wanted him to talk to her. And he had. Somehow, he'd told her a few things he'd never talked to anyone about. That felt like friendship, like trust. But how could all of this have happened so fast? Slim was in the nasty habit of falling in love too quickly, but trust was a thing he'd stopped a long time ago. Until now.

Maybe this world was affecting him more than he realized. He had been feeling changes in his body. Although he was known for the frequency of his lovemaking, his bouts with Nadine had gone far beyond his usual abilities. And he thought that some of his fat was being burnt off. He felt better, healthier, stronger. He knew the power had something to do with it, but could the power, could this world, be affecting his thoughts, his emotions? Progress had said it would, and the changes had all been positive ones. But Slim was the kind of man who liked to understand the whys and hows. He wanted and appreciated the changes, but he wasn't sure he like being fucked with and not knowing why.

His mind, though, kept holding to a single thought. *Nadine.* Everything else, the blues, the Gutbucket, the Glory Hand, was subsidiary to that. But what did he do when the fighting was over? Would things still stay the same between him and Nadine? Between him and Progress? How did he hold on with a whole new world to learn?

"Nadine," he said. "What happens when all this is over?"

She looked at him expectantly. "If we live?"

"Yeah."

She shrugged. "I don't know. I haven't thought that far ahead. I guess, if I have to admit it, I didn't take it seriously until Daddy got hurt. I mean, I did take it seriously, but not in terms of *dying*. If we win, I guess we just go ahead and live."

"You and me?"

She slapped him hard on the shoulder. "Of course, you and me," she said. "You idiot, what did you think?"

Slim could feel the heat of a blush. "I just wondered."

"Well, don't. You're not going to get away from me that easy. We'll just live. Start a new band and play with each other. We'll do whatever we do."

"Talking about doing," he said. "What do we do, now?"

"I don't know. Wait. Why? You worried?"

Slim nodded his head. "Yeah," he said. "It seems like it's been too easy."

"Easy?" Nadine snorted. "How do you figure that?"

"Well, it's just that—that when you read about stuff like this in books, adventures and stuff, other worlds, people are always going from one fight to another. There's always action going on, and danger. The bad guys are always attacking. And if they're not fighting, they're stealing something or planning something, talking about something or doing magic."

"And we haven't encountered that?" she asked derisively. "The black sedan, the theft of the Gutbucket, the Glory Hand, my abduction—these don't count?"

Slim had long been a fan of fantasy novels and, like many readers, considered himself something of an amateur authority on how quests and adventures should be run. "Of course they count! I guess we could call what we've been going through, what I've gone through, an adventure. Or maybe a quest, after the Gutbucket. But it's not happening the way it should. It's too easy and there's an awful lot of talking and thinking."

"I *don't* think so," Nadine said sternly. "Daddy's laid up at Belizaire's, hurt. I was kidnapped and they've tried to kill us all a couple of times. And there's not nearly enough talking and thinking for *my* satisfaction. You call that easy?"

"I dunno. I've just got this foreboding that the other side is letting up, and I don't trust that. We haven't beaten them, we've just foiled them, so far. Something's missing."

"Well, then," Nadine said. "If you don't know, then what are you worried about? This is real life, baby. It doesn't go on as you read in books. We *have* been fighting and planning and we *have* been in danger. What more do you want?"

"I don't know that either, Nadine. I feel like I'm all in pieces. There's things coming out of me that I've never let out before. I'm more together and in better shape than I've ever been, but I still feel all in pieces. I need something to grab on to and center around. Something—I mean, I came here from another world on a lightning bolt. I don't even fucking know if this is all *real.* What happens when it's over? Do I have to go back there? Am I *dead* in that world, or just gone? I need something to hang on to."

"Stop the van," Nadine said.

Slim pulled over to the side of the road and stopped. Nadine got out of her seat and knelt on the floor beside Slim. She looked up at him with almost-tears in her eyes, grabbed his hand and put it under her T-shirt, on her breast.

Like many men who had lived lonely, insecure lives, holding a lover's breast made him feel secure, safe and loved. Nadine seemed to understand that. Many women didn't, or couldn't. Of course, holding on to a breast usually led to further sexual activities. But there was always that first, all-important contact, that holding on, that search for home and safety and peace.

"Hold on to *me*," Nadine said. "I won't let you go back. This is your world, now. *Our* world, and you and I are in it together. This is your life, and this is me," she said, squeezing his hand against her breast. "I understand more about you than you think I do, so just hold on to me, okay?"

Slim nodded and pulled her close. "I have been," he said. "I'm just a worrier. I can't help it. Most of the women in my life have said I wouldn't be happy if I wasn't worrying about something."

"Were you?" Nadine asked.

"Were I what?"

"Happy?"

"No," he admitted. "I haven't been happy very much. Making love and playing a good gig is about all that does it for me. Or used to, anyway. I know that when I'm involved with someone, I should be happy, but I can't be. In my head, I'm always wondering and waiting. How long will it last? How much of my life will I lose when she dumps me? How badly will I have to hurt? Damn it, I know it's not the right attitude. But, see, I've never known anything different. The only way I know how to survive the hurt is to expect it."

"Oh, Slim," she said. "That's no good. That's rotten." Nadine's shoulders slumped. "I'm no better, I guess. The first man I loved hurt me so bad I haven't loved anyone since. Here I am thirty-one years old and you're the first genuine lover I've ever had. Outside my imagination, anyway. You, at least you kept trying to find love."

"I *had* to," he said. "I'm not like you. Maybe I'm not like anyone. You can get by on your own, by yourself. Me, I can't live without a woman. I can't survive. My life just goes all to hell and I walk around like a fuckin' zombie. I get to the point where my whole life is aimed at finding a woman, any woman, who'll put up with me for a while. I fall in love with the first woman who attracts me and shows me any attention. And right from the first I know she's not gonna stay there the rest of my life, that she's gonna hurt the hell out of me. But there's no life for me without a woman to share it with. So I keep on throwing myself into the fire.

"The worst mistakes in my life were with women," he continued. "I've ended up penniless and homeless more than once after they've gotten rid of me. One time I damn near starved to death, didn't eat for a month or more. And I remember every woman I've ever loved, every tit I've ever seen or held or kissed, every time I've made love and every hand I've ever held."

Nadine leaned her head against his shoulder and rubbed his belly. "What about me, Slim? How do you feel about you and me?" She could feel him trembling with her touch.

"I love you," he said. "I love you so much. You know that. And I'm scared shitless. If I lose you, I don't think I could survive it. I don't think I'd want to survive it."

"You wouldn't, umm, *do* anything to yourself, would you?"

"Suicide?" He laughed bitterly and held up his left wrist. "No. See these scars on my wrist?" There were faint scars following the veins, whiter than his skin and chelated. "Those were from a particularly horrible hurt. But I lived, even though I tried hard not to. Since then, I just don't have it in me to do anything like that. But see, after you've been hurt again and again, you reach a point where you can't take any more. The hurt gets so bad and so deep that you don't care if you live or die. I had a friend in my world, called himself Uncle River. He was actually a trained psychiatrist or psychologist or whatever one of those he was. He said that what it is is spiritual, mental, physical and emotional exhaustion. Just using up all your resources until you're empty except for the hurt, and then it's the hurt that keeps you going for some reason. Well, I've been on the edge of that for a long time.

"The last woman I was in love with was everything I thought I wanted. She was smart and strong and sexy. Man, she was sexy. Not what she looked like, but what she did and how she did it. She wasn't what you'd call pretty, I guess, but she had an interesting and a cute face. Sometimes, in the right light she could be real pretty. But she got all tangled up in bullshit and a bad situation. She lied to herself, broke her promises to me, and she was cruel. I mean, she was the most heartless woman I've ever met. No compassion at all. Cold as ice and twice as hard to get to pay attention. It damn near killed me.

"And now here I am with you, and you're the sweetest love of my whole life. I've never been able to trust anyone like I do you, or talk to anyone like this. You're opening me up and it scares me to death."

"Why?" Nadine asked, puzzled. "Isn't that good?"

"That's what people say, I guess. But I'm scared you'll open me up and I'll trust you and give you everything, and then you'll decide you don't want it. That you'll trample all over it. And if I give you *everything,* if I don't hold anything back, then the hurt'll go right to my heart and kill me deader'n shit."

"I don't love that way," Nadine said angrily. "Nothing would have ever happened between us if I wasn't ready to go all the way with it. I'm not interested in any other man or any other life. And I want to know what's inside you. I've never needed a man to get by, Slim. But I do need you."

"That's what they all say," Slim blurted without thinking.

Nadine sighed. "I know, baby. But I'm not all of them. I'm just me. I can only tell you how *I* feel. It's okay to be angry at all the people who have hurt you, but please don't be angry at me before I've even done anything."

"Aw, you're right, Nadine. I'm sorry."

"It's okay," she said. "It's even okay if you want to let the hurt and anger out with me. Talk about it. Yell and scream and shout. Break things for all I care. But don't direct it at me. I'm not going to leave you. I'll be here whenever you need me. Talk about it. You need to. Let me know when you're hurt or angry or scared. But talk *with* me, not at me. Don't chase me off just because you're expecting something that's not going to happen."

"I'll try, Nadine. It's just, I'm all fucked up about things. I don't know anything about love, not really. Lots of times I don't know *how* I feel."

"Listen, Slim," Nadine said firmly. "Maybe you don't think you know about love. But I'm getting to know *you*, and I think maybe you know more about love than anybody."

"Well," Slim said, "I don't know. It's very hard to be me, you know. I have this stupid idea in my head of how it's supposed to be, and I can tell you, it sure isn't anything like I've found in the real world." He paused, thoughtfully. "Until now," he said.

18

*I have spent my days stringing and unstringing
my instrument while the song I came to sing
remains unsung.*
—Rabindranath Tagore

It was two days before the festival. They had talked to Progress regularly on the phone. Belizaire had adopted Stavin' Chain, and Progress was almost healed except for scabs, aches and pains. Around town, posters had been put up, tickets had been passed out and, at the site, the stage was ready. It had been nearly a week since Nadine had been kidnapped. Aside from going to Mitchell's to eat, she and Slim had stayed peacefully in her apartment. There had been no further attacks, on anybody.

Slim and Nadine speculated that Pickens was uniting his forces for the festival. Progress said that he was sure Pickens would have the Gutbucket there, somewhere. The man's ego, Progress said, would not let him do otherwise. Slim raised the issue of trying to find and steal the Gutbucket before the festival, but Progress said the Gutbucket was likely being held in the safest place Pickens could think of, well guarded.

"Where was that?" Slim asked.

"Deep in the helium mines," Progress said.

"Why didn't he hide Nadine, then?"

"Two reasons," Progress replied. "First of all, T-Bone gots a whole special bunch of Vipers that just work in the mines. Blind maybe, no one knows what they are, but they know those Vipers never leave the mine. Chances are, Pickens thought maybe they wouldn't take too well to havin' Nadine down there with 'em. And, too, I don't rightly think Pickens' idea was to keep Nadine. My thinkin' is, he was tryin' to draw you and me in so's he could kill both of us."

"Me?" Slim asked. "Why me?" He'd been astounded that Pickens even thought he was *worth* killing.

"Don't you know, son?" Progress replied. "You the key to all this, somehow." Progress waved his hand in negation. "No, don't ask me. I don't know. But I feels it inside me. And, I'd wager, so does T-Bone. I think even Nadine sees it a little. Son, you don't have to like it, but there it is and that's the fact."

Slim hadn't been able to deny it, and still wasn't able to. He could feel it himself. Every person of power he'd met in this world had tested him in some subtle way, had forced him to think or do things that were somehow sideways to where he was. But what he found odd was that, while he didn't understand it, he accepted it. He was comfortable with it, even liked it in a way. There was that inside him which reveled in the feeling of importance it gave him, like a delightful secret. Not egotism, but wry amusement that someone like him could be a turning point.

Now, though, he wanted to understand it, needed to know why. So he and Nadine were on the road again, headed to Elijigbo's. It seemed to Slim that if anyone knew, Elijigbo would. There was something about the man that fascinated Slim, while at the same time frightening him. But Elijigbo knew more than he had said, and Slim wanted answers.

He pulled the van up, finally, in front of Fluorescent City, but he didn't get out. He sat in the seat, staring straight ahead.

"Slim."

He turned. Nadine was looking at him, concern clear in her eyes and expression.

"Yeah, I know," he said tiredly. "I know. I'm just not sure."

"Of what?"

"I don't know if I really want answers to my questions. I don't even know if Elijigbo *has* any answers."

"What are you scared of *this* time?" Nadine asked.

Slim blushed, but answered. "I don't know," he said shaking his head in doubt. "I've been going along here, thinking I was important. Then Progress tells me that I'm the key to all this. I don't want to find out that it's just an accident, just my being here, you know. I guess I'm a lot like you. I want to know that it's *me*, something I can *do*. Not just the fact that I exist."

"What makes you think it isn't?" Nadine said. "Besides, you're never going to find out anything sitting here, so go on and get your raggedy ass moving."

He hadn't told her or anyone about his conjecture that the enemy was not trying to kill him, because he wasn't sure that was so. But if it *was* so, then he was important, not necessarily as a person, but because he occupied a particular role. He had some power of the blues, it was said, and he had been brought here because of that. T-Bone didn't want to have to deal with whatever would replace him, if he died here. Thus he was leading, perhaps, a charmed life, because of no virtue of his own. But that wouldn't protect Progress or Nadine or anyone else—and that scared Slim. Was he in fact a curse on them, bringing them danger they didn't understand? Would it be better for them if he did depart this world? He just couldn't bring himself to share the guilt of this speculation with Nadine, yet.

. . .

They sat waiting in one of the small white houses this time. The interior was a riot of color. The walls were entirely covered with intricately detailed paintings, in bright hues and a realistic style, paintings which reflected and pondered the religious foundation of the community. Floors were decorated with braided rag rugs and every table and shelf was topped with fresh flowers. No corner, no niche, no forgotten square inch was allowed to go colorless. It was almost enough to hurt Slim's eyes.

"Aha." The resonant voice made them jump. "It's the hardheaded woman and the softhearted man. Greetings, Nadine. Greetings, Slim. Welcome to my home."

"Hello, Elijigbo," Slim said, after he had calmed down, "I've come to ask a few questions."

"Ah, yes. I rather thought you would get around to me. Very well then, ask your questions. I will answer with what truth I know."

Slim hadn't expected it to be quite so easy, so that, now, he wasn't sure what to ask. "There's so much I want to know," he said. "How I got here, what I need to do, why I seem to be so important in all this. Questions I don't even know how to ask."

"Yes, I can see that your mind is troubled. Well, then," Elijigbo said, beaming a wide, dangerous smile. "As to how you got here, I suppose I brought you."

"*You?*" Slim said, stunned and absurdly unsurprised. "Why? How? I mean—"

"Wait. Wait," Elijigbo interrupted him. "Perhaps if I explain a little of who we are and what we are and what we believe, you will be able to understand the answers to your questions. Be patient, please, for I must tell the tale in my own way."

Slim caught Nadine's eye. She was as surprised as he was, though perhaps for a different reason. Would Elijigbo confirm Slim's guilt?

"We are, as you know, the Torriero called Fluorescent City. The name is my own vanity for the modern world. Our lives, such as they are, seem simple to us, and are the way we want them. We raise goats and chickens, sell the eggs. We bake and fry bread and sell that, as well. Many of our men and women weave cloth to sell, and many more go outside the walls to gain knowledge and work at outside jobs. It may seem to you, seeing us like this, that we are isolated, but that is untrue. We have many friends and interests outside these walls. But inside, ah, inside we desire a community which is dedicated to our Gods and our own way of life which we have lived for thousands of years.

"Our Gods, what we call the Orishas, they dance with us, talk with us and are a fact of our lives. Oshum, the Orisha of sweet water, of freshness, love and the sea. Yansan of the wind, the trees and the sunlight. Shango, Orisha of lightning, storms and of sex between men and women. There are these, and many more of their brothers and sisters, whom we honor each day of our lives. Our people dance and let the Orishas ride them, so that we can live and enjoy our Gods coming to dance with us."

Elijigbo fingered the strand of rough, reddish-black beads that hung around his neck. Beads similar to those worn by all the people of the Torriero. "These beads are a sign of which Orisha favors us," he continued. "Each person is favored by a single Orisha, and never any other, though the Orishas may favor many people at the same time. We seek energy. We seek power. A bead, a rock, a song or a dance, the way you play an instrument, all those things and many more have ways to increase energy and power if you know how to search. Do you understand this?"

Slim and Nadine nodded their heads. It was strange concept, but Slim was able to relate it to other religions from his own world that he knew about.

"Very well, then," Elijigbo said. "One of the duties we owe the Orishas, is to hear their warnings of trouble and to use the power they give us to prevent great evils. Not cruelty, for the Gods are often cruel and that is life and the way it is to be lived. But evil. For evil magic is far easier than good magic, so very many people choose a dark path to power. It is our responsibility, as the people of the Orishas, to combat those people and those choices.

"Progress has long been a friend of the Torriero. He is not quite a believer," Elijigbo chuckled, "though there is still hope. But he is a good man who stands with respect for the Orishas. We know, also, of the Gutbucket, of the man whose spirit became an Orisha. It has become a legend for us here, a thing never before seen. So we have, with Progress' permission, studied it, and talked much about it, trying to understand.

"Many months ago, our Houngans felt a disturbance among the Orishas, centered around the Gutbucket. We knew that evil was trying to touch the power of the Gutbucket. We asked the Orishas to come among us and advise us. Only Shango of the lightning came, only he would talk to us. He told us of a man in the other world, the world we know in dreams. A man who, not knowing Shango by name, nevertheless honored and loved him. This man, Shango told us, could take hold of the power and defeat the evil with it. We asked Shango to bring this man to us, to our world from the other. And so, here you are."

"Me?" Slim asked. "But—what do I have to do with this Shango? I don't have any religion."

Elijigbo smiled. "Do you not? Truly? No matter. Each person in the world—your world, too, for Candomble lives there as well. Each person is drawn to the qualities of one of the Orishas. You will see it in their behavior, in their passions and their fascinations. Are you yourself not unusual in your lusts and loving? More ardent, more needful? And have you not loved the lightning, listened to its voice, watched it, walked in it, understood it and tried to take it into your heart and spirit?"

"Yeah," Slim said. "That's true. I *do* love the lightning. And I am pretty odd sexually. At least that's what everyone has always told me. But still—"

"Can you not believe?" Elijigbo asked, looking Slim in the eyes. "It is a simple thing. You are here. Shango brought you."

Slim was forced to believe. There was the bare possibility that there could be some other explanation. But it was *very* bare. The things Elijigbo said had to be true, just by process of elimination. The facts stared him in the face. He was here, in Tejas, and he had been brought here by a lightning bolt named Shango, evidently. "But what about me?" he asked. "Don't I have any choice in this? What about Nadine? Was that arranged by Shango, too?"

"Of course you have a choice," Elijigbo replied. "Are you not a free man, with your own decisions? It was only for one moment, a moment I think you must have asked for, when you were brought to our world. Only in that one moment did Shango control your fate. From that moment on, the things you did were your own choices. As to Nadine, she is favored strongly by Yansan of the wind. And does not Yansan always accompany Shango, coming before and after, moving the storm and carrying the sweet smell of the rain?"

"Okay," Slim said. "I'll buy all this so far. But what am I supposed to do with all this? I mean, I've got the will, but I can't find my way."

"Ah." Elijigbo drew the sighing exclamation out. "That is the most difficult thing, you see. But there will come a time when the spirit of the man who became an Orisha is in your hands. We have seen this. The Gutbucket will be yours. But the man who became an Orisha favors all instead of one. He is a perverse and troublesome Orisha, and must be brought under control. That will be *your* fight, but you cannot do the combat alone, for more rests upon the battle than simple control over the power. To be victorious, you must see the moment and open your heart to Shango. Shango also is a difficult Orisha. He favors very few, very rarely. It has been more than three centuries since Shango has favored any human, in the Torriero or outside the walls. Our records tell us this. So you must open your heart to him and let his power work through you. Only in this way will the evil be defeated and only in this way will you emerge victorious."

"But," Slim said, "how can I let Shango—how can I let him *possess* me? I can't stop being me. I *won't* stop being me."

"No!" Elijigbo was obviously angry. Then the hardness melted from his face. "Pardon me," he said. "I realize that you do not understand. This is not a matter of possession. That is an evil act, not an act of freedom. The Orisha will *share* your body for a time. You will not be pushed out or controlled. You will know what is happening and you will be in control of the dance. Shango will only share his power with you. The Orishas only ride us, they do not control us. In our love for them, we share our world and our lives, we share the dance and the music, so that in their power, they do not forget what it is to be human, and so that in our humanness, we do not forget the greater powers of the world and of life."

"Will you be there?"

"Of course I will. All of your friends will be there. But, Slim, the victory rests on your shoulders. Only you can share with Shango and use his power. Only you can play the Gutbucket and defeat the evil that is trying to come to the world. You need all the people who will be there to help you, but the responsibility is still yours to bear."

"Oh, man." Elijigbo had said the magic, scary word. Slim took it in the heart. "Elijigbo," he said. "I've never been too hip with responsibility. That's what people have always said, anyway. I don't know if I even understand what it is, or what I'm supposed to do with it. I mean, if something's my fault, then it is. But people have always told me that I'm supposed to feel responsible for things before they even happen. I don't know how to do that. How can I be responsible for something I haven't done? How can you let something so important rest on me?"

"There is no choice," Elijigbo said. "You must—"

"Eli," Nadine said, breaking her silence. "Hold it. Slim's telling you the truth. I've seen it in him. He's not stupid or lazy, and he's not trying to avoid responsibility. There are just things about life and living he doesn't know anything about. Things he didn't grow up with and that he can't learn because he doesn't have any concepts to attach them to. Some of that is good. It makes him naive, almost innocent, which is sweet, really. And he's about as honest as he can be and his love is pure, as stupid as that sounds. But I just don't think he's the kind of man who would clean the house or wash dishes or take out the garbage unless someone told him to. I think most of the time he doesn't know *what* to do in real life. He's not stupid or mean, he just doesn't know. He doesn't even *think* about it. I bet if someone tells him what he needs to do, he does it. Right, Slim?"

Slim nodded, a little astonished that Nadine seemed to understand him so well. "Yeah," he said. "I don't have a problem doing stuff, but no one ever tells me. I've literally gotten down on my knees and begged. Tell me what to do. What do I need to do to make things right? All I ever got was, I'm not your mother, or It's not my responsibility. Maybe it's not, but shit, if they really loved me, wouldn't they try to understand that I just don't know stuff?" He was close to tears, not because of sadness, but because Nadine did understand. She moved closer to him and took his hand in hers.

Elijigbo sighed. The sadness in the sigh was obvious. "Yours must be a very hard world, Slim. I'm sorry, truly I am, that you've had such pain and misunderstanding with your life. But you cannot avoid yourself in this. Everything depends on you. Shango chose you for this, and I cannot believe his choice could be wrong. And you will gain from this. You have gained already. There will be much power for you. The Orishas are generous to those they favor. Can you not look at it from that perspective and be content?"

"I'll do the best I can," Slim said. "This world, Nadine and

Progress, the music, the friends I'm making, those things have all become very important to me. I feel like this is where I belong, finally. It's just, I'm scared if you let me be on my own, I'll fuck up."

"Perhaps you will," Elijigbo said. "I can see a deep fear of failure in you. I also see a fear of success which may be even deeper. It must be hard to live in fear of both winning and losing. So, perhaps you will fail. This battle is by no means sure. I do not even ask you to win, you see, I only ask that you do the best you can. If you will do that, then you will not have failed. Can you do that?"

Slim didn't even have to think. "Yeah," he said. "That I can do. I always try to do my best. It just never seems good enough for anybody, but I've never been ashamed. So, yeah, I can do my best."

"Very well, then," Elijigbo said, smiling. "I believe you will, and I believe that with Nadine helping you, you will be victorious." He stood up and spread his arms. "Let us not speak of this further. Will you stay and feast with us this evening?"

Slim stood up. So did Nadine. They put their arms around each other and stood hip to hip. "We'd be happy to stay," Slim said.

They followed Elijigbo out the door to the garden. Dark clouds filled the sky, and Slim thought he heard laughter in the sound of faraway thunder.

19

*Musical contexts are motion contexts, kinetic
contexts. Tones are elements of a musical context
because and insofar as they are conveyers
of a motion that goes through them and beyond
them. When we hear music, what we hear is,
above all, motions.*
—Victor Zuckerkandle, *Sound and Symbol*

"Did you ever do something in your life that changed you?"
Slim asked. "Like drawing a line in the dirt and stepping
over it. And when you do, you're so different that you
look back at it and it was one you on one side of the line, and someone else on the other, so that you don't know which one is really you?

"I mean, the festival's tomorrow. It's like something I've wanted
to do all my life about, play the blues straight, my own way. Be important. Change things for the better. But I know, I know if I do it, I'll
never be the same again. I'll be—I don't know what I'll be. Someone
or something else. Damn it, it's hard to say what I mean. We've been
building up to this thing since I got to this world. And I'm excited, but
I'm scared, too, I've been scared since I got here. Not of fighting or
playing, or the bad stuff like that. But of what it's gonna do to me,
what happens to me, inside, where I live. What do I become?"

Slim and Nadine were lying in bed enjoying each other, the morning sunlight before the heat, and hot coffee. As the event grew closer,

Slim grew more and more nervous. Especially after what Elijigbo had told him the day before. He hadn't slept much or well. They were due to pick up his amp and guitar today, and he wondered if he was even together enough to plug in and play. There was an excitement in him, a part that looked at a positive motion forward. But there was another part, a sensitive, afraid part, that was depressed and scared and wondering what to do.

"It's like being a hermit," he said. "All the time I lived in the city, I thought I wanted to be in the country. So I moved to the country and decided to be a hermit until I could get my life together. Me and my bright ideas, right? What I didn't count on, what I didn't think about, was that being a hermit meant being alone. Man, I'd been lonely in my life, but I didn't realize how totally devastating loneliness could be until I was out there all by myself, no friends, no relatives, nobody but me and my cats. You'd go outside at night and hear complete silence, not a sign that there was any other human being around. Desperate, oppressive loneliness. I mean, I got suicidal after a while, but I kept thinking, nah, I'd screw it up like I screwed up everything else in my life. The bullet would graze my head, probably wound me just enough so that I'd have to work in a convenience store.

"This deal's kinda like that. The loneliness almost killed me, but it came from a choice I made myself. Now, here's *this* change coming. Most of the changes in my life have been for the better. Even the bad ones had some good in 'em. Then I get knocked into *this* world and things got *real* good, almost perfect. I'm scared of losing it all, losing you and losing me."

Nadine snuggled up closer to him and slipped her warm hand between his legs, held him. "Baby," she said, "it's still your choice."

"Don't you get scared, Nadine?"

"Yes—no—I don't know. It scares me. When the Vipers grabbed me I just about peed my pants I was so scared. But to tell the truth, I'm more scared for you than I am with me. I look at you and you're strong and smart and you can play. But I know that, inside, you're really fragile. I know you could break easy, and I know how bad you've been hurt. I just don't want anything to happen to you because of me, or because of what's going on."

"But that's not what I'm scared of," Slim said. "Don't you see? If I get hurt or something, I can deal with that. That heals. I'm afraid of the *change*, that I'll change so much I'll lose you and Progress and this whole crazy world. There's the Gutbucket and there's this Shango, this God or whatever he is. And I'm caught in the middle with everyone counting on me. And all I really want to do is love you and play the fucking blues."

Nadine caressed and held him closer. "You already have that," she said. "You already have *me*. But you have to take care of business, too, you have to pay your dues for being here. This is *your* world now. You have to decide what kind of world you want it to be: our kind of world, or the kind T-Bone wants to make it. There's nothing that says we're going to win, you know. T-Bone's gone a long way with his little empire, and people don't want to live without the things he produces and controls. And listen, even if we get rid of him, there are always more just like him looking for a chance to take over. But he's the worst. Get rid of him and maybe we can save what we have. Maybe we can save those five-calendar cafés and hamburger stands and dancing in the dark. Maybe we can keep the blues free, keep the people free."

"Not much of a revolution," Slim said wryly. "Just hanging on to what we have."

"Better than losing it, isn't it? If T-Bone wins, we'd lose all that. And we'd lose each other, I think. Daddy would die if he couldn't play the blues. So would you, I suspect. Die inside, anyway. You have to figure out what's worth fighting for. Not for me, not for Daddy, for *you*."

"Geez," Slim said. "Isn't that always the way! A lot of the relationships I've had, you tell a woman you live for her, that she's your whole world, and she tells you, 'No, live for yourself. Do what makes *you* happy.' And they never understand that centering your world around them, loving them, that that's what *does* make you happy. That's what gives you the only happiness you know how to find But they always want you to think, want *me* to think. Everybody wants me to think. My brain fucking *hurts* from all the thinking people want me to do. I feel like I'd rather be Rusty the Barbarian or something. Just fight for the sake of fighting, do what has to be done without thinking it to death. I've had to struggle for my life, I'm used to that. But I'm damn sure not used to fighting and struggling for other people's lives, for principles and mystic mysterious causes." He sighed and, for a few short moments, enjoyed the feel of Nadine's hand on his dick. But even her languid ministrations couldn't take his mind off his worries.

"Elijigbo says I have to surrender to Shango. Progress says I have to surrender to the power. And even though no one's said it, I feel that I'm going to have to surrender to the Gutbucket, too, so all of 'em can fight it out inside me. And the only thing I *want* to surrender to is *you*. But I don't know how to surrender, how to give up control. How do you surrender to lightning? To something inside you? To the power and to the ashes of a dead man? And what happens to me when all that's inside me rolling around? Do I surrender to myself?"

"Maybe so," Nadine said. "Maybe you do have to surrender to yourself. You're not very good at accepting yourself. Do you know, when you talk about yourself, all you ever say is how bad you are at this or that, how you fail, what you're afraid of? If someone didn't know you and only heard you talk about yourself, they'd get the impression that all you're good at is fucking and playing."

"That *is* all I'm good at," Slim said.

"Oh, bullshit, Slim. You could be good at anything you wanted to be. Okay, maybe there are things you don't know about. I can get behind that and deal with it. There are thing we all don't know about. Yours are just a little more important to life than not knowing how to tune a carburetor or build a house. You're a nice guy, loving, generous, open. You try really hard to do right, and you're brave and cute and sexy, too."

"How can a fat man be sexy?" Slim said satirically.

Nadine laughed. "Baby," she said, "what kind of woman do you like? Physically?"

"Uhm, well, short, like five-three or so. Skinny, small tits and ass, muscular, distinctive, cute faces, I dunno. I know what I like when I see it"

"But do you ever go for any other kind of girl?"

"Well, no, not really. I mean, that's what turns me on, why go for someone who doesn't? I don't need sex *that* bad."

"Yes, that's my point. Believe it or not, Slim, there are women, usually just the kind of women you like by some amazing grace, who get turned on by big men. I'm one of them, so I know, and I fit your description about exactly, right."

Slim nodded his head. Nadine didn't just fit the description of the woman that turned him on, she could have been the model from which it was written. "You sure do," he said, his hands proving the truth of his words.

"Okay," Nadine continued. "Besides, being sexy, for a woman, isn't in your body so much as it is the way you move, how you act, how you handle yourself. Your balance, I guess. You know what most women find the most sexy, the most irresistible? A man who can make them laugh."

"Oh, come on, Nadine."

She held her hand up. "I'm not lying, I swear. Baby, nine times out of ten, a guy can be hitting on a woman with all the sexiness he wants, and he won't get anywhere. But another man comes up and makes that same women get down on some honest laughter, man, that woman is going to get all hot and wet and slippery. So *you* guess which man she's going home with."

"Geez, Nadine, how do we get into these conversations?"

Nadine moved on top of him. "Mostly," she said, "because *I'm* all hot and wet and slippery, and you better do something about it. I've been getting that pistol down there ready to shoot, but I think you ought to polish the barrel real good, huh?"

"Right. My pleasure, darlin'. Say something hot and mushy to me."

"Oh, shit, Slim."

They did laugh, long and hard.

When they'd gotten out of bed, well and truly satisfied, they packed a change of clothes and headed into town, to Charlie's. When they'd talked to Progress on the phone to check in the day before, he'd told them that most of the folks involved were spending the last day and night before the festival out at the river, just to be safe. Slim thought that sounded like a good idea.

The guitar and amplifier were clean and shiny when they picked them up. Orville had fitted Slim's strat to a slightly used but solid Anvil case. Slim appreciated that. He'd come to Tejas with nothing but his guitar and the clothes on his back, and that was no way to treat a guitar. Orville, to Slim's surprise, was also going to be at the river, his pickup loaded with strings and tubes, mikes and spare parts and tools.

"Yep," he said. "Any kind of festival or gig like this, I works 'em. The roadies are good, but the folks likes to have me around in case of emergencies. I can take care of everything from broken strings to broken necks to blown amps and electrical failure."

"You make any money at it?" Slim asked.

"Naw. I suppose I could, but I don't charge nobody nothin' but parts. I enjoys the music, so it don't seem fair for me to take money for doin' it. It works out pretty even all the same. All those folks brings me their guitars and amps to work on, and they buys their necessaries at Charlie's, so we end up makin' the money."

Slim laughed when they pulled in at the river. It looked as if a very small town had grown up behind and to the left of the stage. A huge, multicolored circus tent stood in the middle, predominating, surrounded by tents, RVs, trailers, semis and a parking lot of cars, vans and pickups. A huge, shining aluminum tipi, two stories, it looked like, stood out from the rest. Heap of Bears, Slim assumed. People were on the move from tent to tent, trailer to RV. Many of them were dressed in the white of the Torriero.

Slim parked the van and, as he and Nadine walked hand in hand to the tent city, they were drawn into the bustling life of the temporary community. The first was the sound of voices intermingling, and the frenetic sounds of people rehearsing on stage. They smelled smoke and the mingled fragrances of foods and cooking. The strongest smell was that of chili, and they discovered why when they walked past a large catering truck with MITCHELL'S—A BLUES TRADITION painted on it, with a woman inside dishing out chili and corn bread to all comers. And there were smells of sweat and beer and the burnt leather smell of sex fully enjoyed and participated in. The sound and smell of the river surrounded and permeated everything.

Vendors were hammering stalls together, preparing to sell everything from I SURVIVED THE CANADIAN RIVER BLUES FEST T-shirts to Indian crafts. One booth they stopped and browsed at, a Mother Phillips booth, according to Nadine, sold sexually oriented products and toys. Slim was constantly amazed at the sexual openness, the enjoyment of good clean lust here in Tejas. It was a good thing, he thought, wishing he had the money to buy a few of the toys that were on display, wondering what others even were.

They walked on through the tents and trailers and booths. Everyone they passed had a smile and a wave and a howdy for them, but nobody stopped. They passed Heap of Bears and two other men, walking slowly, pacing and drumming and chanting, serious, solemn looks on their faces. Slim's impression of the place was of movement, its intense business. The sense of community, of people cooperating and working together, was overwhelming.

"This is wild," he said, looking around rubbernecked.

Nadine bumped him with her shoulders. "Hey," she said. "When we have a big gig, we do it right. This isn't just for us, you know, not just for the Gutbucket and all. This is for all the people who are coming to hear the blues. They're looking for a show, and a show is more than just what's on stage. They want to be able to get good food and T-shirts and records and anything else they can think of. They want to fuck in the grass and swim in the river. They want to see how they think *we* live, see *us* fucking in the grass and swimming in the river. We've got to give them all that. Without them there's no reason to be here at all."

They walked to the stage, thinking that's where they'd find Progress and their other friends. "You ever get freaked out by the audiences?" Slim asked absently.

"No," Nadine replied. "About the worst I ever get is drunks trying to get into my pants or wanting me to sing some horrible crying in your beer song. Why?"

"I don't know," Slim said uncertainly. "Just a feeling. I had some bad experiences in the old days. There's always an endless supply of psychos and loonies and horny little girls that wanna go home with the guitar player. I used to take advantage of that, before I learned better. I'd take two or three home with me at a time. Fuck one and watch the other two love on each other, and then fuck them, too. Hey, I was young and stupid. It was fun and it make me feel good and they'd do anything just for the chance to get their hands on someone that stood up there in the lights playing. That can fuck your head up pretty good. It did mine, anyway, for a long while.

"But along with those you get the loonies. The boyfriends and fathers who wanted to kill you, or at least beat hell out of you because you dared to give their little girl what she wanted. And the people who didn't like rock and roll or blues or whatever you were playing. Now and then, though, you'd get an honest to goodness crazy, a guy with a gun or a knife or a bomb, who didn't think there was anything finer he could possibly do with his life than snuff some hardworking 'star.' No good reason, no logic, no sense to it. Just headlines. That worries me here. It worries me that Pickens might have loaded the crowd with crazies." Who might try to get rid of Slim by messing up those he loved. He wished he could abolish that concern, but he couldn't, quite.

"I don't think so," Nadine said. "That's not his way. Crazies are too independent. T-Bone wants his people to follow his orders and be good little slaves. Besides, he wants to humiliate us, break us, take the music away. I don't think it would satisfy him for some crazy to just kill us. He wants to win, to get control. And we're one of the things he wants to get control of. Then when he has us down, he wants to gloat. He's a nasty man."

They walked up the steps to the stage. "I hate him," Slim said. "I really do."

"Why?"

"Because he wants you," Slim replied, blushing a little with the ardency of this feelings. "Ever since we went to his office and he made it clear he wanted you. I've hated him since that moment. I think you *were* what he wanted when he kidnapped you. I don' think he wanted to kill anyone the way Progress says. I think he just didn't plan it very well, or he underestimated us. But whatever it is, I think he wanted you." And that was nudging closer to the truth. T-Bone might want to have Nadine, and make Slim watch. Then give him a chance to vacate this world.

"Maybe," Nadine said. She pointed to a crowd of men gathered around the sound board. "There's Daddy," she said.

Progress turned as they approached. The side of his face was still bruised, but the gold-toothed smile was back, and shining more broadly than ever. "Howdy, chillen," he said. He turned back to the men at the board, muttered a few instructions and turned back to Slim and Nadine.

"You okay, Daddy?" Nadine asked.

"Sure I is," Progress replied. "A little worse for wear, but nothin' permanent. I been worse and hurt more. How about you kids?"

"Shaky," Slim answered. "But so far, so good."

"I talked to Eli," Progress said. "I know what he told you. You okay with that? You livin' with it?"

"Okay?" Slim shrugged. "Nah. Not really. I don't see that there's much choice, though, so I guess I just get through it the best I can."

"Good for you," Progress said, slapping Slim on the back hard enough to nearly knock him over. "How about you, Nadine?"

"I'm fine, Daddy. Just a little worried about Slim."

"Yep, I can see that. Anyhow, why don't we go have us a little bite and get set up. You're gonna need some playin' time, Slim. I knows that amp you done got. It's fine, fine equipment, but you're gonna have to cozen it a bit. The man who built it, Dusty Hills was his name, he sorta enchantivated it. He was lookin' for a way to amplify the power, you see. But the thing has its likes and dislikes, so it can back up on you if you don't treat it right and take it in hand." Progress chuckled, shaking his head. "Ole Dusty," he said, "he was a good boy, but a mite crazed."

"Oh, good. Just what I need. An amp with a mind of its own. Like I don't have enough to deal with."

"Now, son," Progress said, patting Slim's shoulder in a fatherly fashion that Slim basked in. "Don't awfulize it. I knows you think you got a hard road, but you're ridin' the clutch. You gots to let yourself up a little. You'll have the best of the backroom boys behind you, and me and Nadine'll be right up there with you."

"Yeah, I know," Slim said. "Nadine and I, we've talked a lot, so I guess I'm as ready as I'll ever be. Just a little scared."

"Well, son, to tell the absolute truth, I guess we all are, a little. But sometimes you just gotta kick it in the get along. You gots to know what you're doin'. You got the power, plenty of that. You got the amp and you gonna have the Gutbucket."

"Oh," Slim said, almost bitterly. "Let's not forget Shango."

"Yep, that, too. Ole T-Bone, he ain't never gonna be able to beat all *that*."

"Daddy," Nadine said. "Isn't it enough just to get the Gutbucket back? Do we have to go after the rest of it?"

"You talks like it was easy, girl. Slim's gonna have to steal the Gutbucket back, and that ain't no cinch. But if he does it, we gots to go all the way down with it. If we don't, T-Bone'll never give up whippin' on us, or tryin' to. He's a damn tush hog, bullyin' everybody. I don't much likes it but we're gonna have to kill him too dead to skin."

Slim laughed. "Okay," he said. "But listen here, talk's cheap but it takes money to buy whiskey. How in hell am I suppose to steal the Gutbucket?"

"Not sure, son," Progress said. "But T-Bone, he might be bad and he might have power, but he's kinda stupid, too. No imagination. He's the kinda man would ride a horse every week, but he'd be pissed off 'cause he had to go the same direction as the horse. That's what I'm countin' on. His stupidity."

They'd walked and talked their way to the big circus tent. It was filled with chairs and tables and people eating and a smell of food that was almost overpowering. The three of them sat at a table and, after a man in Torriero white had taken their orders, Progress continued his talk.

"The way I figure it," he said, "is that T-Bone's gonna have a few of his boys outta sight, holdin' the Gutbucket. But we've got a whole slew of folks gonna be up on that there stage buildin' up the power for the blowout. T-Bone ain't gonna sit by for that. He's gonna be around. I got some boys I hope are gonna distract him. While he's boggin' off, that's when you makes your move, you and Nadine."

"What move do we make?" Slim asked.

"That ain't up to me, son. That's gonna have to be up to you and Nadine. You're the ones takin' the risks, you're the ones got to be in control of it. You and Nadine make a mighty fine team. Use that and go from there. Trust your feelings. You been doin' fine so far, but the hard part's comin' up, and I ain't *even* talkin' about stealin' the Gutbucket."

"That's *not* the hard part?" Slim asked incredulously.

"Nope," Progress replied. "Not for you. Remember, even after gettin' it, you still gots to play it. You gots to call down the power and bust a move wide open."

"That's right," Nadine said. "All the things we've been talking about. The surrender."

"That's it, son. Remember, when I first told you 'bout the power. I told you you was gonna have to surrender to it, that you was gonna have a hard time with that. You've changed a lot since you first fell in here, but that hasn't changed out of the way. You've given a little, but you still got a ways to go with it. You still got a heavy load to carry. I'm sorry about that, truly I am. I didn't know when we first met down at the creek that you was gonna have as much weight on your shoulders. I wish it was different, but it ain't. It's all on you. We'll be backin' you up, but you still the one's gotta step out in front with it."

Slim sighed. "You know," he said. "It's funny, but in a way, that's what I wanted. Not with my mind, maybe, but with my heart. As long as you and Nadine believe me, I can do it, or at least, I can do my best. Being scared isn't nothin'. I've lived most of my life scared of one thing or another. Still managed to get up and around. I guess I will this time, too."

"There you go," Progress said.

Their food came at last, and they ate silently, listening to the conversations around them. Folks were worried, they could tell, but generally in good spirits. Slim heard his own name mentioned several times, and that puzzled him. How could these people know him? Or was he, in fact, a mysterious figure, a name they'd heard mentioned as being a part of it all? Did they, any of them, know what was really going on? Were they all good guys, or were there a few Vipers in the crowd?

As he ate the last of his hamburger, Slim tried to calm his harried thoughts. He should be excited. He'd be up on stage tomorrow, playing the living blues for a festival crowd that wanted to hear it. If he lived. He'd never thought much about his own mortality, nor did he now. People, he thought, spent far too much time worrying about dying, and didn't leave much room for living. Right now, he had about everything he wanted. Room to move, music to play, a woman to love, friends and adventure. He had a whole new world to discover. So why, he wondered, was he so much more interested in trying to figure out what was going on inside himself?

"We best be heading for the tents," Progress said. "We gots one big tent, figured it'd be safer that way. It's partitioned off, so you kids'll have privacy. Belizaire's comin' along later on. Mother Phillips is here, takin' care of her business. Heap of Bears is off in that metal eyesore of his, drummin' and walkin' and whatever else he does, puttin' his own whammy on the whole shebang. Eli is—well, he's Eli, you know how he is. He'll be there when we need him. It ain't the best situation in the world, but we figured it was the safest. For now, we'll get you settled in and then you can have time to rehearse a little."

"What are we gonna play?" Slim asked. "I mean, it doesn't seem to me like this is the kind of situation where anything will work if we just jam. And I haven't played with any of y'all before, so what's what?"

"That's gonna be up to you, son. It's your gig, you gots to pick the songs. We can play along with most anything, just compin', you know. When it's time for you to stand out, though, you gots to be goin' with what you know. You the one's gotta do the pickin'. Me and the boys and Nadine, I s'pect we all know about the same songs, so we'll just stand and rehearse and then you and us can figure out what we wanna do. Fair enough?"

"I suppose so. It's just that, right now, my mind isn't thinking much about songs."

"Aw, son," Progress said. He smiled broadly and, even in the dim light of the tent, his teeth flashed brightly gold. "Don't worry about it. It's just one-take Johnsons. Just do it. You was born for the blues, son. I can feel it. You just been sidetracked by all this mess. Once you start playin', you'll know where you are. Just remember, life don't be no rehearsal. Don't hurt nobody who don't hurt you first. Don't hurt yourself, dress nice and go on all the rides. Nothin' to fret about. This be a barrelhouse town, son. These folks a-comin' out here, they're wantin' the real blues. That's gonna inspire you to come up with what you need. Just use your common sense."

"You got it," Slim said happily. "Though no one's ever accused me of having common sense before. I dunno. I'll crank it up to patent applied for and kick ass. Don't know any other way to do it."

"That's the spirit," Nadine said, tickling him.

"Yeah—why, they've trifled with the wrong alert, steel-nerved chap, this time."

"Now wait a minute, baby," Nadine said, intensifying her tickling by going to the use of both hands on his ribs, which she knew from experience were a particularly tickle sensitive part of his body. "Let's not strain the old brain pan with attic wit, huh."

"Oh, just you wait, Nadine. Right there—I'll think up a retort.

I'll come back at you like lightning—you'll be sick at your stomach with sheer envy at my wittery."

"Say," Nadine said, trying to hold in her own laughter and generally having as dismal a success at it as Slim. "I bet you think you have almost human intelligence, don't you?"

"Hey, it takes a lot of thought to appear swayve and deboner."

"I'll deboner you, sucker. I don't mind you crying on my shoulder, but your nose is dripping on my neck."

Slim turned to Progress and held his hand up to his mouth confidentially. "I don't know about you," he said in a stage whisper, "but I think there's some cahootenizing going on here."

"That goes for me, too," Nadine said in mock indignation. "Though we're enemies, we're bonded by the bounds of friendship and true love."

"Right," Slim replied. "We're fellow bounders."

The two of them fell into each other's arms laughing wildly. They paid no attention to anyone else in the tent as their hands squeezed and tickled and touched. Nor did they see the happy smile on Progress' bruised face, or hear his sigh of relief. Nor did they hear him say to himself, "Good, things are back to normal, almost."

20

The blues, like the dream, continues to retain its rights—even if its future is uncertain. We see in it an appeal to close the shutters on a withered concept of virtue and a harsh and oppressive civilization; we see in it a demand for non-repression, elaborated by the images of a capacity for fantasy that has not been crushed. We see in it one of the few modern . . . poetic voices through which humanity has fiercely fought for, and managed to regain, a semblance of its true dignity.
—Paul Garon, *Blues and the Poetic Spirit*

Slim stood on stage, ready to play. Nadine was on his left, ready to sing with him. Progress held his right down, playing rhythm guitar. Belizaire stood in the background, hefting the biggest, heaviest-looking bass Slim had ever seen.

It looked to be made of bone, but no bone could possibly be that large or flat. Two of Elijigbo's drummers held the floor down. Progress had asked him if he wanted a keyboard player, but Slim had declined. He'd always found keyboards disruptive and dissonant in the kind of blues he wanted to play.

An odd hush had fallen over the festival town. Many of the people had gathered on what Slim had always thought of as the threshing floor, where the gate usually stood or sat. He knew they were waiting to see what the new boy had. He and Nadine had made love and smoked a joint beforehand, but he was still nervous. It was a new feeling for him. The stage had always been home for him, the place he was at his best. He'd always been ready and steady on the stage.

In the old days, friends like Fogarty and McKee and Sunflower had said he was the only human being alive who never suffered from stage fright, and that fact, they said, made them wonder about his humanity. It had been a good joke, then. But now, he was nervous on stage for the first time in his life.

Songs. He needed songs. The sound men were tweaking the boards, the band was ready to play, Nadine was ready to sing. And Slim's fingers were itching.

"Son," Progress said. "You know what you wanna play?"

"Yeah, I guess. You wanna make a list?"

Progress pulled out a frayed old notebook and a stubby, chewed pencil. "Okay," he said. "Shoot it to me."

"Let's see," Slim said. "You tell me if you don't know any of these. Uhm, 'Dust My Blues,' 'Alberta,' 'Two Trains Runnin',' 'Lend Me Your Love,' 'Worried About My Baby,' 'Ridin' in the Moonlight,' 'Spoonful,' and maybe 'The Red Rooster.' That seem like a good set?"

"S'copacetic with me," Progress said. "Ain't none of 'em we don't know well enough. What you wanna start with?"

"How about 'Dust My Blues'? Who did it here in Tejas?"

"Man named James Son Thomas," Progress said.

"In my world, it was a cat named Elmore James. Bad, bad player." Slim hitched his guitar up to playing position, "Let's do it," he said.

He started out with the twelfth-fret hammer and slide that Elmore used so much, setting up the rhythm and the groove for Nadine to jump into.

"I'm gonna get up in the mornin'," she sang. "I believe I'll dust my blues."

Slim played a little passing riff in the change from E to A. Just enough to accentuate the positive.

> *"I'm gonna get up in the mornin',*
> *I believe I'll dust my blues.*
> *I gotta leave my baby,*
> *I got no time to lose."*

Slim hammered on the twelve again, listening to the monitors to see how he sounded, then he smoothed down as Nadine went into the second verse. Sometimes he was a busy player, injecting grace notes into the spaces, but something was making him lay back. The amp? It sounded good, distorted just right to add a little dirtiness to the tones. But he felt a reluctance to play any of the passing riffs he was used to, any notes that weren't the right ones. That seemed all right, though. Not worth fighting about.

Nadine was tearing the song up. Slim had never heard a woman sing it before, but Nadine was getting down low and wet, making her voice cut through. He was impressed. He'd heard some mighty fine blues singers in his time, but Nadine had the kind of voice that a player dreams of working with, the kind of voice that jumps right into the groove and grabs people by the balls, be they male or female. Now, he could understand her deep need, her attitude about the power and wanting it to be all *her* behind the music.

He could feel the power rising in him, softly and easily, growing in his gut and flowing out into his mind and fingers. He could feel it passing into the strings, into the guitar, and from there, into the amp. And somehow, by some quirky feedback loop between the speakers and the pickups on the guitar, the amp was feeding the power back to him. He could see how people would think the amp was fighting them. It was uncomfortable and devious, but he laid back and tried to accept it. When he relaxed and let it go, he could loosen up more, and play in his own style.

The song ended, and he called out, "Red Rooster," and the band segued right into it. The music snapped and popped and growled and slinked and left a little more room for him to play. He started adding grace notes and using the strings to get the chicken scratch and cat strut sounds that he used to make the song his own.

Nadine almost crooned the old song. Her voice was low and soft and deep. He watched her knees bend and her ass shake as she reached down into herself to grab on to the arrogance and slyness the song needed. He watched her thrust her hips out as she slywalked to the groove, bending and shaking with the words. He quickly pulled his pocketknife out of his pants. He'd filed down and polished the backside, and when his solo was ready to stand forward, he used it to play slide, trying to duplicate on strings the rhythm of the song, and the slow, languid way he played slide, it came out as what he called "fuck music." He called it that, he and others, because you couldn't hear the groove and the lowdown slide without thinking of steamy, hot sex. He liked it, and the smile on Nadine's face as she laid back to give him room told him that she liked it as well.

They finished off the "Rooster," and he started fingertapping the nine-note hook riff for "Spoonful." He laid a heavy sustain and vibrato on the lingering eighth note. He'd been told he had a strange vibrato. Most players shifted and bent the string up and down. Slim had taken his vibrato from violin players, stretching the string back and forth sideways. People had tried to tell him that, with steel strings, it took too much strength for too little effect, but he liked the subtlety and distinction of it.

He stepped up to the mike and motioned to Nadine to let him sing. He didn't do it often, but "Spoonful" had always been one of his favorite songs. He tried to pitch his voice low and quiet, where he thought it sounded decent. He knew he couldn't come close to anything anyone would actually call singing, but he had heart and enjoyed it. It was, after all, just a rehearsal. It wasn't as if he hadn't sung before. He could pass if he didn't push it, and there were a few songs he could pull off without falling down.

> *"Well, it might be a spoonful of diamonds,*
> *And it might be a spoonful of gold,*
> *But just one spoon of your precious love,*
> *Satisfies my soul . . . "*

After the first verse, Nadine stepped up and began to sing with him. To his astonishment, she pitched and adjusted her voice somehow, and managed to sing in harmony with him, and it worked. No one had ever done it before, but it worked. He felt, as he and Nadine sang, that the power was about to explode inside him. His dick got hard and his hands seemed to glow red and itch. It felt good. So good that, when his solo came around he cut loose completely, finding a speed and a groove he'd never been behind in his life. He played for twenty-four bars and didn't want to quit, so the band let him go on jamming.

Offstage, people were dancing and smiling. Some few stood and stared, caught up by the power in a sort of helplessness. Dust devils formed and spun around the threshing floor, whirling between the dancers, picking up leaves and twigs until they assumed a kind of transient solidity. The trees bowed and swayed and rustled, leaning toward the stage as even they began to swing with the groove.

Nadine stared at him wide-eyed as he hammered down on the riffs that were evolving under his fingers. It was as if each note he played was the culmination and sum of every note that had come before, and the partial exposition of each note that was yet to come. Slim's eyes were closed and he was playing to Nadine, unaware that the playing had, for that moment in time, brought the entire festival city to a laughing, dancing halt. He had surrendered without knowing it, he was in control without awareness. A mystic would have called it enlightenment, but Slim wasn't conscious of any great happening. In giving his heart to Nadine, playing for her, he opened the rest of himself up to the power, and let it flow out of him. He only played.

He took his scale down to a diminished seventh, remembering the Climax Blues Band version of the song. For the first time in his life, he played into what most people in his world would have called jazz. He didn't think about it, didn't call it by any name, he just played through, following the notes that seemed to build by themselves. The playing was slower, more tentative, because of unfamiliarity. But it seemed to smooth the frenetic power his playing had created. The dust devils fell apart into powder, the dancers slowed and stopped. People began to once again go about their business. Slim finally felt the power leave him. He let go of it without reluctance, completed, and the band let the song end.

Slim turned to Progress. "That was pretty good, huh?"

The band broke into wild laughter. Belizaire fell to the ground, his raucous guffaws ringing out over all the others. Progress was breathless and teary-eyed from it. Even Nadine was laughing. Slim looked around at them, puzzled.

"What is this?" he said. "What's so funny?"

Progress worked hard to catch his breath. "Oh my," he said, the laughter still in his eyes and barely gone from his voice. He unstrapped his guitar and stood it in a stand. Slim did the same. Progress walked over to him and put his arm around Slim's shoulders.

"Son," he said, still chuckling. "You just knocked this whole festival into a rocked hat. You really don't know, do you?"

"Know *what?*"

"You just here and now played with more power than anyone I ever did see. You had every single man, woman and child here in the palm of your hand. You coulda done *anything.*"

Slim walked around in circles. Then he grabbed Nadine's hand, held it, and faced Progress again.

"All I did was play," he said. "I was just playing for Nadine, 'cause she sang with me."

"That's just the point, son. You didn't *care* about the power, so you just let it go, you surrendered. Once you did that, nothin' else mattered. Whoo, boy! You did some playin'. I ain't never seen nobody reach out the power like that."

"Was it good?" Slim asked timidly.

"Good?" Progress said incredulously. "*Good?* Son, if you'd had the Gutbucket in those hands, you'd have about torn the place up entire. They'd have been dancin' and standin' all the way into town. Good?" Progress laughed again. "Yep, it was good. It was good enough that, fearful as I is, I can hardly wait for tomorrow, when it's our time to play."

"Don't we need to rehearse more?" Slim asked.

"Not after *that.* I don't think none of us is ready to play no more behind that. You just be thinkin' of good songs you can pick." Progress shifted his attention to Nadine, who had been standing quietly at Slim's side. "Nadine, honey," he said. "Seems like as if you set it up for Slim. You want to try to figure out how you can do the same thing tomorrow?"

"Sure Daddy," she said. "My man and I won't let you down."

Her man, Slim thought. He liked the sound of possessiveness in her voice, liked the attitude the phrase conveyed.

"Well, chillen," Progress said tiredly. "I gots to go get me some rest and talk to some folks about this and that. You two go on ahead and have some fun. Meet some of the peoples that done come out here." He walked off with Belizaire, leaving Slim and Nadine standing alone on stage.

"So, what now?" Slim said.

Nadine shrugged, the motion of her shoulders giving her breasts a delightful bounce. "What do you want to do?" she asked him.

"Well," he said. "I have two things in mind."

"Oh yeah?" she said, looking at him through one cocked eye, her suspicions clear.

"We could go skinny dippin' and make love in the river," he said. "Or we could go get something to eat. Now me, I don't know which I'd rather do. I'm hot and horny and I'd dearly love a swim and a swive. On the other hand, I'm starving to death, too. What do you think."

"Race you to the river," Nadine said, already starting to run.

She won the race. But Slim, despite his extra weight and short legs, wasn't far behind.

21

*They intimidate each other, shrug off and ignore
each other, groove on and with each other. Equal
moves from all directions come out of this
pressure, further insuring the same total nibbling
at the entire cosmic scene—where everything is
relevant because everything is visible, and nothing
is relevant because visibility is nothing and
nothing is everything, everything appears as hint
because nothing is there, and there are no hints
because everything is there. And the blues is all.*
—Richard Meltzer, *The Super Super Blues Band*

"**N**adine?" Slim said.

"Yes, baby."

They were lying naked on a blanket at the edge of the
river, watching the sun go down and enjoying their wet coolness in
the diminishing heat of the day. Mother Phillips' gang were still playing in the water, so no one in particular paid any attention to them,
and their nudity went unnoticed and uncommented on.

"Did I do good?" Slim asked shyly. "With the playing, I mean?"

"Slim," Nadine said. "I think you played just great."

Slim looked closely at her face. He seemed to see pride and admiration in her eyes. At least he interpreted it as such. It wasn't some-

thing he had ever seen in any woman's eyes before when they had looked at him. "Thanks for singing with me," he said.

Nadine chuckled good-naturedly. "Well," she said, "I couldn't leave you up there all alone."

"Yeah." Slim laughed, too. "I know I don't sing too well. But it's fun, you know. I really enjoy it. And when you sang with me, it was the first time in my whole life that I felt like I was any good at it—that I thought it sounded okay. It was really a nice thing for you to do. Thank you."

"You're welcome," Nadine said. She moved to lie on top of him, looking down into his eyes. "I could see you wanted to sing," she said. "I know what it's like to want to so bad. And I wanted to play and see if we *could* sing together."

"Yeah?" he said. "How come?" He shifted beneath her so that all the bumps and grooves of their bodies fit into each other more comfortably with her pressing down on him. The small bumps of her breasts and nipples adjusted themselves, with a little help from her, so that they matched his own sensitive nipples, kissing tip to tip and teasing. They had already made love in the water, so there was no real need in either of them, just a sheer enjoyment of the feel of each other's bodies. Slim stopped, only for a moment, to wonder how they'd become so comfortable with each other that they could be naked on the shore, intimate, in front of other people without being self-conscious about it.

"Why'd you need to see if we could sing together?" he persisted.

"Promise you won't tell anyone until I'm ready to?" she said, blushing.

"Who would I tell?"

"Okay. I guess it's not that important. See, I have some songs that I've been writing. No music, just lyrics. But they're written for a man and a woman to sing together. I was hoping—well, that you and I might be able to do them together after all this is over. You can write the music, I know you can. And the words are pretty good, I think."

"Great," Slim said, excited. Creativity in women, their assertion of intelligence and skill, had always turned him on and, in his own clumsy way, he'd always tried to encourage it. "Why don't we do one of them here tomorrow?"

"But—"

"No, listen. Progress said for you to think of a way to set me up, to help build up the power. Right? Neither one of us can do it alone. And I can't think of any way that's better for me than us singing together. Man, that would make me about bust with it."

"But there's no music," Nadine protested.

"Oh, come on. Music's the easy part. Just come up with an intro and a hook riff and set it for a standard twelve- or twenty-four-bar progression. It'd take about five minutes to fix it with the band so we could at least play a rough version of it. It's not the music that gets the power for us, it's the singing together."

"But wouldn't it be just the same if we sang a song we already knew?"

"Probably," Slim said. "But I want to hear *your* songs."

"That's really what you want?" Nadine asked.

"Yeah. Everybody keeps saying that it's all up to me. So there, I've made a decision. Let's do it."

"Okay," she said, sighing. "For you it's okay." She wriggled against him. Though there was still no need for sex, there was a definite trend growing.

"Now that's what I like to see."

Slim and Nadine looked up at Mother Phillips' wizened body. The old woman stood with her hands on her hips, smiling down at them.

"Nothing I like to see more than good, clean lust," she said, sitting on the sand beside them.

"I see you two have gotten all the shyness out of your systems. My, I do enjoy seeing young people in love. Are you happy with each other? Everything fit?"

"So far, so good," Nadine said.

"Wonderful!" It was hard to be unhappy or worried around Mother Phillips and her unbridled enthusiasm and joy for life. "I just knew you two were meant for each other," she said. "Why don't you come to our tent and we'll have a few beers and some grub. You hungry?"

"Starved," Slim said. Nadine nodded her head in agreement.

Mother Phillips stood and brushed her wrinkledy butt off. Nadine got off Slim and they stood beside the old woman, dressing, then following, hand in hand, as Mother Phillips led the way to the tent where her group was quartered for the duration.

"Would you kids like to get married?" she asked offhandedly. "I can do that, you know. The nation of Tejas, in its wisdom and nearsightedness, lets me have a license to commit marriages and funerals."

Slim was taken aback. He hadn't thought about marriage at all. But when Mother Phillips mentioned it, he suddenly knew that was what he wanted more than anything.

"Nadine?" he asked, hoping.

"I'm game if you are," she said, laughing happily.

"You're both pretty gamey if you ask me," Mother Phillips quipped. "But how about getting married? You want to?"

"I think we do," Slim said. "Yeah. I think we'd like that a lot." He put his arm around Nadine's shoulders and pulled her close to him, their hips bumping as they walked.

"Well, come on then," Mother Phillips said. "Why don't you get some chow. I'll get these old bones around and tell everybody and get things ready. Oh my, this is going to be *some* festival."

. . .

The wedding was to be onstage, under a full moon. Slim wondered if Progress had known the moon would be full when he'd set up the festival date. Probably, he decided. Mother Phillips had sent some of her people back to Tralfaz for a pickupload of fresh oak leaves, pine branches, flowers and bushels of fresh vegetables. Then they had dressed the stage until, now, it looked like a quiet forest clearing and smelled almost too wild and fresh to bear. The moon and stars provided all the light that would be needed.

People had gathered on the threshing floor, a marriage evidently a big event for the temporary community. All the celebrants, save Slim and Nadine, were gathered on the stage under a circle of pine branches and flowers. Elijigbo's band played a soft, strange music that echoed off into the night and the river. Some of Mother Phillips' people accompanied them on simple wooden flutes and bells.

Except for Progress and the band, everyone was naked, both on stage and down on the threshing floor. Slim and Nadine walked hand in hand toward Mother Phillips from offstage. Their small fears and apprehensions seemed to evaporate with the sound their feet made in the crackling leaves that covered the stage. People cheered as they walked. Then Slim and Nadine stopped, to stand, still holding hands, before Mother Phillips.

The old woman seemed to glow in the moonlight as she nodded her head, smiling. She turned and poured a clear red wine into a large wooden goblet.

"Spirits of the East," she said, turning in that direction, "close the circle. Bless and protect this gathering." She poured a little of the wine onto the floor, and then took a small drink. "Spirits of the South," she said, repeating her previous motions, "close the circle. Bless and protect this gathering." She did the same for the West and the North, then handed the goblet to Slim and Nadine to drink the remaining wine it contained.

A group of women stood forward and began to chant in harmony:

> *"Mother of all,*
> *Oh, Goddess divine,*
> *Whose spiral spins,*
> *Through all of time,*
> *Be with us now,*
> *And never part,*
> *Forever dwell here in our hearts.*

> *"She is the source,*
> *The mystery deep,*
> *The inspiring song,*
> *Protecting sleep,*
> *From her we come,*
> *To her return,*
> *None greater is,*
> *Than she who lives."*

Many of the people on the threshing floor joined in the chant, giving it a power that affected Slim more than he would have expected. Several women of varying ages stepped forward and began to recite in joyful voices.

> *"Maiden Mother,*
> *Mother of all,*
> *Goddess Mother,*
> *Three aspects of our Great Mother's face,*
> *Be with us now,*

Fill us all with
Your power and grace.

"*Goddess Mother,*
Swift and smart,
Bring your joy,
Into our hearts,
Mother of all,
Full of life,
Surround us now,
With brilliant light.

"*Goddess Mother,*
Old and wise,
Teach us your secrets,
Of Earth and sky."

The women stepped back and left a void of silence in their wake. Mother Phillips stood once again in center stage.

"We ask the Goddess to bless and protect us," she intoned, "as we bind these two, male and female, in body, heart, mind, and soul. We ask our community to help and support them as they bind each to the other. We ask the Gods of all beliefs to smile on them as they struggle to live lives bound in love. And we ask our Mother the Earth to share her bounty with them, so that their lives may be full."

She turned solemnly to Slim and Nadine. "Do you swear, now," she said, with only a small twinkle in her eye, "to love only one another, to share hearts and lives, neither outshining the other, but as equals before the Goddess and the community?"

"We do," they said, together.

"Do you swear, now, to treat our Mother, the Earth, with love, to treat the people of the community with respect, and to treat each other with gentleness and compassion, always trying to understand each other?"

"We do."

"Then, in the name of the Goddess, in the presence of the community, and with the blessing of our Mother the Earth, I declare to all present that you are now bound together, in love and in life. You are married."

The crowd on the threshing floor began to cheer and the party was full on. Slim looked at Mother Phillips.

"Is that all?" he asked, bemused.

"Yep," she said. "There's not a thing hard about it. It just takes making the vows in front of the community."

"Thanks," he said.

Nadine had reached down and, almost unconsciously, was playing with his dick. He reached for her breast and looked around. Nearly all the people on stage and in the crowd were in various stages of lovemaking. Even Progress, still mostly dressed, was nuzzling Mother Phillips' neck as she worked to undo the buttons on his jeans. Bowing to the inevitable, Slim and Nadine slid down onto the oak leaves, making slow, gentle love along with the community. Each couple present made love in a world of its own, yet each was aware of every other, and there was an energy, a power that built and covered them, an energy that felt as old as the Earth itself.

As the orgy, or so Slim thought of it, wound down, some of Mother Phillips' people began passing out plates of raw fruit and vegetables, washed in the river, chilled, sliced and delicious. Mitchell brought up two huge pots of steaming chili and pans of corn bread. Someone turned the stage lights on and Elijigbo's band began to play dancing music. People that Slim knew, or had met, and many he didn't and hadn't, came up, one by one, to give him and Nadine presents and good wishes. A pile quickly grew beside them, of clothing, crafts, guitar equipment, coupons and promises for services, invitations, bedding, even a few certified offers for gigs and one recording contract, open ended.

Slim had never experienced the kind of love and affection, the neighborliness and friendship that was being offered to him here. He wasn't even sure yet how he felt about being married all of a sudden, nor did he know how to return all the love that was being given him in any solid, emotional manner. To Nadine, yes. But to the people of the community who were opening their hearts, he didn't know how to either accept or repay the gift. Simple thank-you's were only tiny moments in time. They didn't express the continuing emotional commitment that people seemed to be offering. It gave him, to his vast surprise, a sense of responsibility to them. He knew he had to do his best to get the Gutbucket back and to find a way to win the victory they all wanted. And after that, he just didn't know.

He wanted, and wanted very badly, to be a part of this community, of this world. He just wasn't sure how to do it. He'd been a loner, a hermit, too long. Nadine would be here to help, he knew. But he, himself, was going to have to let go of some of the things that had always held him apart from people. He was going to have to let people be a part of his life, learn to accept their feelings. Well, he thought, that would be okay. It made him feel good in a way he hadn't felt before.

The party went on into the late hours. That the festival proper began the next day was not a consideration for most people. For them the festival had began with the rehearsal and had come together joyously at the wedding. The next day's activities were simply a continuation of a celebration well begun. But Slim and Nadine, tired and seeking privacy, went to bed some time before the party wound down to a sweating, lubricated halt.

22

Polarity and intensification—in these Goethe
believed he had discovered the two principles
governing all the phenomenon of animate nature.
Now we find them in twofold activity of the
forces that give all musical phenomena, in so far as
they are temporal succession, their characteristic
organizations; in the tendency that closes,
establishes symmetries, equalizes every weight by
a counterweight; and in the tendency that drives
on, accumulates, is responsible for constant
augmentation.
—Victor Zuckerkandle, *Sound and Symbol*

The day came like fire and smoke.

Mother Phillips blessed the opening of the festival at the break of dawn. Slim and Nadine woke with the sun and even after the late night and the excitement of the wedding, they were filed with energy and wide awake. During the night, the small part of it during which they had slept, a townful of people had come rolling in to the river. And even as the festival got started, more and more were still coming, so that the threshing floor was nearly filled for Mother Phillips' benediction. The tent city was bustling with people buying and looking and eating. Elijigbo's white-clad followers were acting as guides, security, clergy and all-around facilitators.

A natural-bearded, grizzly-growly DJ named Earthman Jack took the stage, acting as the festival's MC. He quickly, blurrily, introduced a band called Cannon's Jug Stompers, who began to play the bouncy, humorous, insinuating jug-band music that seemed to just fit the early morning. Slim and Nadine stumbled around, minds awake, but bodies still in shock from the early hour and the late night and the abuse that they had inflicted on themselves in celebrating the marriage. They headed in the general direction of the chow tent. Most of the people they met greeted them with smiles or waves or handshakes, asking them how they were doing.

It was tremendously exciting. Slim had played his share of outdoor festivals in the old days; the Human Be-In, one or two of the Monterey Festivals, Big Sur, more than a few of the Golden Gate Park love-ins. This festival, *this world,* reminded him of those. The affection, the lust, the good humor of the community invoked some of the spirit he had loved in the sixties. But, where that was childish and rebellious, many times drug-induced, the temper here was sober and adult. The drugs were still around, still being used, but they were no longer the big deal, the symbol they had been in that other time and place.

Slim had sorely missed the old days. He'd never really gotten over their ending, always searching for a person or a place that still held some of those cherished feelings and beliefs. It wasn't that he lived in the past. He'd kept up with the music and the times, simply because he believed if he didn't, the world would pass him by. But the music and the times had lost an innocence and an honesty, a purity and a colorfulness, that he'd loved in the sixties.

It was *his* generation, the way he'd grown up. It was what he believed in, down deep in his heart. When he'd walked in the solemn procession down Haight-Ashbury, following the painted, flower-bedecked coffin holding the soon-to-be-sacrificed symbols and remains of "Hippy," he'd cried. And he had not been alone in his tears.

And when he'd returned to the streets nearly twenty years later, when he'd seen that nothing remained of the life that had existed there, that there was only a uniform cityness where a monument should have stood, he'd cried again. This time feeling very, very alone.

But this time, this place, this world, this *Tejas* had the same feeling in many ways, the same joyfulness, the same freedom. It was the sense of community, of extended family. Except for Pickens and the Vipers. Thinking about it, remembering, gave Slim much more reason to win the fight they were in. His own beloved time had been polluted and destroyed by men and a society very much like Pickens, and what he was trying to build. And Slim was damned if he was going to let them take *this* world away from him as well.

"Hey, Nadine," he said. "You think I could get a hamburger this early in the morning?"

"Baby," she replied, "after yesterday and last night, I think you could probably get anything you wanted."

"Yeah? That's nice, huh? Let's go eat."

Nadine laughed and put her arm around him as they walked. When they entered the chow tent, people applauded. Slim blushed.

"Man, you're cute when you're embarrassed," Nadine said. Which, of course, made Slim blush even more deeply.

Someone must have guessed at his habits or, more likely been informed, because as soon as he and Nadine sat at their table, a waitress brought over hamburgers and fries for both of them.

"See how nice it is not to have to work?" Nadine said.

"Yeah. But your breakfasts are awfully nice, too."

"For you, maybe. You don't have to cook them. You just get to eat."

"I'll tell you what," Slim said. "After this is all over, I'll cook you breakfast. How's that?"

"Hah!" Nadine said. "Your clever little strategy has backfired. I'll take you up on that. Will I live through it?"

"Sure. Of course. I'm a good cook."

"Really?" Nadine said. "I'm surprised. Most men can't cook."

"I know," Slim replied. "I have no respect for men that don't know how to cook. I mean, how do they survive? And if they're married, don't they ever like to give the women in their lives a break? I know that most men just seem to take it for granted that women cook the meals. Me, I can cook everything from hamburgers, to Mexican food to gourmet. I don't *like* gourmet crap, but I can cook it."

"Good," Nadine said. "You can cook for both of us, then."

"Really?" he said. "Can we get drunk and puke on each other all night, too?"

"If that's what turns you on, sure. As long as you clean up the mess."

"Ye Gods," Slim said in mock seriousness. "I wonder if you can refuse to inherit the world."

"I think once you're born, it's too late." Nadine munched on her hamburger for a while, small giggles escaping past mouthfuls of meat.

"Listen," she said. "Let's get serious, okay? What about today? How are you feeling abut it?"

"Oh, I don't know, baby. I think we're gonna kick ass. I have to think that. I *can't* let Pickens win. There's just too much at stake, too much to lose."

"You scared?" she asked.

"Damn straight."

"You think he's here yet?"

"No," Slim said. "I think Progress would have told us. Besides, I'm not so scared of him as I am of the Gutbucket and what Elijigbo told us."

"You did good yesterday," Nadine said encouragingly.

"I know. But today is today. It's a whole different gig. I never killed nobody before, Nadine. I never even thought about it. Now, I'm supposed to kill Pickens. I'm supposed to open up to the Gutbucket and let some crazy-ass God share my body. How am I supposed to do that?"

She shrugged. "Just do it, I guess. I don't know what to tell you. I don't know how I'm going to do any of what I'm supposed to do either. I just know we have to. There's no choice."

"I hear *that*. You have any suggestions?"

"We could go back to bed for a while. Work up a good sweat and then go listen to the music awhile."

Slim looked at her, at the innocent, fine-featured face, the clear green eyes, the expression of utter love and devotion in the look she returned to him. "Oh, Nadine," he said. "How do you always know the best thing to do?"

"I don't," she said. "But I know *you*. I know how you like to make love, what it means to you. I know that's the only time you feel safe and secure. And that's okay. I love it, too, with you, and I'm happy I can make you feel that way. If it was just fucking, it'd be different. But it's not. There's something there inside you that makes it extremely special, no matter how often it is. You have a way of letting all your love out when we make love. It's like, at that moment, you trust and love completely. You don't want to be anywhere else or with anybody else. Right then, you're completely there, totally together, the three-lock box. It can make a woman feel—well, *loved.* I don't know much about it, but I suspect that's not the way it is for most people."

"I don't know, either," Slim said bashfully. "I can't explain it. It's even more than that, but you're the first person to even begin to notice it or understand it at all. A lot of women, all they can see is that I want sex all the time. They don't see the other side of it, don't see the love and desire I'm trying to express to them. Do you know," he said, "that in my whole entire life, I have never cheated on any woman I've ever been with?"

"I believe it," Nadine said.

"I've never needed to, wanted to. I've never even *thought* about it. It was never a matter of having to resist the idea, I never *had* the idea. The women I've loved were my friends, or I wanted them to be, thought they were. And you just don't treat friends that way, you don't treat the people you love that way." Slim was close to tears, but he wasn't sure why. Somehow, everything that had happened, everything that was still going to happen, was causing all his walls to collapse, letting out all the pain and hurt and anger. It was making him give it up to Nadine.

"Come on, baby," she said sympathetically. "Let's go on back to the tent. We can still talk about it, but I think it would be easier if were in bed."

She was right. He could let it *all* go when he was in her arms, when he felt safe. She held his dick, and he held her breast and told her everything, things he'd never told anyone. He told her the things he had done right, and the things he had done wrong, the things, right and wrong, that had been done to him. He poured out all the hurt and anger and frustration that had built up in his heart over the years. He tried very hard to be completely honest, not glossing over things that made him look bad, and not blaming or badmouthing the women that had passed through his life. Before he'd finished, both he and Nadine had shed a lot of tears together.

"Slim," she said, holding him close, stroking his dick and enjoying the unconscious thrusting of his hips into her hand. "Why are you telling me all this right now?"

"You sure you want to know?" he asked sadly.

"Yes, I do. Why?"

"Well, if something happens, you know. If I screw up and get killed, if I die, I want to know that there's one person in the world that knows me and understands me and loves me anyway, just because I'm *me*. Does that make sense?"

"Oh, baby," she said. "Hasn't anyone *ever* understood you?"

He shook his head slowly against her shoulder. "No," he said. "All anyone's ever done is misunderstand me. I've tried to talk about it before, but after you get hurt a few times you give up and just hope you can pull it off for a while without getting caught. But all the time there's this little guy inside you, crying and hurting, wanting someone to understand and care."

"I care," Nadine said. "I love you. And I think I understand, I know what hurt can do to a person's heart. You and I, we're not so different."

"You remember what I said at Belizaire's? About black people and white people in my world?"

"Yes, I remember. What about it?"

Slim looked down at his pale white hand against the rich caramel of her breast, studied the deep brown and red of her large, erect nipple. "Well," he said. "I just wondered—do you think I'm funny-looking because I'm white?"

That seemed to crack Nadine up completely. She let go of his dick and curled up, holding her stomach and laughing. Then she regained her grasp, reached down and took him in her mouth for just a moment, then stretched out against him. He could feel her shaking a little.

"Oh, Slim," she said, still giggling. "Yes, I think you're funny-looking. But believe me, it doesn't have a thing to do with the fact that you're white."

"That's okay, then," he said. "I was just worried."

There was no answer to that except to make love. It was, after the talking, a marvelous, affecting experience, and when they were satisfied, they slept.

. . .

"Wake up, chillen." Progress stood above them. The gold smile wasn't in sight. "Wake up," he said. "T-Bone's here. It's time."

"Okay," Slim said. He stretched and yawned as Progress walked out, then he and Nadine rose and began to dress. As they did so, Slim happened to look absently up at the plastic window in the wall of the tent. A wasp was crawling on the upper edge. It moved jerkily, a half-inch forward, halt, then another half-inch. Precisely below it, about an inch away, was a small wolf spider. It matched the wasp's movements, step by step, scuttling along sideways, never taking its eyes off the wasp above. The spider was, at best, about the size of the wasp's head.

He's gonna bite off more than he can chew, Slim thought of the spider.

Suddenly, the wasp stopped and stood still. The spider, in small increments, crept upward and to the side of the wasp, constantly watching it, looking it in the eyes. Then the spider stopped as well, no more and no less than a half an inch from the wasp's face. It froze. It didn't move, it didn't pounce, it simply stared—and stared. Then, to Slim's amazement, the wasp fell, simply dropped. Before it hit the ground, before it had even traveled two inches downward, the spider had pounced, landed on its back and fallen to the floor with it, where it began happily and calmly eating what was, for the immature spider, a gargantuan meal.

"Well I'll be damned," Slim said, a wide, bemused smile lighting up his face.

"What is it, baby?" Nadine said sleepily, struggling with her pants.

"Oh, nothing really," Slim replied. "I think the Gods or the Goddess or someone just tried to tell me something to help me out."

Nadine looked at him puzzled, shrugged, and continued dressing. "Okay," she said. "That's nice."

Slim chuckled to himself at her nonchalant attitude, putting it down to satiety and tiredness, the sleep that still held her.

I hope I'm not turning into a mystic, he thought. *But that was a sign.* The wolf spider hadn't attacked. It hadn't pounced, it hadn't bitten, it didn't even have any venom to bite with, as far as he knew. It was as if it had hypnotized the much larger wasp, as if it had a power that had captivated and paralyzed it, stunned it. Even as it had sat quietly and eaten the wasp, the wasp hadn't moved, hadn't fought its consumption.

Slim had always admired the wolf spider's eyes, or, at least, what he assumed were its eyes. He didn't know enough about spiders and their construction to be sure. But he knew that when the light struck the spider's distinguished face, there were bright reflections of red, blue, yellow and green, metallic glints and shinings that made the spider beautiful in the sunlight. But he had never in the world suspected that the spider, despite its exceptional eyesight, used its eyes for anything beyond seeing. And he knew, somehow, that the small stalk and kill he'd just witnessed was no accident.

The Gods or Goddess, whoever *they* were, wanted to tell him something. He felt it was something more important than just the lesson in the disparity of sizes between the wasp and the spider. But, at the moment, despite the inspiring feelings the sight had given him, he didn't understand what it signified. Perhaps later on the meaning would become clear, but for now, there was business to take care of. And despite his confusion, the small spider's victory did make him feel good.

It was dry and cloudy and not too hot as they stepped out of the tent. The band on stage was pumping out a good shuffle blues, and the audience on the threshing floor was clapping and shouting with the music. Progress was pacing the grass in front of the tent, hands clasped behind his back.

"There you is," he said. "Good, good. We're ready for it to come down. Are you?"

"Yeah," Slim said. "Strangely enough, I think we are. What's the plan?"

Progress rolled his eyes. "Well, son, to tell the God's honest truth, we ain't got no plan beyond doin' it. Bunch of us is gonna buzz around T-Bone and his men, distract 'em, like, while you and Nadine goes and gets the Gutbucket."

"How do we do that?"

"Same way you found Nadine, son. Use the power to hook on to it, let it pull you along till you're there."

Progress looked closely at Slim and Nadine, his face almost fierce. "Once you got it in your hands," he said, "just come on. Don't stop for nothin' nor nobody. The band'll be waitin' on stage. The folks playin' knows to step down when we got the Gutbucket ready to go. Once we got it, we gots to play right then. *Right* then. You got your playlist figured out?"

Slim nodded and pulled a folded piece of paper from his back pocket. "Yeah," he said, handing it to Progress. "I hope you know them all."

"Hmmm," Progress mumbled as he looked at the list. "'Standing at the Crossroads,' 'Who Do You Love,' 'Hoochie Koochie Man,' 'Ridin' in the Moonlight,' 'Come to Mama'—good, that's Nadine's best song—'Seventh Son,' 'Take Me to the River.' Yep, we knows all these. But what's these last two on the list. They got no names?"

"One's a song for Nadine and I to sing together," Slim said. "No sweat, just a standard progression in A, a little hopped up and jumping. The other—I dunno. See, if we're building up the power like you say, I figure I'd better wait and see. If the power's working, by the time I get there and get ready to cut loose, I'll know what to play. I can't pick a song here and now, and have it be right, then."

Progress nodded. "I think you're right, son. You just do what you gotta do. Kick out the jams, the band'll be there along with you. All these folks that been playin' on stage, they been buildin' up a mighty power for us. Belizaire and Elijigbo and Mother Phillips been holdin' on to it so it don't run out like it usually would. There's a big pile of it waitin' to be let go when you open the gates."

Progress walked closer to them, put his arms around their shoulders. A touch of the golden smile returned. "Listen here, chillen," he said. "I'm real proud of you two, I want you all to know that. I'm as happy as I can be that you got yourselves married, and I'm lookin' forward to watchin' you go through life together. So you be careful, you hear?"

"You bet, Daddy," Nadine said. She grabbed the front of Slim's shirt and shook him gently. "I won't let anything happen to this big lug."

"I lug you, too," Slim said, barely containing his laughter and an impulse to grab Nadine's breasts and shake them, which he knew tickled her.

"All right, then," Progress said. He looked at his watch. "There's a new band comin' on in a few minutes. Sonny Early and his boys. When you hear that, you'll know it's time to move. You'd do best if you get on the outside of this crowd before you start seekin'."

Progress walked away without another word. Slim and Nadine watched him, and then began their own walk, skirting the edge of the threshing floor and the swaying crowd that stood listening as the band wound down their last song.

"What do you think?" Nadine asked.

"I dunno," Slim replied, "I feel okay. Feel good about it. I think we'll be all right."

They threaded their way through the brush and found an isolated clearing a little way from the crowd and the music. They sat down on a huge, ancient, fallen cottonwood trunk. Slim started humming the fishing song he had used to find Nadine. She listened for a few moments, picked up the melody and started humming it with him. He worked at calming his thoughts and emptying his mind. Someone on stage began playing an accordion, and Slim noticed the dark clouds getting thicker, covering the sky. A soft, warm wind began to blow and he felt a hard tug on his power, in his gut. He and Nadine stood, and he led the way down to the river, along the bank, east, following the way the power was pulling him.

They walked for about a quarter of a mile; then there was a hill ahead, at the edge of the river. One edge had been eaten away to cliff and rock. It was stony and steep, but there was a path that appeared to lead to the top. Slim began climbing the path, drawn to the top of the hill. The Gutbucket was up there. He could *feel* it.

Nadine grabbed his arm and stopped him. "Wait a minute," she said. "If they're up there, they'll be watching this trail. Come on, there's another way."

She led the way away from the river and around the side of the hill. Slim noticed small, round holes in the boulders they walked through.

"What are those?" he asked.

"Oh, the holes?" Nadine replied. "The Indians used to grind their corn and wheat here at the river. They'd dump it in the hole and bash it with rocks. Over the years the holes got so deep they abandoned them and started new ones." She stopped and looked around carefully. "Here it is," she said, pointing to a narrow cleft in the rock wall. "Up there."

Slim moved carefully to the cleft. He saw that, past the narrow entrance, it opened out and slanted gently upward to the top of the hill. He squeezed through the opening, Nadine following, and began slowly climbing.

Slim tried to walk as quietly as he could through the dry grass and brush of the hill. Surprisingly, he found it was easier than he thought it would be. They weren't entirely silent, but silent enough so that when they reached nearly to the top of the hill, they could hear quiet, mumbling voices.

Nadine crept up beside him. "Let's get closer," she whispered.

"Why?"

"Because we're sneaking. When you're sneaking, you're supposed to get as close as you can. Don't you know anything about sneaking?"

"To tell you the truth," Slim said, "I don't."

"Well, come on," Nadine said, creeping forward.

Slim followed her. The voices grew louder as they approached what appeared to be a circle of stones. They hid behind one and looked surreptitiously out to the center. Three men sat on boulders around a small fire. One of them held a guitar.

Slim nearly stood and went forward to the guitar when he saw it. It was a pearl-gray strat with a beautiful maple neck. The pickups weren't the white plastic Slim was used to, but were blue-chrome tubes. The guitar seemed, to Slim, to glow with an almost-blue light. The Viper was holding it with what Slim saw as a total lack of respect, letting the butt end drag in the dirt. Now and then, he would reach down and pluck one of the stings far harder than he should have, as if trying to break them.

The guitar called to Slim. He had to get it, had to play it. He could almost feel it in his hands, the smooth slide of the neck, the bends of the strings. He could hear in his mind exactly how it would sound, what he could do with it, how far he could go.

As he watched, as the guitar called out to him, the pouch he'd worn around his neck since Belizaire had given it to him grew warm and heavy. The gris-gris man had said he'd know the time to use it. Now, with a little help and inspiration from a wolf spider, he thought he did know.

"Nadine," he whispered. "Go around to the other side of the circle and come out."

"Why?" she asked.

"I need you to distract them. I have an idea that I think will work."

"What if it doesn't?"

"If it doesn't, there's only three of them. We can kick their asses. I'd rather try to do it easy, though."

"Okay," she said. "But you better be right."

Nadine slipped quietly around the stone circle. Slim took the bag from around his neck and opened it up. It contained a red dust with bits of white stone or bone mixed in it. It felt warm in his hand and seemed drawn to the fire in front of the Vipers.

He looked back into the circle and watched. Soon, he saw Nadine step out from between the rocks and walk into the circle. The Vipers jumped up and faced her. She inhaled, making her small bosom evident, and smiled, as if she had come upon them by accident and was about to ask directions to the festival.

They smiled too, but not the same way; they surely saw her as a fit candidate for rape, just to wile away the time while they were waiting for the real action. They were about to get up and catch hold of her, knowing that it would probably require two of them to hold her while the third did his business with her. That was okay; they'd take proper turns, and it would be more fun that way. It wouldn't even matter how loud she screamed, way out here. Screaming just added to the pleasure.

When their attention was focused on Nadine, Slim ran into the circle. He hurled the gris-gris bag into the fire and yelled to Nadine, "Don't breathe!"

The fire exploded in a thick red cloud that completely filled the circle. Slim and Nadine held their breaths for what seemed like hours. Finally, the cloud thinned, dissipated and they drew dusty, cinnamon-scented air into their strained lungs.

The Vipers stood frozen, motionless. Slim passed his hands in front of one man's eyes. They were unseeing, unmoving. He didn't know if they were dead or alive, and he wasn't going to wait to find out. He reached down eagerly to grab the Gutbucket out of the Viper's hands.

There was a lightning bolt in his hand. He was aware that it wasn't literal; he had not been struck physically. It was only a thought, an image. But it was enough to freeze him in place, so that he stood for a moment as still and sightless as the Vipers.

DON'T BE A FOOL!

That was the voice of Shango; Slim recognized it, though he had never heard it before. The God of Lightning, who had brought him here. Why was Shango trying to stop him, now that he was on the verge of success?

Slim didn't know, but neither did he doubt the warning. He stood still, gazing at the Gutbucket—and his vision blurred, shifting. The guitar changed, and assumed the form of a giant Glory Hand.

Now he understood! It was a trap! They had fashioned another awful fetish to take him out, and masked it so that he would grab it without thinking—and be vaulted back to his own world. In his moment of seeming victory, he would be nullified—and Nadine would be left to the brute mercies of the three Vipers, and all that was good in this world would become the object of T-Bone's cruel exploitation. Everyone would lose, except the enemy.

No wonder their siege of him had eased up recently. They had been preparing the worst trap of all, baiting it with the one thing he couldn't resist, the Gutbucket itself. They had set it up here, seemingly inadequately guarded, knowing he would have little trouble nullifying the Vipers.

How close he had come to falling for it! But for Shango's timely warning—

But there was no time to react to that. He knew the Gutbucket was close, because he had oriented on it. It had to be right here, just beyond the masked Glory Hand.

Slim stepped around the fake guitar. Now he saw that the boulder the Viper sat on was fake, too; it was a box covered over with material the color of stone. He reached for it, pausing, but got no additional warning, so he touched it. He pulled away the material, and there beneath was another guitar, looking just like the fake one.

He reached in and put his hand on its rounded surface.

The reaction, as he touched and held it, was almost unbearable. If Nadine hadn't been holding on to him, he would have fallen to his knees. He found himself, suddenly, with no warning, no transition, in another life, another time, another *mind.* In a matter of minutes, or, perhaps, seconds, he lived an entire lifetime.

He was a poor black child, barefoot, sitting on a rough wooden porch looking up at a fat man playing a guitar and singing. Then he grew into shoes and a guitar and learned to let his own music out. He saw himself—no, his other self, the Gutbucket, playing at parties and on porches. Passing into teenage years, he discovered sweat and sex and playing rough blues at even rougher roadhouses. He felt the pain of drunken fistfights and the gentle, urgent touch of lover's hands. He grew into a man with blues in his heart and whiskey and women on his mind. He felt the warm, liquid rush of heroin and the stumbling hunger of a weakening old man who knew it was slowly slipping away, trying desperately to hold on. And he felt the numb, orgasmic collapse of death and waiting, the painful awakening into the Gutbucket and the search for a player to give it all to.

Slim opened his eyes and the Gutbucket was silent in his hands. He had drawn it out of its cavity during his vision, and now was holding it in both hands. There had been no real sense of surrender, no combat, but he felt older, and he knew the Gutbucket had accepted him. He didn't feel diminished, or that he had lost control, but he had lost something. He didn't know exactly what it was, but he didn't miss it. He was left with his own mind and a knowledge of the blues, a feeling for the music he'd never dared imagine he could have.

"Slim," Nadine said, shaking him. Her voice seemed frightened, tentative. "Oh Slim."

He looked around himself, dazedly. The Vipers were beginning to shake and tremble, trying to break the spell the gris-gris had put on them.

"I'm okay," he said. "Run like hell."

They turned and began running down the trail they hadn't gone up, swerving and jumping around bushes and rocks in their way. Slim held tightly to the Gutbucket. He could hear the Vipers beginning to run clumsily after them. Nadine was in front, weaving her way through the rocks and trees that grew at the bottom of the hill. They had a long way to go back to the festival, through the crowd and onto the stage.

There was a heavy bass and drum line coming from the stage. Slim could feel it pounding in his gut as he ran. The Gutbucket felt almost alive, as if it were squirming in his hand. Not to get loose, but to cut loose, to play. How long had it been since Rosie's death, Progress had told him? Thirty years? Forty? Slim suddenly realized that the hunger to play he carried in his own soul could never match the hunger that he could feel emanating from the Gutbucket, wanting to take him over. And so, he thought, it began.

They approached the edge of the crowd. Nadine was still running ahead of Slim. The people saw them running, saw the Vipers chasing them and, as if it had been arranged, a path opened up for them. The three Vipers were close behind, but as Slim and Nadine got to the inside of the crowd, people closed the path behind them, so that the Vipers had to push and shove to squeeze their way through a crowd that was more than willing to push and shove back.

Slim estimated the distance to the stage at just less than a quarter of a mile. That was a long way to run and a lot of people to go through. He was already winded from the run they had just made. For a second, he thought he would fall. But he felt a burst of energy from the Gutbucket and the guitar itself seemed to pull him along.

A Viper stepped into the path ahead of them. Nadine didn't pause. She just ran straight over him. People in the crowd grabbed the Viper and pulled him back in. Another stepped out after Nadine had passed. Almost without volition, the Gutbucket came up and the headstock slashed the man in the throat. The Viper dropped and Slim spun around to catch his balance and then kept running.

Time seemed to slow. Running was a painful dream, the distance left to cover looked like miles. Slim struggled against the oppressive sense of exhaustion and futility that was trying to overcome him. He also fought against the attempts of the Gutbucket to enter his mind and thoughts. Lose or win, he swore, he would remain himself. He didn't notice when the band on stage stopped playing and Progress and the boys stood out. He didn't see the Vipers in the crowd ahead of them draw back. What he did see, what stopped his running, what pulled him up short, next to Nadine, was the short fat man all in white, standing in the path ahead of them, holding what looked like a very big gun. T-Bone Pickens had shown himself at last.

23

The blues is just a feeling, but in musical terms,
it's much more than that. The history of Rock 'n'
Roll as we know it today makes a bee-line
through the Mississippi Delta and the Texas
Panhandle to Memphis and Chicago and all points
in between. Elvis heard B. B. King in his Memphis
youth and Mick Jagger and Keith Richards, John
Lennon and Paul McCartney, Van Morrison and
Eric Clapton heard John Lee Hooker and Albert
King over the ether and across the Atlantic and
Angus Young heard it all the way to Australia.
And Ed Van Halen heard it from Eric Clapton
and Steve Stevens heard it from Curtis Mayfield.
From heavy metal to hard rock, from Led Zep to
the Beatles, the influence of the blues is seminal.
Lo and behold, the blues itself, in its original form
and with a herd of true-to-the-roots believers, is
alive and well and traveling all over the country
and the world in the form of bent-note crusaders
playing the clubs and colleges, the small halls and
the outdoor festivals, carrying it on, true to the
twelve bar.
—Noe the G, *Blues, the Anatomy of a Feeling*

"Y'all might just as well stop right where you are," Pickens said, handling the gun the same way he'd handled his money. "I admit I'm surprised you managed to get this far, but I never leave important matters to underlings. It's all over, now."

He stepped closer and pointed the gun at Slim. "Hand it over, boy. And keep in mind, I'll blow your ass off if I have to."

Slim stood, trying not to stare at the gun. All this, and T-Bone was going to win, just because he had a fucking gun? Slim decided, one way or another, that this slime wasn't going to get the Gutbucket. He hoisted the guitar up to his chest and held it with both hands just under the headstock. He could see men in black pushing their way through the stubborn crowd, gathering in a circle around him, Nadine and Pickens. He looked up, and saw Progress and Belizaire on stage, but was unable to read the looks on their faces. A blackness came down around him, like tight steel bands round his chest, making it difficult to breathe, to think. Why should he fight, why should he struggle? He couldn't beat a gun, Nadine might get hurt. *He* might get hurt. Why didn't he just give the Gutbucket to Pickens? He'd never be able to play it . . .

Then something took him. He stood and screamed *"No!"* Swinging the Gutbucket up onto his shoulder, he brought it down and around like an axe, an axe that, with all Slim's weight of body and soul behind it, crashed into the side of Pickens' head with a solid *thunk* that was almost painful to hear.

The gun exploded and Slim felt an immediate, hot-poker pain in the fleshy part of his upper left leg. He fell to the ground and the Gutbucket slipped from his hands. A Viper stood over Pickens, who was lying on the ground holding his head. Blood leaked from between the man's fingers, and Slim was almost surprised to see it was as red as his own. The Viper reached for the Gutbucket, but Nadine stepped up to him and kicked him viciously in the face. He went down and Nadine grabbed the guitar and shoved it back into Slim's hands.

"Come on, baby," she said urgently. "We still have to get to the stage and play. It's not over."

Slim looked up at her stupidly. "He *shot* me," he said. "The son-ofabitch *shot* me."

He held the palm of his hand up to her. "Look at that," he said. "I'm bleeding."

She grabbed the bloody hand he'd held out to her and pulled him to his feet. "I know," she said. She put his free arm around her shoulders. "Lean on me, baby. Come on. We've got to get there and finish it."

She started pulling at him. "Okay, okay," he said, trying to go along with her. He couldn't run, but he did manage a quick limp and drag. His leg hurt like hell, burned and throbbed, but they made it through the crowd. He had some rough moments climbing the steps to the stage, but when he reached the top, Progress and Belizaire were there to grab on to him and help carry him along. Elijigbo brought a chair out to stage center and the men sat Slim down on it.

Progress took the Gutbucket from him and quickly tuned it. As he handed it back he asked, "Can you play, son? You *gots* to."

Slim couldn't answer him, but he shook his head yes, anyway. Belizaire took out one of his multitude of pouches. He cut a slit in Slim's pants over the bullet hole, and spread a greenish powder on the wound.

"Dis take de pain away," he said. "I tink you do fine, me. You play now, eh?"

The hurting in Slim's leg eased and he smiled up at the gris-gris man in gratitude. "Thanks," he said. "Let's play now. Let's kick some Viper ass. Plug this fucker in."

Progress handed him the business end of a guitar cord, the other end of which was already plugged into his warmed-up amp. "Okay, son," Progress said. "Hold up your part of the sky."

Slim was unable to answer him. The sudden burst of power that resulted from the mating of Gutbucket to Amp nearly knocked him out of his chair. It was—magical, orgasmic, joyful and terrifying. It was the full potential of the blues, all their power, waiting for Slim to tap into it, as it tapped into him. It blew him away for a moment, then he let it seep into all the cells of his body and mind until it felt as if his muscles and stomach were laughing. *Is this surrender?* he thought. If it was, man, it felt good.

Belizaire patted him on the shoulder. "You do fine, now, eh? Bon?"

Slim nodded his head, grinning like a natural fool from the rush of the power through him.

"Good, then," Belizaire said, sprinkling more powder around the stage. "*Laissez les bontemps rouler.*"

Slim felt the power, could almost *see* it as a blue light, pouring into him, into the Gutbucket and into the Amp. He could feel and see it flowing into every member of the band on stage, into Nadine, who gasped and went weak in the knees. Even Progress, Belizaire and Elijigbo closed their eyes and shuddered as the pent-up blues power of all the wizards who had played before them rushed into their bodies and souls and electrified, blues-ified and motivated them. It was as if a giant generator had been switched on, releasing gigawatts of pure power.

Slim could no longer feel the pain in his leg. His dick was hard, his spine was stiff and his heart was pounding. Sweat was covering his body, and he was filled with a bright heat, nearly more than he could handle, but the reinforcement from the Gutbucket and the Amp, though contributing to the flow of power, also helped to control it.

He took three Dunlop blue Tortex picks from his pocket and slid two under the pickguard of the guitar, ready to speed grab in case he lost the one he held in his fingers. He grabbed on to the maple finger-board and began picking out the chords to "Standing at the Cross-roads."

"Let's do it," he yelled, turning up the volume.

Nadine smiled at him, though there was still concern in her eyes, and she began to sing the verses. Slim rocked back and forth in the chair, oblivious to everything but the Gutbucket and the power that was pouring through him. He could hear the band through the floor monitors, hear Nadine's luscious voice as she belted out the song. The double drums shook the stage, the Earth pounded like a mad heart, and Belizaire's bass hammering shook his belly. Progress' rhythm guitar was smooth and sticky and deep like Tejas red mud after the rain. But, through it all, he heard the growling of the Gutbucket. It was a voice that spoke for him, with him and through him, helping him to say what he wanted to say, what he'd always wanted to say. He controlled it. Having surrendered to it, accepted it, he'd won.

But where was Shango? he wondered. Where was the God that was supposed to jump in? So far the cat hadn't been much help. Except when he'd been about to throw it all away by grabbing the fake guitar.

The band slid into "Who Do You Love?," one of Slim's favorite songs. He let his fingers play with the A-flat scale, playing with a mind of their own as he looked around for the first time since taking the stage.

The people on the threshing floor were caught, enchanted. He could tell. They were swaying and dancing and joyful, entranced, enhanced, and hot at a glance. Slim could see Vipers moving through the crowd, directed by a bloody but unbowed T-Bone. The men in black seemed unaffected by the music. At least it seemed so until one of the Vipers tried to climb the stage. Slim let loose with a vicious riff and a fierce wind seemed to bounce the Viper backward from the stagefront.

Slim looked up at the sky, at the giant Tejas horizon. It was clotted in with dark clouds, and he could see flashes of lightning building deep inside them. Then he looked down at his fingers on the strings—and he played, flashes and sparks jumping between fingertips and strings as he changed notes. A storm was building, and he played as he'd never played before. He'd finally caught hold of the feeling. It was all his—and yet, it wasn't. He could understand, now, Nadine's fear of the power, the sense that it wasn't *her*. He wondered if he'd be able to explain to her that, yes, there *was* something foreign in it, but it was still *him*, that there was a joy in it. A joy that came from the Gutbucket, partially, but which was definitely all his.

But none of that mattered. The only thing that mattered was that the band played on, that Slim kept running on the strings and laying down the riffs and licks. He was playing riffs and runs he'd never learned, never even heard before. They were there, in him, a part of the life he'd absorbed, or a part of the Gutbucket, it didn't matter. In the middle of "Come to Mama," he started fingertapping a complex double-string lead line he would never have thought of or imagined for the song. Nadine turned and stared at him, her mouth open in awe. And he could feel a strange sense of surprise and astonishment coming from the Gutbucket itself.

He let the solo go, let it fall from his fingers like drops of rain as Nadine started singing again. Her voice was low and husky and, as he listened, he realized she was using the power. It was gentle, tentative, to be sure, but it was there, and growing. He looked closer and he could see it in the position of her legs, the looseness of her shoulders, the tight clenching and rocking of her ass and hips.

He poured all he had into his playing, trying to channel some of the immense power he felt into her, through her. He tried to touch her, to make love to her with his fingers on the strings and the sounds they were making. As he did, she seemed to grow taller, straighter. Her voice began to match the Gutbucket, until the two were harmonized and working together as a unit.

He was deeply into the middle of the music when he heard a whizzing noise go by his ear. He kicked the trance and looked into the audience. Pickens and the Vipers were standing with guns drawn and aimed. Having failed in their attempts to get on stage, they were shooting at the band from the threshing floor. But, somehow, Slim could see the bullets as they flew through the air. He let his playing fall slightly behind the backbeat and time slowed.

He didn't stop to consider Nadine's singing, or where he was in the song. He started a lead riff, bending notes like crazy, whole tones at a time, hoping the strings wouldn't break. It was a twisted, dissonant lead that he ordinarily wouldn't have played, but as he bent the notes, the bullets were deflected from their path and disintegrated in small balls of sparks and flame.

The look on Pickens' face was one of sheer, black rage. He'd been thwarted at every attempt and, perhaps, pushed beyond what little sanity he might have once laid claim to. Slim knew, without knowing how, that Pickens would soon turn on the crowd that surrounded him. He knew that Pickens and the Vipers would instigate a bloody massacre, a slaughter that though it would win no victory for them, would just as effectively destroy the blues.

Slim signaled to the band to stop the song they were playing, and called Progress over to his chair.

"It's no good," he told the old man. "Pickens is gonna bust out bad. I can feel it. Nadine and I should sing our song, and then we should go to the finish."

"Up to you, son," Progress said, adding, "what's the gig?"

"Nadine's song is just a twenty-four bar in A, like I told you before. The finale—the way I figure it, you remember what I played at Elijigbo's. That's what I think I want here, the boogie."

Progress nodded and walked back to the band to explain the plan.

Slim adjusted the mike stand that stood in front of his chair. "Nadine," he said, off mike. "It's time for you and me to jam."

Nadine looked down at the Vipers who were staring up at them hatefully, still holding the useless guns.

"I see what you mean," she said. "All right, baby. Let's *do it*."

Slim fingered the intro to the country blues he'd come up with for Nadine's song. The band slipped in almost easily and they started to sing, their voices harmonizing as before.

> *"Tejas women*
> *Walk on legs*
> *That reach up to the sky.*
> *They run on clouds*
> *To touch the light*
> *That shines within their eyes.*
>
> *And when they stand in moonlight,*
> *Your heart flies to the stars,*
> *And just along about midnight,*
> *They'll take you very far.*
>
> *Tejas women*
> *Know the way*
> *To keep you hangin' 'round.*
> *Tejas women*
> *Don't need your heart,*
> *What they want is further down.*
>
> *And when she stands before you,*
> *Your life is in her hands,*
> *And when you've tasted her sweet lips,*
> *Buddy you'll understand."*

It sounded good for a first time through. Slim could feel the power build to a nearly unbearable level. Then—he went black. His fingers still played and his voice still sang, but he wasn't there with them. He was, abruptly, in world of thunder and lightning and wind.

Shango had finally returned.

There was a presence, or something much like one. Huge and old and powerful, Earth wide and ebony black. Images filled his mind and soul. The planet Earth, wreathed in a constantly moving, charging and discharging field of magnetism and electricity. But there was a sentience behind it, a sentience whose attention was now turned to Slim, sitting and playing on a small stage.

He saw, for a moment, overlapping visions of both his world and the world where Tejas existed. Then his mind was sucked into a vortex and spun. He felt himself come apart, molecule by molecule; then he was brought back together in light and heat. He felt—gratitude?—love? Whatever it was, it was now inside him, a part of him. Perhaps it always had been. It moved with his rhythms, or he with it. He wasn't sure which and it didn't matter.

He was once again shown the double image of the worlds, and he was offered a choice. But he knew, and communicated to the being, to Shango, that there was no longer a choice. He was a man of Tejas, a man of the blues, and would remain so.

Then he once again felt the Gutbucket in his hands. The song was over and he had come back to consciousness, fully rooted in the world he loved, awake with the sound of thunder. Lightning crashed in the sky and he cried out into the microphone, "*Boogie, chillen!*"

He started out slow and alone, building the grove till it was rock-hard boogie. Loose and free, at last, he slapped the strings carelessly, trusting to the power and to Shango. He played with it a little, hitting harmonics and octaves, wandering and finding the feel. When he had a hold on the groove that was solid and immutable, he started to sing:

"Hey-ey-ey-ey-ey-ey-ey,
Hey, hey, hey,
Working the midnight job, yeah,
Walkin' down easy street,
I hurt, hurt, hurt.
Everybody been talkin' 'bout,
Talkin' 'bout,
A strange love,
But I dropped in that night,
I did the boogie, chillen,
Did the boogie low,
I did the boogie high,
Did the boogie, chillen."

The lightning began popping and crackling as he sang and played. It rose and fell from the ground, surrounding the threshing floor. Pickens and the Vipers began to look afraid and Shango rode Slim's soul.

"Hey-ey-ey-ey-ey-ey-ey,
Hey, hey, hey,
It's late right now,
Ooooh, oh, oh, yeah,
I went down one night,
I hurt, hurt, hurt,
I really hurt,
I hurt, hurt, hurt,
I hurt,
I gotta tell ya,
Hey-ey-ey-ey,
Hadda boogie,
Boogie, chillen."

Slim began to fly on the song. Shango held his soul, the Gut-bucket held his mind, and the Amp brought it down to a right, tight focus that fed it all into the sky.

> *"Do you wanna boogie,*
> *Yes, do you wanna boogie?*
> *Do the boogie, now,*
> *Hey,*
> *Hey, hey, hey,*
> *Hey, hey.*
>
> *Let me tell you something,*
> *I went down one night,*
> *Went down,*
> *Oh, I hurt,*
> *I hurt, hurt, hurt,*
> *I hurt,*
> *I hurt,*
> *Hey-ey-hey,*
> *Did the boogie,*
> *Feel good,*
> *Feel good, good, good,*
> *Feel good,*
> *Feel, feel feel,*
> *Feel good,*
> *Do the boogie,*
> *Boogie, chillen."*

He slammed down on the strings when the solo struck him. A white-violet bolt of lightning flashed to the ground and struck a Viper. The man in black screamed and fell to the ground, burnt and smoking, his gun a twisted mass of metal fused to his hand. Slim fingertapped a quick pop riff and lightning walked along the ground, taking out five Vipers in succession. He moved down to the bottom strings and the thunder roared from his fingers, shattering glass in every car, van and pickup in the parking lot. He slid to the sixteenth fret and picked the glass up off the ground and fused it back in place, laughing.

He could do anything, he thought. A mistake. As soon as the thought crossed his mind, a shock coursed through the Gutbucket, stinging his fingers. A warning not to get carried away.

He began playing an easy repeating riff, copying himself in octaves up and down the scale. Lightning played in the clouds, lighting up the sky in white and violet and pink. He wondered why people never realized that lightning came in different colors depending on intensity. As he wondered, the thought came—from Shango, he knew—that the colors were also emotions. He intensified his playing and consciously shifted into violet and blue.

Nadine raised her arms and stood shaking and screaming to the music. As she did, a cold wind began to blow, and Slim knew that Yansan was also present, and that Nadine had finally accepted the power. He started fingertapping again, playing faster and faster. Though the sun had set and the black clouds blocked the moon and stars, lightning was flashing so quickly that the threshing floor was lit as brightly as day, but with a strange light seldom seen by humans for more than a split second.

He focused his attention on Pickens. Doubt showed on the fat man's face, then fear. Pickens began to run.

It was time to end the song.

Slim waited until Pickens had reached the edge of the crowd, and then he motioned to the band and put all he had into the concluding chord.

Strings slapped and whipped off the guitar. A huge, twined bolt of lightning exploded from the ground. It threw Pickens up into the air, then arced back down, striking him in the chest. For a moment, only a moment, he was a person-shaped glow of violet and blue light. Then he was gone.

Slim unplugged the Gutbucket, laid it gently down beside his chair and collapsed.

When he woke, his leg hurt like a sonofabitch. He was in the tent where he had watched the spider. Nadine, Progress, Belizaire, Mother Phillips and Elijigbo stood looking down at him.

"Gee," he said weakly. "I had this strange dream, and you were all there."

Nadine laughed. "I think he's all right," she said.

He sat up painfully. *"The Gutbucket!"* he cried.

Progress smiled. "Right next to you, son."

Slim reached down and felt it, picked it up. It was warm in his hands and he could feel a pain of broken strings, but it remained silent. He held it out to Progress. "Here," he said.

Progress shook his head. "No, son," the old man said, just a glint of gold showing in his half-smile. "It's yours, now. You wouldn't have been able to play it at all if it wasn't meant for you."

"Really?"

"Yep. Just treat it right and don't misuse the power. That's the heart of the blues you holdin' there. Don't you go forgettin' that."

Slim turned to Elijigbo. "What about Shango?" he asked.

Elijigbo shrugged. "Gone," he said quietly, almost sadly. "The task he came for is done. If you call on him, or he needs you, he will come again. But he is a solitary Orisha. He will not bother you."

"Then I'm okay?" Slim asked. "We won?"

Progress nodded vigorously. "Yep," he said. "Thanks to you and Nadine. You're gonna have a mighty sore leg for a while, and your fingers need to heal, but you okay mostly."

Slim held his hand in front of his face and looked at his fingers.

They were cut and bloody from the strings that had snapped on the final chord. He felt the pain only as he saw the wounds.

"Nadine," Slim said, almost frightened and whispering. "Is everything all right?"

She shook her head side to side and laughed. "No, stupid," she said. "Everything's *not* okay. You've got a fucking bullet hole in your leg, no food in your gut, you're about five shades whiter than you should be, you need a bath and we have a honeymoon to get started on. Now, you want the *full* report, or are you ready to go home?"

"Oh, I'm ready," he said. "I've been ready for years."

"Then grab your axe and get up off your butt and let's go."

He leaned on Nadine as they walked to the van. But, to tell the truth, he didn't even really feel the pain in his leg.

24

*All along there have been good reasons to play—I
like it, a lot of other people like it, it's fun. But
beyond that, it can help us out in all kinds of
ways. Music really is a way to reach out and hold
on to each other in a healthy way. It's helped me
to open up and take a chance on loving people,
instead of just isolating and suspecting everybody
I run into.*
—Stevie Ray Vaughn

*Man you go through a lot when you're out there
playing. I done been through so much ... I could
write a book . . . . man, I could tell you some facts.
Blow your mind.*
—Albert King

It was the first day he had been able to get out of bed. Progress
and Belizaire had told him to stay there, and then they had gone
fishing. Nadine insisted, and when Nadine insisted, it was no
use even trying to argue with her. Besides, she had ways to keep him
in bed, and it hadn't been a hard order to follow since his leg wouldn't
support him. But he'd woken up this morning and decided to fix
breakfast.

It had been two weeks since the festival, since he had . . . No, it would do him no good to remember what he'd *had* to do. Better to remember what he had been *able* to do.

He played. He was finally a bluesman, all the way. But, more importantly than that, he had the good, sweet woman who was still asleep in the bed they'd shared almost constantly for the last two weeks. They'd made love, they'd talked and they'd played silly games that made them laugh. And they knew each other, knew there was little difference between them.

He slid thick slices of ham onto two plates, put some hash browns beside them, then took easy-over eggs from the frying pan and placed them carefully on top of the ham slices. As he put the plates onto a tray and was turning to get the coffee, he heard noises from the bedroom. He smiled, knowing that when Nadine woke fully and had eaten, she would want to make love. And today was the day he was getting out. They were going to go see about getting some gigs.

"Nadine?" he yelled. "Honey, is that you?"

The only answer he got was the sound of a yawn and a stretch and the image in his mind of what Nadine's breasts and stomach looked like when she stretched. He put two cups of coffee on the tray, picked it up and headed for the bedroom. He still limped, but carried it all easily.

When he went in the bedroom, Nadine looked up at him, tousle-haired and sleepy-eyed. The sheets were drawn down to her waist, leaving her upper body bare. It was an almost painful sight, seeing her naked, caramel skin limned in yellow sunlight from the open window. Slim had always thought women looked awfully soft and cute and vulnerable when they first woke up. A wave of desire washed over him, and he realized how very much he loved this woman he'd been through such a lot with, through *everything* with. Everything he now felt was important in his life, anyway.

"Rise and shine," he said happily. "After this, you can bring me breakfast."

"Why?" she said. "I've been getting your breakfast the last two weeks. Besides," she said, smiling wickedly, "I think I *like* it this way."

Author's Notes

PIERS ANTHONY

I answer an average of 150 letters a month, always hoping that will diminish. All of the collaborations in this series grew out of that correspondence, because I am sympathetic to the situation of others, especially hopeful writers. I know how difficult it can be to make that first sale and publication, having taken eight years to make that breakthrough myself, and I know how hard it can be to maintain a career in writing, having been blacklisted in the 1970s for being right. My position is now secure, but that seems to be the exception rather than the rule, in this business. There are those with talent and good will who nevertheless struggle, and Ron Leming is one of them. Thus, I have done what I can to help him get established. In a better world, such as the one he created in this novel, no such help would have been necessary.

I first heard from Ron in 1989 as a reader of my novels, and a professional writer and artist in his own right. Over the years there were a number of intelligent, thoughtful, feeling letters from Ron, as he explored the truths of the world as he perceived them. But his mundane situation was deteriorating, and there came a point when he was broke, having no money to buy food. He was slowly starving, literally. Somehow the social services manage to miss a number of real folk, and not necessarily by accident. I phoned the police in his region of Texas to ask them to check on Ron, and they told me that such a request had to be originated from my home state, Florida. So I called the local police, and they told me that such a request had to go to the home state of the person concerned. It was, in short, a runaround. I pushed the issue, and finally the police in Ron's area agreed to check into the situation. But they never did.

I do what I can for my readers, in my fashion, but there are constraints. I gave Ron two pieces of advice. One was to check with the Author's League, which offers financial help to writers in need regardless of their membership or lack of it. The other was to write the first draft of his novel in pencil on scrap paper, because though he had no computer or typewriter he did have time. The creative process does not require an expensive computer system; I wrote my own novels in pencil for seventeen years before switching reluctantly to the computer. He followed both bits of advice, and that impressed me; there are those who seek help but who aren't interested in actually helping themselves in practical ways. So when the Author's League help was not enough, I loaned him money myself, to get him out of his immediate fix. And when he completed the novel, but couldn't sell it, I took it over collaboratively, adding my name, expertise, and experience to it. Thus did *The Gutbucket Quest* come to be the present volume.

I don't like to interfere in the lives of others, but sometimes it seems warranted. I am not certain that what I am doing with these collaborations is right, either technically or socially, but hope that it is. I think that this novel would not have existed had I not acted as I did, and perhaps that is my justification. My concern is of course for human need, but also more specifically for human expression. The world may not care whether *The Gutbucket Quest* exists, but I do. It has helped to broaden my horizons, because though I have always liked folk songs, my knowledge of the blues is close to nothing. Thus I would never have produced a novel like this on my own. The language differs from what I would use, but I believe in authenticity. I hope others appreciate the novel for its totality, rather than taking narrow issue with its vocabulary.

And those interested in further information about me may check my Web site at www.hipiers.com.

Author's Afterword

RON LEMING

It's been a hard life. I sit here now, a few years after this book was written, an ill, broken man. A completely different man than the one who wrote this book. I've lived one of those lives that leads some people to wonder why I'm still alive, and others to wish I wasn't. It's been one misfortune after another, ending up, at the present moment, with me suffering from chronic fatigue syndrome, extreme poverty, crushing loneliness and wondering if I'll still be alive by this time next year. I'm rich only in one thing. I have the best friends in this world. Piers once called me a Sad Sack, after the comic strip character, saying that no matter how good my intentions, things always went wrong for me. He was accurate in that assessment.

My life has been called a tragedy, a disaster and a great crying in your beer song. I've gained and lost weight, been in accidents, done drugs, quit doing drugs, been drunk and been abused. I've laughed sometimes, cried most times, beaten my head against the wall and had my head bashed by others. I've seen oceans, mountains, forests, deserts, watched a shitload of TV and made friends with hawks and squirrels. I converted to computers only to discover I was a born computer geek. I've attempted suicide, had homicide attempted against me, had gall stones and kidney stones and driven on sharp stones that shredded my tires. If anyone has a right to sing the blues, it's me.

I've loved some wonderful, horrible women. Annette, the love of my life, whose insanity led her down paths with dark tolls and even darker nightmares and who is unable to love or be loved. To this day I wish she was still speaking to me. I miss her friendship and advice.

Donna Gail, who taught me that tomboys had hidden charms and how abusive and hateful drinkers can be. Sweet Michelle, who abused the living hell out of me while at the same time opening my mind and imagination up to things I had never considered before. Sammi, whose father was an old riding bud of mine and whose need for love was almost as deep as mine. Her body betrayed her and she died before we even had a chance. And Jenn, my little Jenn, my present love, who is the only human being I've ever met who's been abused more than I have, and whose mind and soul and hunger are fully equal to mine. We wait on new beginnings, hoping to change the ending.

I recently reviewed a pre-release of Carlos Santana's *Supernatural* album. I predicted it would go straight to the top, and it has. I mention that because it's inspiring for me to see things and people I love rise to the top despite any odds, while I can only wish to have that same luck. Music is a big part of my life. I create. I don't just write, though that's my first love, I CREATE. Whether it's art, writing, music or building furniture, the act of creation is the central anchor of my life. Though it's evolved from paper to the computer screen, it's still creation, and it's all I have. It's what I get up for in the mornings, when I can get up. It's what I live for. My life is a piece of art. It may be sad or tragic art, it may not be a piece of art you like, or admire, but it's a creation, just the same. It's only regretful that love, the greatest act of creation, has always been the one thing that was denied me.

I am Native American, and my people have a belief that we are born as animals, and that life, if lived rightly, is the process of becoming a human being. Piers Anthony is the most human of all the beings I've ever known. He is an unfailingly honest, deeply caring, thoughtful man whose life, mind and talent have been vastly underestimated by those whom he frightens with his life and work. It's been said that what we don't understand, we fear. If I may change that slightly, I would say that what critics don't understand, they criticize. Piers has saved my life more than once, and perhaps saved my soul as well.

Though his work always has something to say, if one is willing to listen, he is a creator who understands that the act of entertaining people, taking them out of themselves and away from their problems can be one of life's greatest callings and hardest jobs. He has been a mentor, a friend and a hero to me.

I could not create a work about the blues without mentioning some of my other heroes. First and foremost, there is always Carlos Santana, who in a different world, at a different time, would be a spiritual leader of great power and compassion. He put three words together which I adopted into my own philosophy of life; Love, Devotion and Surrender. ZZ Top, the voice of Texas and the state's best ambassadors, whose music inspired much of this book. Jimi Hendrix and Stevie Ray Vaughn, who both died before they could truly create the music that burned in their souls. John Lee Hooker, the shaman of the blues, who understands the magic and power of the music. Buddy Guy, whose every note is like a chisel, chipping away from the stone everything that isn't the sculpture. Climax Blues Band, who in a fair world, would have been kings. Eric Clapton, whose song "Tears in Heaven" taught a cold world how the blues could touch hearts and souls. Cab Calloway, the clown prince of blues, who engendered laughter and dancing wherever he went. Roy Buchanan, who taught me everything a bluesman needs to know, whose lessons still sneak up on me unawares when I'm working on a midi and find myself inserting a grace note into moments of silence. And last, but certainly not least, my greatest hero, Muhammed Ali, whose life taught me that, no matter what the consequences might be, you must stand up for what you believe, and stand up proudly and honestly.

Life has been hard. I have never expected life to be easy, or fair. It's neither. But I have never expected to reach a point where simply surviving, staying alive is a struggle. Suffering from an incurable illness that isn't even well understood is a daily war that you don't even have the energy to wage. I spent a large portion of my life caring for the handicapped, but it wasn't until now that I understood what it's like, facing the spectre of death and knowing that it's never going to go away, that it's permanent, and there's not a thing you can do about it. It does not do good things for either your attitude or mental stability. It's been said that that which does not kill us makes us stronger. Those who say such things never seem to mention that, quite often, though things don't kill us, they make us wish we were dead.

I would fail in my duty to myself if I didn't ask you to visit my Web sites. *Rosewort*, a magazine of horror and dark fantasy, at http://www.geocities.com/Soho/Den/3712; *Dragonglass*, a magazine of science fiction and fantasy at http://www.50megs.com/users2/bone; Niversa Films at http://www.geocities.com/Hollywood/Park/1287; and Silly Ole Bear Web design at http://sillyolebear.freeservers.com. These sites all contain parts of my life and soul and heart.

Ron Leming
Amarillo, TX
October 29, 1999